Books by Delphine Boswell

Unholy Secrets   April 2018

Silent Betrayal   November 2018

Bitter Wrath   August 2019

Whispering Remorse   Winter 2019

Published by Jujapa Press

BITTER WRATH

A Dana Greer Mystery Series

DELPHINE BOSWELL

jujapa
hansville
press
washington

ISBN-13: 978-1-7321976-3-3

Library of Congress Catalog Number: **2019910569**

Published by:

Jujapa Press
PO Box 269
Hansville, Wa 98340

Cover image by fiverr artist: netherxel

Acknowledgments

As with my last two novels in the Dana Greer Mystery Series, an idea was needed to spark a beginning. Personally, I had wanted to be a nun, since an elementary-school child, but things didn't end up quite the way I thought they would. I think, it was this desire plus having grown up Catholic that inspires me to web a sense of Catholic culture into each of the books I write.

For this reason, I initially thank all the nuns who have crossed my path over the years and who taught me what such a life of dedication must be like.

To those who were beta readers – Wayne Ude, Julie Mattern, and my daughter, Ashley Boswell - I owe a debt of gratitude. Each offered a unique view of not only the content of my book but also of its plot, structure, and style.

Thanks to Clark Parsons of Jujapa Press for being my genie out of the bottle! His long, tedious hours spent getting my book into print are much appreciated.

Lastly, I thank my family who offered me respite on days when, as writers, we become thirsty for reassurance and motivation.

For those I have unintentionally overlooked, know that you, too, were part of my process.

And, as I look forward, a special thank you to my readers, who bring me the greatest joy knowing my words have traveled the distance to reach each and every one of you!

Prologue

Grotto of Lourdes Cemetery, a popular tourist spot established in 1892, was known for its majestic shrine, where it was said miracles had taken place, All were in view of the archangels, seraphims, and cherubims, who looked down upon the people.

The crutches, canes, braces, and even soiled bandages of those afflicted with various diseases and ailments lay in a glass case as a reminder of the power of prayer. To this day, pilgrims journeyed from miles away in hopes of a cure.

Charles Filmore, the groundskeeper, wiped the sweat from his brow. Dusk turned the clouds to a splash of purple, pink, and bright neon orange. One more grave to fill, and he could return to his wife, Tilly, of thirty-seven years. The business had provided him with a constant income, and he found the job of cutting, trimming, and weeding to be rewarding.

His least favorite part of the work was digging and filling the grave sites. Something about the finality of life frightened him and sometimes offered him a piercing heartburn in his chest. He figured tonight would be no different. He grabbed his shovel from his rusted 1939 Dodge TD-21, one-ton pick-up and headed toward the opened grave next to the statue of the Archangel Michael. The porcelain figurine bore a chipped nose and a missing hand that formerly gripped a sword. At his feet was a slain devil.

Charles edged closer to the rim of the grave, a pile of heavy, wet soil on the blade of his shovel. Last night's storm made the ground squishy, and his work boots sank into the soil. About to toss the wet dirt into the deep hole that bore the burial vault of a recently deceased parishioner, Charles blinked hard. Nearing nightfall, he assumed his eyes might be playing tricks with him. He pulled his flashlight from his back-overall's pocket. He blinked again and shone the light into the dark abyss. There staring back at him through inches of freshly fallen rain, he tried to make it out.

"God almighty! Jesus Christ, no," he called into the lonely air. Taking his time, as his stiff body didn't work quite as well as it did when he was twenty, he got down on his hands and knees. With his shoulders hunched over his humped back and his head as low as it would go, he propped himself up on the palm of his hand. Aiming the shaking flashlight downward, he saw there, atop the vault, what appeared to be a young woman, lying face-up, dressed in the habit of a postulant, all in white. Her legs and arms were splayed in the form of a letter *X*.

The ground bore tracks, ripped up grass and wet mud, that could have been caused if the body was pulled into the gravesite. Blood covered her white veil as if it had been crushed against something. The position of the body convinced Charles that someone had to have pushed her into the grave. It was then that Charles identified the young girl. "Sister Mary Margaret, Sister." He continued to call out her name, an echo reiterating in the cold night air. "God, in Jesus's name, no!" he cried out. The woman never responded. He tried yet one more time although he knew his screams were in vain.

Charles remembered the day not quite a year earlier. Mary Margaret had been granted special permission to join the Order of Carmelites at the mere age of thirteen. She had been the oldest of ten children, and her mother could no longer financially care for the family. Charles sat down on the wet, dew-covered grass, and wept silently into his hands. His chest burned as if he had swallowed a cup of acid. Bile rose in his throat. Who in God's name would do such a thing to the young, beautiful nun?

Chapter One

A black DeSoto with shiny silver hubcaps pulled up to the train station, and Charles Filmore, whose shoulders were bent low, making him appear almost folded in half, stepped out. He forced his body to straighten and gave a quick glance to the passengers at the curb, who waited for their rides, anxious to get to their destinations. There were couples and families standing hand-in-hand with small children.

Dana waved with her white-gloved hand until the man hobbled toward her. She wore her favorite red suit with matching heels as she knew it made her easier to find in the blur of otherwise dull colors around her.

"Dana Greer, I assume," he said, in a scratchy voice, running his fingertip through his long, scraggly beard.

"Yes, and you are?"

"Charles Filmore. I'm what you call a jack-of-all-trades, but my primary job is taking care of the cemetery and the grotto." He twisted his back until his bones made a snapping noise and reached for Dana's suitcase. "Let me get that for you." Before Dana could stop him, he headed toward the car's trunk. "You go ahead and make yourself comfortable."

Within seconds of the trunk slamming, the elderly man got into the driver's seat after a few huffs and puffs. He straightened a large pair of black-and-white dice on his rearview mirror. "Afraid we have a bit of a ride ahead of us, Miss Dana. Winter Willows is an island in the Sound and with limited ferry service, I might add." He proceeded to put the key in the ignition, and they sped off.

"Why's that. . .the limited ferry service?"

He chuckled. "Once you see the place, you'll completely understand. Other than a small fishing industry and some quaint shops, the good, cloistered sisters make up the community."

"Cloistered, you say? I had no idea."

"When you're lucky, you might get a peek at one of the good sisters gardening or praying in the backyard of the convent. Other than that, they stay out of view."

Dana felt her jaw lower. "Sounds like utter dedication," Dana said, remembering herself as a child and how she had hoped to don the habit of a nun one day. Most of the girls in her second-grade class felt the same. Sometimes during play, they would put doll blankets on their heads to replicate veils and robes to complete the habit. How may of these same girls went on to actually profess vows was a moot point as Dana had lost contact with her childhood friends, in particular, Connie Eton and Eleanor Woods.

Dana opened her shoulder bag and pulled out a colorful brochure. "I picked up one of the fliers at the train station. Winter Willows. . .a tourist site? Is that correct?"

"You better believe it. We locals try to forget that, I guess. Maybe that has something to do with the ferry's schedule. . .don't want to bring over too many, too often." He laughed at his own joke. "Seems ever since the late nineteenth century, miracles started happening at Grotto of Lourdes. The lame walked, the blind could see, well, you get the idea. Sounds like a Biblical passage, eh? Word spread and soon most of the Pacific Northwest heard of us."

Dana threw her blond curls over her shoulder and stared out the passenger window—tall evergreens covered the landscape as a light mist of rain fell. After leaving the heat and humidity of Texas, she knew she would like it here much better. "That's quite a story. Any explanation as to the miracles? I mean, people obviously must have believed?"

Charles turned on the windshield wipers and his headlights. "Wouldn't you if you could suddenly see for the first time in your life? Like Lourdes in France, our little shrine, complete with a waterfall is said to have healing powers."

"Well, I'm looking forward to my stay," Dana said.

"Wish it were under better conditions, but Father Merton tells me you're the one for the job. Solved at least two other crimes connected with the Church huh?"

"Yes, I am under contract by the archbishop of the diocese wherever a crime is committed."

"A shame, ain't it? I mean, crimes in the Church and all."

Dana removed her gloves and placed them on her lap. She pulled her compact from her bag, powdered her nose, and fluffed up her hair. She clicked the case shut. "My mother used to tell me that a Church is no different from a hospital. One treats the sick and the other the sinner."

Charles nodded with some effort; his neck could barely move. "Guess that ain't a bad way of looking at it." He turned and a truck carrying a load of logs honked him. "Ah, go to hell," he said. Shortly after, he added, "Sorry for my language. Gotta get to confession this weekend." He tried to turn his head toward her and raised his bushy, grey eyebrows. "You Catholic?"

Within seconds, Dana could feel her face warm up. She hated that question. She was one of those fallen away Catholics who had good intentions of coming back one day but hadn't quite gotten around to it. "Born and raised," she said, hoping the man wouldn't further the topic.

Charles cleared his throat, but his voice remained raspy. "Well, all I can say is I'm sure glad you're here. Still can't believe it. Only a monster could kill a young sister."

"I plan to do my best to get to the bottom of this." A comforting source of confidence came over Dana as she reminisced about the Bernadette Godfrey and the Douglas Clifford cases. This one a bit different, she thought, in that it involved a young nun. "Charles, the girl. . .the postulant—."

Seemed the man was anxious to explain, as he began to fill Dana in on what had transpired. "Sister Mary Margaret. . .a mere girl. . .only thirteen-years old."

"Rather young to enter an order, isn't it?"

"The Carmelites sought special permission for Mary Margaret and were granted the dispensation, yeah, that's what they called it, to take the girl into the order as a postulant until the age of eighteen.

The plan was that she could decide if she wanted to pursue the novitiate later on if she so chose."

Here stood the segue Dana waited for to get into full investigative mode. "Might I ask what the special circumstances were surrounding her admittance?"

"I don't quite get it myself. Something about it just don't seem right." The rain poured down in pellets now, sounding like tacks hitting the roof of the truck. Charles increased the speed of the windshield wipers and gripped the wheel tightly. "Better I tell you some about the family. It might make sense then. The girl's father left the family about a year ago...an old drunk and womanizer. Talk has it he went to the mainland and busied himself with those ladies of the night."

Dana shook her head.

"The man hasn't been seen from since."

"How terrible."

"The Missus was expecting, her tenth, at the time. Deborah never was quite the same after the birth of her last child. Those in the Church took it upon themselves to find good homes for all the children. Mary Margaret, being the oldest, was sent to the cloister."

"And the young girl's mother...is she still on Winter Willows?"

"Oh, no. She's on the mainland at the St. Dymphna Asylum for the Mentally Ill."

Dana knew about the saint. Having collected holy cards ever since a child, Dana well remembered the saint's history...a young girl whose widowed father wanted her for his wife. When she refused, he murdered her. Interesting, Dana thought, that Mary Margaret and the patron saint of the mentally ill had both been the same age and both murdered.

Could it be that Mary Margaret had refused one of her pursuers and had been dealt the same fate? A jump to a conclusion, too early to know, but Dana would not rule out the possibility. When Dana settled in at the convent, she would make a list of those she needed to speak with.

While she was lost in her thoughts, she overhead Charles say something about the pastor visiting the woman on a weekly basis. "Father Merton, the pastor."

Charles tapped his bent and deformed hands on the steering wheel. "Oh, you'll soon meet him. Father lives in the basement of the Church. He's frugal old soul. Does anything to save a nickel. Moved out of the old rectory years ago and gave it to a large family in the parish. Tells you the kind of man Merton is."

The wind suddenly picked-up speed, and a metal trash can in front of one of the homes rolled out to the center of the road. A woman scurrying down the sidewalk tried to close her umbrella, which turned inside out. Newspapers tied in bundles in a truck at the curb fell out onto the pavement.

"Jesus Christ, quite a storm coming."

Dana could hear the man mutter, ". . .swearing, gossiping, taking the Lord's name in vein. . .confession Saturday." Something about the man's sincerity struck Dana as endearing.

She attempted to get Charles to continue. "So, the girl. . .the postulant, Mary Margaret. . .was she happy with the option to join the convent? I mean, she was so young. Did she even have a choice in the matter?"

Charles snickered. "Let's just say, at thirteen years of age, the sisters felt she needed some over-seeing, protecting, chaperoning. . .that kind of thing. Ain't too many want to take on the responsibility of a teenager when it ain't their own."

"I hope you don't find me presumptuous, Charles—."

The man rolled down his window; a gust of wind blew passed him. He rolled the window back up and took a deep breath. He continued to tap his fingers against the wheel. The man began to hum the refrain of a Latin hymn that Dana was familiar with but could not recall the words. He turned his gaze toward her. "Go on," he said. "Don't detectives like to ask lots of questions? Shoot away."

Dana, pleased the man gave her clearance to continue, asked, "So, you're saying Mary Margaret was difficult to handle? Did she like boys?"

The man laughed, wiping the corners of his mouth with a large, white handkerchief he pulled out of his pant pocket. "I like the way you make the word plural. . .boys, exactly. The question remains of which one do we speak? You see, Miss Dana, the girl had no role models with her father gone and her mother suffering from mental illness." The man bit down on his lower lip and thought for a moment. "I shouldn't be talking ill of the deceased. Jesus, God, forgive me."

"That makes sense. I mean, an adolescent whose interests turn to the opposite sex. I can see why the sisters felt they were doing the girl a favor, protecting her from the outside sources of temptation."

The man laughed. "No way the devil's getting through those walls."

Glancing over at the old man's face, Dana could tell he appeared to be in discomfort.

Charles moved his crooked back restlessly in the upholstered driver's seat and sighed loudly. "Ain't no fun gettin' old. Well, my wife, sweet she is, keeps trying to get me to retire, but who would do what I do around the place? I mean I weed, I trim, I mow. . .even bury the blessed dead."

"You must be much appreciated for all you do." Dana felt a twinge of sadness for the man who accepted his responsibilities with such grace despite bearing his pains.

The closer they got to Winter Willows, the heavier the rain became, and the sky darkened to a steel grey. The wipers made a swishing sound, trying their best to keep up with the downpour, like a fast-moving metronome. The branches of the evergreens swayed like long fingers combing the air.

Charles clicked on the radio. Archbishop Fulton J. Sheen's "Life is Worth Living" radio hour came on. The priest began to speak about the snares of the devil. As an elementary student in Catholic school, Dana recalled her religion lessons, that spoke to that very topic. Dana thought at the time that it must be impossible to be holy as no matter where one might turn, Satan was waiting in the shadows, ready to snag anyone he could with his sharp pitchfork. Becoming a nun, she would thwart his powers to overtake.

Charles turned up the radio a notch. "I enjoy listening to this show. Father always has a great message."

"Speaking of priests, is Father Merton the only one at Grotto of Lourdes parish?"

"In addition to Father Merton, we have a young man, fresh out of the seminary by the name of Tanner Bennett, who joined the staff about six months ago. He's only twenty-three. Apparently graduated ahead of his class. He looks a hell of a lot younger, though. He's often taken for a mere teenager when he's out of his cassock. His uncle is an archbishop in Rome. Father Tanner rose in the ranks quite quickly from what I hear." Charles made two left-hand turns, and the Winter Willows' ferry could be seen in the distance.

"Hmm," Dana said, thinking maybe the young man's connection to the archbishop helped him gain permission for Mary Margaret to enter the convent.

"There she is," Charles said, pointing to a green-and-white ferry. "With only two going out a day, we'd better step on it." The crooked man did his best to extend his leg and pressed his foot down on the accelerator. Within minutes of the ferry's blaring horn, he drove his DeSoto up the ramp. "It's only a five-minute ride over to the island. Do you prefer getting out on deck, or would you rather wait it out here?"

Ever since Dana had almost drowned, falling off her uncle's boat when she was seven, her heart palpitated whenever she came near water. She remembered the view as if peering into a dirty aquarium only this time she was on the inside struggling to get to the top. She thrashed in an effort to rise until her uncle yanked her ponytail and brought her onboard. "I'm fine," Dana said, "let's wait in the car."

Several more cars parked behind them. The engines idled and turned off—silence spread like that of a sanctuary at midnight.

Charles's eyes began to close when Dana interrupted with, "I do have one more question," breaking the solitude like cracking a piece of ice with a hammer.

He jumped. "What were you saying?"

"How long was Mary Margaret in the convent before her death?"

The man studied Dana's face.

She wondered if the man would answer her question as he remained quiet for some time. He ran his finger like a fan across his mouth, first one way and then the other. "Just a bit over seven months."

Dana refrained from going any further with her questioning. She decided now was not the time.

The three honks of the ferry and the rattling of the white metal gates announced they had pulled up to shore. Charles drove off the ferry and headed North. Like a postcard one might send home to a loved one, a wooden sign with carved black letters read:

Welcome to Winter Willows

The homes, like colorful sprinkles on a cake, zig-zagged the slight hillside in pastel shades of pink, green, yellow, and blue under the dim skies.

"What a beautiful view," Dana said.

Along the shoreline, next to the dock, a large brown-brick building stood, its name: *Willow Fisheries*. And in the distance stood the Mount Carmel Cloistered Convent surrounded by a concrete wall at least twelve feet tall. The DeSoto's engine rumbled up the hill, slowly making its way around one *S* curve after another until it stopped at a large wrought-iron gate. Charles stepped out and stretched his back, hunched and stiff. He spoke into a speaker, and the entrance flung open. He drove about another half mile until they arrived at the cloister. He parked in front of a pair of large wooden doors with bald eagles as knockers.

Dana got out of the car and stood back to admire the impressive grounds, the architecture in a simple, federal style common to the early nineteenth century. She found herself staring at the peaceful surroundings: the Church; the cemetery; and in the middle, towering over both, the cloistered convent. She questioned how evil could have stalked these holy grounds. What right did it have to show its ugly face and to capture and murder one of the young religious within? She prayed she'd find the answers.

Charles shuffled up behind her and interrupted her thoughts. "Hope you enjoy praying?"

At first, Dana assumed the man might have read her mind.

"The good sisters…they pray non-stop. I should add they pray behind grills. . .even attend Mass that way. Hard to believe so as to keep themselves totally separate from the outside world. Gotta give those women credit."

"I imagine that would have been difficult for the young postulant. Teenagers are known to be incredibly chatty." Dana smiled at the man.

"Maybe Mother Anne Baptiste can answer that better than I can. She heads up the cloister; all the nuns report to her."

"But—."

"She can talk! Besides being in charge of the convent, she is also the only nun who handles the rare moments when matters necessitate making contact with the outside world."

"I see. Thank you for telling me that, Charles. I wouldn't want to break any rules while I'm here."

Dana hurried toward the trunk to get her luggage. She questioned how the poor man was capable of the yard work he described when he had such difficulty moving about.

"Please, let me," Charles said. "A lady ain't got no business lifting heavy things." He placed her suitcase on the porch to the convent. He shook her hand and began to walk toward the DeSoto. "Was a pleasure meeting you, young lady." Under his breath, he said, "Gotta get to confession."

Dana paused for a moment before she spoke. Her curiosity had gotten the better of her. "There is one more thing—?"

He looked over his shoulder.

"Sister Mary Margaret. . .with her family scattered as it is, did anyone attend her funeral?"

The man moistened his lips and bit down on the inside of his cheek. "Not a one other than the sisters and Father Tanner. Why'd you ask?"

"Why? Just wondering," Dana said, but she knew that often the perpetrator of a crime showed his face at the wake whether out of guilt or curiosity. "No clue there," she mumbled under her breath.

Charles slammed the trunk to his car and focused his attention on the burial grounds next to the convent. As if speaking to himself, he said, "Such a pity." Before driving off, he struggled into the seat of his car.

*

About to grab the head of the bronze eagle's door knocker, Dana took a slight step back when one of the double doors to the convent opened.

The prioress's eyes opened wide as she lowered her glasses from the bridge of her nose and slipped them up again.

"Hello, Sister. The name's Dana Greer. Charles Filmore brought me here."

The nun said nothing, only motioned for Dana to have a seat in the front-room parlor. The sister then left, rather in a hurry.

The only thing about the dark, dreary room that looked the least bit alive was a tall vase in the window filled with yellow snapdragons, orange lilies, and pink gladiolas. Dana bent to take a whiff of the large bouquet when she was interrupted.

"Dana. . .Dana Greer?"

Dana turned abruptly and found herself looking into the face of a nun with the complexion of porcelain, dark chocolate eyes, and thin black brows. "Oh, sorry, I found myself admiring the flowers."

"Please do. A Mrs. Carmichael, one of our dear parishioners, sends them weekly. She runs a small flower shop in town."

"How nice of her," Dana said. "It sure makes the room cheery."

"I'm Mother Superior, Sister Anne Baptiste."

The woman's voice so soft-spoken, Dana wondered if her demeanor interfered in her ability to govern or to take charge of a group of sisters.

As if reading her mind, Mother said, "I'm one of forty-three sisters at the convent, three novices, who have professed temporary vows, and. . .well, it's two postulants now with the passing of Sister Mary Margaret." The nun grabbed hold of the rosary beads at her side and beneath her breath said, "Eternal rest grant unto her soul, Lord."

Dana found herself bowing her head with the nun.

"Well, well, more of that later. Let me show you to your cell, where you'll be staying."

Dana picked up her luggage and followed the nun who appeared to almost glide across the grey, marble floor, her habit making a soft swishing sound as it touched. Voices, like a choir of angels, sang in the distance, the lyrics in Gregorian chant.

"Sorry, if I'm interrupting your prayers, Mother."

"No, right now the sisters break into groups of ten or twelve to sing in the chapel." She brushed the edge of her veil aside. "You see, we never choose to leave our Lord alone at any time—twenty-four hours a day."

Dana thought about a young girl attempting to abide by such a rule and could not understand how Sister Mary Margaret must have followed such a routine with a strict set of obligations.

Alcoves lined the hallway, as far as Dana could see, with small statues of the saints, a small light illuminating each. Dana recognized them all from her collection of holy cards saved over the years: St. Francis of Assisi, clutching a lamb and a goat; St. Luke, holding a roll of bandages in his hands; St. Nicolaus with a group of children; St. George with his dragon; and St. Teresa of Avila, one of the original Carmelite nuns. The dusk of the day shone through the ceiling-to-floor walls of stained glass, representing all fourteen Stations of the Cross in vivid shades of burgundy, green, and gold.

A few nuns passed them as they walked. Their hands bundled in their sleeves, their eyes cast downward. A heavy scent of incense filled the space. It reminded Dana of the High Masses she had attended while a student. Every morning before classes began, the students lined up in single file and followed their respective teacher into Church. Dana had made her mind up that she wanted nothing more than to be a nun when she grew-up. The unfortunate incident on her uncle's boat when she was only seven years old directed her away from her dreams. She was left feeling dirty, unworthy, unholy. What convent would ever accept such a soiled soul? she had asked herself. Her uncle had since passed away, but Dana's memories remained alive.

"Right this way, Dana, up these four steps. Your cell is the only one on this level, so you should have your privacy. It even has its own bath, which is unheard of in the other cells." Mother Anna Baptiste opened the door with a silver key, and the two women stepped inside. A small bed, which looked more like a cot with a lumpy mattress, a two-drawer night table with a lamp, a cloth chair, and a wooden one beneath a built-in desk were the only furnishings in the room. Above the bed was a crucifix, and on one of the walls hung a painting of Mary announcing to Elizabeth that she was with child. "I hope you'll be comfortable. There's an overhead ceiling light, as well."

"I'm sure I will like it here, Mother. Are there any rules or guidelines I need to follow, so as not to be an inconvenience during my stay?"

Sister thought for a moment. "You're most welcome to attend morning, afternoon, and evening prayers with us in the chapel. We have silent breakfast daily after the six a.m. Mass, lunch at noon with a spiritual reading, and dinner at six, also with a reading. I suppose the hardest thing for you will be to join the sisters in solitude as we only speak during recreation in the parlor between three p.m. and four. You're welcome to be a part of these times," the nun grasped the edge of her veil and looked at Dana, "or not, as you please."

"Thank you, Sister. I may well partake as time permits."

Mother nodded. "You're almost in time for lunch if you like."

"Mother?"

"Yes, my child?"

"Do the other sisters know that I'll be staying here among them?"

"They've been told," she said, placing the room key in Dana's hand and closing the door quietly.

Dana was about to set her suitcase on the bed but decided against it when she noticed the spread was lily white; instead, she opened the case on the floor and slowly folded her belongings and put them in the night table.

The time as good as any to meet the other sisters at lunch, Dana locked the door to her room, and followed a group of about six nuns headed toward the refectory. She entered the room, where bowed brown heads were all that could be seen. "Excuse me, Sister," she said. "Might you tell me where the best place to sit would be? I'm Dana Greer, perhaps, you've heard."

The young nun dressed entirely in white, obviously a postulant as had been Mary Margaret, pointed to the end of a long table covered with a green linen cloth, next to a podium, where stood an elderly nun with a large book in front of her. No sooner had Dana sat down then the nun began to speak.

"Sisters, welcome to the table of the Lord. May he bless our food, our lives, and all who serve. Amen."

Quietly, everyone in the room motioned the Sign of the Cross over their chests, and dishes began to be passed. Grilled cheese sandwiches and a small helping of potato chips filled each white, China plate. An elderly nun with broad shoulders and a manly stature began to read, her voice deep, her posture arrogant and stiff:

'Our reading is from the book of 'All Saints in Glory.' Sister Therese of the Little Flower found at the ripe age of fourteen that doing for others brought much more happiness than thinking of one's self. Fifteen-years-old, she was, when she entered the Carmelite convent."

Dana nibbled on the toasted bread, her mind beginning to wander. Almost the same age as Sister Mary Margaret, Dana thought. Yet Dana questioned how such a young girl could be happy here. If Charles Filmore was correct and the girl was as boy crazy as he said, it struck Dana more than odd that the girl would be satisfied living a life of seclusion, such as this. Her mind distracted by her own thoughts and not listening to the nun's reading, Dana noticed the elderly woman put her finger in the pages of the book as a place holder. She quit reading and scowled at Dana.

"Miss, would you care to continue?" the nun, said in an exacerbated tone.

Dana looked up-and-down the table, a blur of black and brown.

"Yes, you," the nun said, pointing a long, shaking finger at her.

The nun continued reading for about a half hour when all the sisters processed out of the dining room, except for the elderly nun.

"Miss," she said. "You must be the investigator?"

"Yes, Sister. Sorry to have disturbed your reading. Something about Saint Therese being almost the same age as Sister Mary Margaret—."

The elderly nun's face grew red with a sheen of sweat on her cheeks. "Sister Mary Margaret was not chosen for the order. I'll have you know! The Carmelite Convent was nothing more than a roof over her head." Sister closed the thick book with a thump. ". . .much like yourself, I presume."

Dana, taken aback, could not think of a response for the nun, who glared at her through her smeared wire-rimmed glasses.

The nun curled her lip, gathered the long folds of her habit, and stormed out of the room, leaving Dana standing with her mouth ajar.

*

Although Dana told herself not to be rattled by what had happened in the refectory, she was. Only in the convent less than an hour and already she felt as if she made an enemy. She recalled having felt so welcome in Ellie's home when she investigated the murder of Douglas Clifford, a small, blond-headed, ten-year old who looked more like a cherub than a hardened criminal. No sense reminiscing about the hospitality of Ellie, she thought. Father Merton had made arrangements for Dana to stay with the nuns, and Dana's mother had always told her to respect the wishes of those in power. There was no way she could ask to be sent somewhere else at this point, and furthermore, not all the sisters had to be as rude as the one she had just ran into.

She planned to go to recreation hour at three. In the meantime, she propped herself on the bed and closed her eyes.

When she awoke, the room pitch black, she felt disoriented. She quickly turned on the light on the night table, realizing she must have fallen into a deep sleep ever since lunch. That's when she heard a rattling like someone tugging on the knob to her room. She opened the door and looked up and down the hall. A black shadow scurried in the darkness until out of sight. Only the sound of distant chanting could be heard, coming from the chapel, where small groups of sisters rotated throughout the day and night in praise of God.

Chapter Two

Dana awoke early following the smell of oatmeal. The hallways were empty as she expected, the nuns directly exiting the chapel, others gently closing the doors to their cells. All headed toward the dining hall. In twelve years as an investigator, Dana remembered well the words of her former mentor, "Sometimes it is in the silence that the loudest clues in a case speak." That's exactly what Dana hoped to observe: the sisters interacting with each other, no words being spoken, only body language to study.

Dana found an empty seat across from the two postulants dressed in white from head to toe. She attempted a smile, but only stoic faces stared back at her.

A sister, with an obvious crook in her back, measured out a cup of oatmeal from a small wooden ladle and poured it into each of the bowls. Another sister with a tasseled, black shawl, served the second table. Each nun nodded in turn. Mother Anne Baptiste, standing at the podium, led the women in prayer before the meal.

Without wanting to appear too obtrusive, Dana's eyes furtively glanced from one nun to the other while she tried to swallow the lumpy breakfast cereal, which tasted more like moth balls. She felt a slight kick under the table but realized it was meant between the two postulants as she caught them laughing silently to each other. With her head semi-bowed, Dana continued to peek at the two young girls, who seemed to be preoccupied with each other's behavior. Dana wondered how Sister Mary Margaret got along with these two women, who appeared to be not a day over eighteen years of age.

From what she had heard of convent life, even in the holiest of places, cliques did exist.

The breakfast hour ended in twenty minutes. The clatter of bowls and silverware filled the formerly quiet room, and the majority of nuns processed out. A large number turned back toward the chapel, but others walked the long marble hallway to their cells. A few remained for kitchen clean-up. Dana planned to meet some of the sisters during the afternoon social hour, but right now, she headed toward the basement of Grotto of Lourdes Church to pay an impromptu visit to Father Merton.

Dana stepped out into the fresh air, taking a deep breath. She hadn't noticed how intense the scent of the incense in the convent's walls had been. That and living behind the metal bars of the grills everywhere that separated the outside world from the inner sanctum of the convent added to the claustrophobic feeling she felt.

The Church door open, she stepped inside and genuflected in the main aisle. Flickering candles shone upon the faces of the porcelain statues of Mary and Joseph. One stood on either side of the main altar as if soldiers keeping guard. Large urns of fresh zinnias and dahlias stood at their feet. Must be the same woman who filled the parlor with her beautiful bouquet. In the sanctuary, as if flying down from the tall ceiling, were a group of angels, their wings entangled with one another. Dana relished her presence in the church, a faith she claimed to be a part of, yet a side of her telling her she didn't belong. Next to one of the confessional doors along the side wall, she noticed a door leading into a hall. A small plaque above the door read:

Private Residence of Father Merton

If needing assistance, please ring bell.

Dana did as instructed, not expecting the bell to ring as loudly as it did. . .more of a gong. Pleased that she did not have to repeat her actions, she heard a man's voice say, "C'mon down."

Dana thought it a bit odd that the man would invite someone into his living space without knowing who stood at the top of the stairs, but she did as he asked. The priest, out of garb, wore a yellow polo shirt and a pair of khaki pants. In his lap, he cradled a chocolate dog that looked more like a stuffed animal with a red collar.

In a woeful voice, Father Merton said, "Yes, my child, what is it you desire...to have your confession heard?"

Dana smiled slightly yet half expecting the priest would have been better informed of her coming. "No, Father, the name's Dana Greer. I've come to investigate the case of the young postulant."

The priest's manner perked up. "Mary Margaret, ah yes. Pleased to meet you. Here have a seat." He motioned to the chair across from him. "This here is Francine," he said, holding the dog up for her to see. "Named after St. Francis, she is." He planted a kiss upon the dog's fluffy head. "One of the parishioners was kind enough to give me the dog."

The damp chill from the cinder-block walls filled the small sitting room. Dana sat down on a maroon velvet chair.

Father sat opposite her on a mismatched chair upholstered in blue and yellow stripes. A crucifix hung from the wall, and a small bookcase was filled with motivational books, a catechism, and several theology books. Atop it stood a statue of Mary, her blue gown etched in shades of gold.

"Feel free to cover yourself, Miss. Most aren't comfortable with the temperatures in my place." He fumbled with a turquoise, knitted sweater in his lap and stretched it over the dog's head and paws. "We say, 'Offer it up for the sins of the world,' don't we, Francine? I always tell my visitors."

Dana had heard that expression many times from the sisters in the elementary school she had attended. She often wondered if the strangers she offered sacrifices for ever were aware of all she did for them.

A purple wool blanket lay on the back of the chair, and Dana did as the priest suggested, tossing it over her lap.

"Father Neil, from your last assignment in Texas, tells me you're quite the detective. I'm pleased to know that, as I have my misgivings about how Mary Margaret left this world. Not sure the archbishop is convinced either. According to our caretaker, Charles Filmore, there were deep ruts leading toward the grave site as if someone dragged the young girl to the burial site." Father got up and reached for a bag off his bookshelf. "Plus, only a day or two after the murder, Charles brought me this." The archbishop asked that I keep this until you arrived." From the opened bag, he pulled a piece of broken concrete covered in what appeared to be dried blood.

"Charles found this? He didn't mention anything about this on our drive over to the island."

"He's quite shook up about it…going contrary to the coroner's report that the girl accidentally fell that dark night. That's when Charles called the archbishop once again, and he, in turn, invited you onto the case. Archbishop Boretti asked that I keep this as possible evidence until you arrived." He put the concrete back into the bag and handed it to Dana.

"You mean this object has been held, passed around? That pretty much destroys it as a piece of evidence." Dana remembered in a previous case she had solved, a key piece of evidence had been thrown away. She told herself that, unfortunately, not everyone understood the importance of keeping a crime scene untouched.

"I'm sure Charles meant no harm…just wasn't thinking. We sure need someone around here, though, who has the gift of an investigative mind." He smiled.

"I am confident that's what I have," Dana said. "I work under contract with whoever is the archbishop of the diocese, where the crime was committed. In this case, it's Archbishop Boretti of Seattle."

"Know the man well," Father Merton said, nodding his head long after he commented. "We were in the seminary together years ago."

"Nice," Dana said.

"The case is in good hands then," father said, smiling. His facial expression suddenly changed as he added, "I'm puzzled, though. I mean, who would do such a thing to a child?" He thought for a moment and continued, "I hate to say it, but it's not that the girl wasn't barking up the wrong tree."

"It's difficult to believe a young girl who was welcomed into the order of cloistered sisters could have had such an untimely death. As to 'barking up the wrong tree,' I'm afraid I don't understand, Father."

Father bit down on his upper lip. "We must note, Miss Greer, that the child had friends, not necessarily the best of friends. Why it certainly wasn't as though she had a vocation to the convent."

Dana ran the palm of her hand across her cheek. "A calling, you mean?"

Father raised his voice to an angry pitch. "Precisely! A father who walked out of the family and a mother who suffered mental illness after delivering her last child…you must understand that the ten children were taken in by others who offered to raise a child or two. You see, Miss Greer, Mary Margaret had no desire to enter the convent; she was placed with the sisters at the suggestion…or should I say urging of Mother Anne Baptiste."

Dana fiddled with her pencil. "Against her will?" She readied herself to write down the priest's answer into her notepad.

"Oh, praise God, yes. To be exact, the girl had many boyfriends. Where do we begin, huh?" Father set his dog onto the floor and threw his arms outward. "Raising an adolescent is never an easy task, let alone one as popular and beautiful as she."

"What grade was the girl in? Rather young, I'd say for having many boyfriends."

"Rumors had it that the eighth-grade girl was sought after by just about every boy in her class."

"But isn't that the reason the sisters took her into the convent...to protect her from worldly temptations?" Dana was about to say that that is what she heard from Charles Filmore but decided not to bring up their discussion.

"I suppose, but it was too late for that." The priest ran his hand across his chest. His lips and chin trembled. The tendons stood out in his neck. "Perhaps I shouldn't tell you this, but did you know the sister was with child when she came to the convent?" The priest's grey eyebrows shot up. His face revealed shock as if finding out the news himself for the first time.

Dana involuntarily stood up, raising her chin and lowering it. Her face flinched. "No, I had no idea. Did the sisters?"

The priest's dog jumped on father, looking for comfort. Father gently put his hand on Dana's arm. "Please sit back down. Let me get you a cup of tea." First, Father Merton patted the round cushion in the corner and called to his dog, "Francine, come." The dog scampered over to her bed and scratched at the pillow until finding the perfect resting spot. Then, father stepped through the arch to the kitchen while Dana waited. Several minutes later, father returned with two steaming mugs brewing with the smells of apples and cinnamon. He offered Dana a cup. "My favorite," he said.

Dana smiled and nodded, but somehow the news of Sister Mary Margaret's pregnancy left her chilled to the bone. This was something she hardly expected to learn. She closed her notebook and put it in her bag.

"Now, where were we?" Father Merton asked.

Dana was left speechless, frozen. When her mind should have been filled with a multitude of questions, hers became immobilized, unable to think. Something about the case suddenly going from that of a young girl taken in by a group of protective nuns to that of a promiscuous teenager prompted Dana from saying anymore. When she was called to investigate the case by the archbishop, no mention was made that the young girl was pregnant when she entered the convent's walls. She set her teacup down, excused herself, and promised to speak with the priest at another time.

*

Dana could hear the chattering, much like canaries in a cage, coming from the parlor as she entered. Recreational hour and some of the sisters sat alone, knitting, crocheting, or embroidering. Others sat in small groups huddled together like a flock of . crows. Dana sensed the uneasiness she felt, her stomach growling, her esophagus burning. Father Merton's unexpected revelation left her shocked. She should have stayed, asked the unanswered questions, but she found herself too jolted to do so.

Dana debated whether to discuss the shocking news…the news Father Merton had shared…with Mother. The woman, blue yarns strung between her fingers, sat alone in the corner of the room.

The nun looked up as Dana approached.

"Mother, I'm sorry to disturb you, but might I ask you a few questions?"

"Concerning the case?"

Dana nodded.

Mother wrapped her yarns into a ball and placed them into a tapestry bag. "Please follow me." Mother led Dana down the hall toward her office and closed the door. "Have a seat, dear."

Dana rubbed her hands, clenching and unclenching them. "I spoke with Father Merton. He informed me Sister Mary Margaret was with child when she entered the convent."

Mother pursed her lips. "That man...sometimes he speaks when it would be better if he kept his lips shut."

"I understand your feelings, Mother, but I am under contract with the archbishop to solve this case. That means asking questions that might be uncomfortable to answer."

"I know. I know. You are here to do a job. What can I help with?"

"Did you know sister was expecting when she came to the convent?"

"Hardly. No one was aware until she realized it herself. She came to me in tears one night, telling me she was with child. I suggested she confess her sin to the priest."

"But you agreed she could stay with the sisters until when?"

Sister sighed. "I did not offer her a choice. I said she *would* stay with us until she reached the age of eighteen. If at that time, she wanted to pursue a vocation, she would take her temporary vows."

"I'm confused, Mother. If the postulant had decided to profess vows, what would become of her child?"

Mother smiled. "That was the tradeoff, Dana. If the girl decided she had a vocation, we promised to raise her child until the age of eighteen."

"In a cloistered convent?"

"There have been more peculiar arrangements made…trust me."

Dana twirled her pencil in the air. "And, if she decided not to profess vows?"

"She could leave with her child in five years."

"Sounds, from what you said earlier, you gave her no choice but to live in the convent?"

Mother tossed her chin upward as if thinking of what to say. "I hate to be so blunt, Dana, but when the siblings were separated, no one on the island was willing to take Cindy…Cindy Sullivan."

"And the siblings were separated due to the mother no longer being in the home?"

"Exactly," Mother said. "All of the children were sent to different parishioner's families. Cindy, well, a teenager was harder to place. I was able to clear Cindy's admittance through the Roman Curia, the administration of the Holy See. We agreed to let the child become a postulant until she reached the age of eighteen."

"Mother, how did Cindy feel about being so young and pregnant?"

"If you're asking whether she wanted the baby, the answer is yes." Mother pulled a white handkerchief from her side pocket and dabbed at her lips. "Why, when she learned the baby was stillborn, she cried almost nonstop for the entire week prior to her death. The sisters and I did the best we could to help her through her loss."

"Still born?" I had no idea. Chills raced up and down Dana's arms.

Chapter Three

Still in shock over what she had learned yesterday, Dana paid another visit to Father Merton. Had he known the nun's child was stillborn, or was he intentionally keeping the news from her? She was not here to play cat-and-mouse games.

"I hear you, my child," Father Merton said. "The child was born dead."

Dana edged closer. "You mean you're not surprised by my news?"

"It was during one her weekly confessions, shortly before her untimely death, that she gave me the news about her child."

"Was sister pregnant at the time of her death?"

The priest shook his head. "From what I learned, no. She delivered her child only a week before her passing. She confessed she wanted to keep her baby and that the sisters told her she could."

"If her murder—."

Father threw his hands into the air. "Murder? Better be careful how you use that word around Henry Gillion. He's the Sheriff's coroner from the mainland. The priest lifted Francine from her cozy bed in the corner of the room and placed her on his lap. "Seems Henry has a totally different perspective on what happened the night Sister Mary Margaret died. Like I said before, he ruled the death as a result of an accidental fall."

"Interesting. I need to speak with him and to see the scene for myself...now, if possible."

Father dialed the phone.

*

Henry Gillion, due to arrive on the evening ferry, had not yet arrived. Father Merton and Dana waited at the cemetery. The grotto stood in the background as the sun began to set. The rays from the blood orange sun shone above the grotto, making the grounds look technicolor. A cool breeze blew through the trees; nightfall was in the air.

A rumbling sound could be heard in the near distance as a sports car left a wake of dust. Henry Gillion had arrived.

Father Merton introduced Dana.

The man was a carbon copy of Gregory Peck, complete to his tweed jacket and yellow sweater vest. Tall and thin, the coroner was quick to speak as if in a hurry.

"So, Miss Greer, father tells me you're wanting to know my thoughts about what occurred on the night Sister Mary Margaret passed away. As I told the sheriff from the mainland, it was a gruesome sight to be sure, but the gravesite had not been closed. Anyone with an ounce of sense could see exactly what must have happened. Dusk, around eight p.m., and the girl lost her footing and slipped into the open grave."

Dana interrupted with, "Is that why Archbishop Boretti called and asked me to investigate?"

"Probably just following protocol, but you can take my word for it. It was an awful accident. I'm sure the nun had a broken back and a crushed skull; her white veil covered in blood."

"No autopsy?"

"Must not be a Catholic. Catholics don't believe in autopsies, Dana."

Dana was called to look into the event, which told her the archbishop wasn't necessarily buying into the coroner's account.

"Oh, one other thing, Mr. Gillion. Was sister with anyone that night...other than nuns, friends?"

"You mean witnesses? No one came forth that I know of."

"Now, if you don't mind, I'd better be going. Meeting someone at the Fireside Inn for dinner."

"That's right. You came over on the last ferry...must be spending the night," Father Merton said.

"Staying at the Vincent's."

"The Vincent's?" Dana inquired.

"The doctor and I go way back."

"Hmm, good friends then?" Dana asked.

"The best," Henry said, as he shook hands with Dana and the priest.

"One more thing before you dash off, Mr. Gillion."

The man opened his mouth and stopped suddenly.

"I'd like to see the death certificates for Sister Mary Margaret and her child."

"Of course, I'll get copies made from the sheriff's office. Should I send them to you, Father…at the rectory."

"Sure, Henry, that'll work."

As his car stormed down the narrow, dirt road out of the cemetery, Dana said, "Where exactly is the gravesite, the coroner spoke of?"

Father pointed to a newly plotted piece of land. "Right there," he said."

"If you don't mind, Father, think I'd like to stay a bit longer and look over things."

"Be my guest. I've got to take Francine on her last walk for the night."

Dana raised up her index finger. "Oh, and one more thing, Father, who are the Vincents?"

"Ned Vincent is the island doctor. He was the one who delivered sister's baby."

Ned Vincent…someone Dana needed to meet.

After father left, Dana walked around the new grave that, as of yet, did not have a tombstone. The sun set and dusk began to darken the sky. The thought of someone accidentally slipping into the open grave was not unheard of if the nun had been alone as the coroner indicated. But was she? Another question she'd have to consider. She roamed around, noticing a concrete mausoleum nearby, complete with small, stained-glass windows. Carved into its side was the year 1894. Two years since, she thought, the cemetery was established. The grass around the building was much longer than that in the cemetery. Dana figured a mower couldn't get close enough to the mausoleum to cut it, and it probably needed to be sickled. Dana walked around to the other side and around to the front. There in the right corner of the building, she found a rough edge. Could it be that this is where the broken piece of concrete came from? She removed the item from its bag and like a puzzle piece, the broken concrete fit neatly into the place.

Could the blunt piece have been used to hit Sister Mary Margaret over the head? Could whoever murdered her have cast away the concrete once the merciless deed was done? If so, could this mean the murder was not premeditated but rather done in a moment of anger and rage? If this was the case, could the murder weapon have been too handy not to consider? Certainly, its strength would be great enough to result in blunt force trauma. Who would sister have been with that night? More importantly, why would she be here in the cemetery, especially after having just given birth? These questions needed answers. She intended to find them.

Chapter Four

As often was the case, Dana found herself rising early…the excitement of a new case to be solved. She quickly dressed and made her way to the chapel for the six a.m. Mass. The nuns stood in their pews behind a tall, metal grid that separated them from the priest and the altar in the sanctuary. The grille represented to the cloistered nuns their separation from the outside world.

In harmony, the nuns sang "O, Sacred Head Surrounded," the familiar Lenten melody that Dana recalled from her days in the Church. Engaged in making her way from Punkerton, Texas to Winter Willows, Washington, Dana had completely forgotten that Easter was less than two weeks away. The somber time in the Church when prayer, fasting, and sacrifice made up the order of the day. Somehow finding herself in the middle of a murder investigation completed the mood of gloom.

A tall nun with black-rimmed glasses resting on the bridge of her nose guided the sisters in song as she stood at the podium in the front of the chapel. Her arm extended upward, downward, and from right to left.

The tinkling of a bell rang, and a young priest led by two altar servers entered the sanctuary. This had to be the newly ordained man that Father Merton had spoken about. The priest's body posture exuded an air of confidence…perfect stature; sandy, brown air tousled as if he hadn't cared to comb it; and his vestment ironed with perfect pleats and folds as if it had never been worn. He set his large, red-covered missal down and kissed the altar as he began to sing the

Latin words of forgiveness, "Kyrie Elision," in a crisp and articulate voice that obviously had years of seminary training.

Dana found herself disengaged from the service and more interested in studying her surroundings. Standing on one side of the grid with father on the other, Dana sensed the humility, the lowness, and the suppression that the simple piece of metal represented. More than likely, it accounted for and added to father's arrogant assurance.

When the young man entered the pulpit to address the congregation, he peered through the openings in the grid as if looking for a lost soul. "My dear sisters," he began. "Today marks the third week anniversary since one of our own was found on the grounds of the Grotto's cemetery. The grotto is a place of miraculous healings, a history of such, and that day, instead, the remains of Sister Mary Margaret were found tossed into an open-grave site."

The sound of rustling gabardine could be heard in the pews and the movement of rubber-soled shoes on the stone floor.

"This, my friends, is the work of Satan, alive and well. He bears no shame or regret from entering these holy grounds and murdering one of God's own." His words sounded more like a memorized speech rather than an empathetic lector.

This time sad outbursts acknowledged the priest's words, and veiled heads nodded. Sniffles and sighs temporarily stopped the priest words.

He continued, "Let us remember this holiest season of the Church by recalling the faithful souls departed…Sister Mary Margaret and all the others waiting to enter their final reward." The man stepped down.

The tall nun at the podium led the sisters in prayer.

When the Mass ended, Dana waited at the end of the divider. She pried a metal gate open and hoped the priest would take note of her presence, so she might speak to him. She waited outside of the sacristy where, in minutes, she saw the altar boys tossing their Mass garments into a heap in a cardboard box. The two boys were obviously twins and looked to be about sixteen years old. One grabbed a letter jacket with the letters WWH and the other a black leather jacket from some hooks on the wall. One of the boys pulled out a pack of Lucky Strikes from his pocket and stuck the unlit cigarette into his mouth, dangling it from his lower lip. "Let's get the hell out of here," he said, to his brother. Shortly afterwards, the young priest came out, wearing a pair of jeans and a red polo. He looked more like a golfer than a priest who had just engaged in Mass.

"Father, may I speak with you?"

The man cocked his head to the side, his eyes narrowed. "I'm sorry. Guess, we haven't met."

"Name's Dana Greer. I'm here…."

Moving toward the exit with a too quick smile, the priest said, "I know. Father Merton told me about you. Be sure to let me know if I can help." With that, he turned around, ready to leave the chapel by the side door.

"Father," I'd like to speak with you."

He peered over his shoulder. "Perhaps, some other time you could. You know I live down the street with my ailing mother...in the peach-colored house."

"No, I didn't know that." Dana had never heard of a priest living anywhere other than a rectory.

In a nonchalant voice, he replied, "My mother suffered a stroke and is paralyzed."

"Sorry to hear that. Certainly, I wouldn't want to bother you at your home. Is there somewhere else we might meet?"

The priest turned and stared blankly at Dana. "I'm leading the sisters on a Lenten retreat next week. I've got to prepare for that." In an irritated voice, he said, " Now, if you'll excuse me...."

More than the excuses, there was something about the man's demeanor that spoke of a "leave me alone" attitude. Dana hoped she hadn't overstepped her boundaries, but quickly realized it was not her request, but the shortness of the priest's remarks that came across offsetting...almost rude.

"If you should find the time to speak with me, could you let Mother Anne Baptiste know? I'm staying here at the convent while I conduct my case."

Father Bennett's eyes squinted. His jaw tightened. "So, I've heard."

Father Merton must be told about this man's arrogant attitude, Dana thought.

*

Dana headed toward the parlor, where she hoped to make a to-do list, something of a habit with her, offering some direction. Murder cases tended to be complex. When she stepped into the room, darkened by the closed, heavy drapery, she saw a woman positioning a vase filled with fresh red roses and baby's breath.

The woman came up to Dana. "Hello. The name's Betty Carmichael. I own the *Buds and Blossoms Floral Shop* in town. It's the light blue house. The shop's downstairs, and the boys and I live upstairs."

"The boys?" Dana asked.

The woman with the chubby face and heavily rouged cheeks stood there admiring her floral arrangement. "My sons, Jesse and Jimmy. The day God gave me those twins, he gave me triple the trouble, I always say. They're as different as night and day."

"Altar servers, correct?"

The woman's eyes opened widely. "Why, yes. Have you met them?"

"Not yet but I would like to." Dana intended to add these names to her soon to be written list.

"The one, Jimmy, is an all *A* student and wants to enter the seminary so badly."

"And, Jesse?"

"Jesse's a cat of a different color. You know I had to force him to get a job to keep up with his smoking habit. Can you believe a pack costs twenty-five cents? He works at the *Chilly Treats Soda Shop.*

Think he enjoys meeting the girls more than he does dishing out ice cream. I just pray he doesn't go ahead and get one of those pretty lasses pregnant."

Pregnant, Dana thought. Could it be Jesse who was involved with Sister Mary Margaret?

The woman chattered on, "You know Jesse was dating Sister Mary Margaret before Mother Superior saw to it that the girl entered the cloister...went out of her way to get permission from Rome."

Before Dana said anymore, Betty, clenched her teeth, and filled in the blanks. "Unfortunate as it is, you know there are those in Winter Willows who'd like to think *my* Jesse had something to do with the young nun's death. How dreadful an accusation, isn't it? It's even affected my sales at the shop."

"People can be mean, but why would they say such a thing?" Dana's mentor when she first got into investigative work, Fiona Wharton, used to say, "Don't be afraid to ask dumb questions. Just expect to learn more than you ever hoped for."

"They were dating off-and-on, but Cindy called it quits when Jesse asked her to go steady with him. He wanted her to be his girl, but no, no, she liked playing the field."

The woman's words echoed the exact sentiments of Father Merton. Sister Mary Margaret was far from innocent.

Dana could tell the woman realized she may have already offered too much to the conversation.

She ran her finger over one of the rose petals, then abruptly said, "Better be off. Nice meeting you."

When the woman left, Dana sat down on the floral couch and pulled her notebook out of her bag. She began to write:

- *Speak with Fr. Merton about the young priest's attitude.*
- *Try again to speak with Fr. Tan Bennett.*
- *Arrange to speak with Dr. Vincent.*
- *Speak with Betty's son, Jesse.*

Dana put her pen and paper away. About to leave the parlor, she took a quick whiff of the roses. No sooner had she turned than she caught a black shadow out of the corner of her eye. She rushed to the hall and saw the back of a large, broad-shouldered nun rushing through the corridor. Could it be the sister who spoke disgruntled of Sister Mary Margaret's admittance to the cloister?

Chapter Five

This time when Dana entered Father Merton's residence, Francine came running over to her, jumping on her legs. She picked up the dog and hugged him closely.

"Looks like we both made a friend," father said.

Dana handed the dark brown dog to the priest as he motioned for her to be seated.

"What brings you by, dear?"

"Why, I don't want to be perceived as a school-girl tattletale, but I met your associate after Mass the other day at the convent."

"And what do you have to say about the young man?"

Dana grabbed her lower lip before she spoke. "I found him to be quite short with me…rude actually and a bit arrogant, I might add."

"Wow! That's quite the list, but I will say, it doesn't surprise me much."

"Why's that?"

"With an archbishop for an uncle and in Rome no less, I'm afraid the poor boy's

head has gotten a bit too big."

Dana turned her neck sideways. "Are you saying these are the only reasons to rationalize his behavior?"

"Heavens no, Dana. He's also an only child, and the pride of his mother's heart. Worse part of it is he knows it."

"No matter then, but I would appreciate it if you might speak to him. I am here on behalf of the Church and should expect a level of respect."

"No doubt about it, dear. I'll address the matter with him at once."

"Thank you, Father."

"On a happier note, I have some good news for you. Henry stopped by and brought these." The priest put Francine down and walked over to his bookshelf. "The death certificates you were asking about." He handed the two copies to Dana.

SEATTLE HEALTH DEPARTMENT
SEATTLE, WASHINGTON

Certificate of Birth Resulting in Stillbirth
According to the records of the Seattle Health Department

Name Jewel Sullivan

Was delivered in Winter Willows, Washington on February 15, 1953

To Cynthia Sullivan

HEALTH OFFICER SIGNATURE *Henry Gilliam*   ISSUED March 1, 1953

Certificate of Death

CERTIFIED CERTIFICATE OF DEATH

I <u>Henry Gillion</u> County Coroner of <u>King</u> county, in the State of <u>Washington</u> hereby certify the death of <u>Cynthia Sullivan</u> DOB <u>April 6, 1940</u> Age <u>13 years</u>

Cause of Death <u>Accidental Fall</u>

Married ___ Single <u>X</u> Widowed ___ Divorced ___

Date of Death: <u>March 31, 1953</u>

Date Recorded: <u>April 10, 1953</u>

Document #: 483351520

Book and Page: G 1530 P 422

Application: DOA-4356

STATE
CERTIFIED

This is to certify that this document is a true abstract of death recorded and filed with the county.

Signature of County Coroner: *Henry Gillion*

Print Name: <u>Henry Gillion</u>

Witness Signature: *Ned Vincent, MD*

Date: <u>April 9, 1953</u>

"Looks authentic enough."

"What's that supposed to mean?"

"I still plan to determine if the child sister delivered was a stillborn, or was she born alive?"

"What are your thoughts about sister's death certificate? It verifies what Henry said about her death being an accident."

"I see Ned Vincent is the witness on the document."

"Henry and he are the best of friends," father said. "Furthermore, why would he not be? Doctor Vincent is the only doctor on the island."

Dana mumbled under her breath, "For sure, I'll be paying *him* a visit."

Chapter Six

Dana waited in the vestibule of Grotto of Lourdes Church until the eight a.m. Mass was over. After the final hymn was sung, she walked toward the side door that led into the sacristy. Within minutes, she spotted the young priest already changed into layn's clothing. He straightened a wrinkle in the collar of his blue shirt as he made his way out. Dana thought it odd that the man did not wear his black cassock but, rather, chose to dress as any other man might.

Nonchalantly, he passed right by Dana, again appearing to be in a hurry.

"Father, please wait," Dana called out.

He stopped walking and turned abruptly toward her. "Oh, so it's you."

"Yes, the name's Dana Greer."

Squinting and with a hard smile, he said, "Ah, yes, the interloper."

"Pardon me."

"Father Merton tells me you've been reporting me."

"So, I have. I've come to solve a case, hired by the archbishop, not to be treated as an interference."

The priest laughed loudly. "Then, do what you've been called to do as will I. I don't have time for investigations, plain and simple. Let me be the priest, and you go ask your questions elsewhere."

"I'm afraid it's not all that simple, Father. Everyone who knew Sister Mary Margaret must be interrogated."

"Well, if I were you lady—."

"Dana's the name."

"If I were you Dana, I'd talk with Henry Gillion, the coroner."

"Already have."

"And, let me guess. He claims Sister Mary Margaret was in the cemetery after dusk and accidentally fell into an open grave site. If you ask me, that's a problem for Charles Filmore. The old duke never should have left the grave without covering it up. More-and-more, it's my opinion, the old cuss should lose his job...should have been fired on the spot."

Dana crossed her arms. She found it difficult to believe the priest would be speaking so disrespectfully. His critical attitude put her in defense mode. "The issue here is not Charles Filmore; it is Sister Mary Margaret."

With a shake of his head, his tousled hair falling across his forehead, he said, "I have a question for you, *Dana*. Why don't you believe what you've been told?"

"Not all that simple, Father. I hardly doubt I'd be brought out here by the Church

to investigate this happening if there weren't some question as to how sister's life ended."

"Have it your way, lady. All I ask is that you leave me out of it and, I might add, Father Merton. He's not my father and has no right reprimanding me!"

"Then, let me ask you one last question."

He threw his arms outward. "Go for it."

Dana reached into her bag and pulled out the sharp-edged piece of concrete. "Think this might be capable of murder?"

A red blush worked its way up the priest's neck and covered his face and the tips of his ears. "What the hell is that? You want to be arrested for carrying a concealed weapon?"

"That's exactly what I wanted to hear, Father. Let's talk again soon, shall we?"

*

"Tan, Tanner?" the woman's voice echoed from her wheelchair as the rubber tires rolled along the wooden floor. Her cigarette was a mere nub.

"Yes, Mother, I'm coming." The old bitch. He set his pen down, his final plans for the nun's retreat not quite finished. He adjusted the violet stole around his neck. "Running late, Mother, for Mass. Don't want to keep the sisters waiting."

"But my coffee...have you made any? I haven't had my coffee this morning...black with two lumps of sugar."

The young priest scowled at his ailing mother. How he wished she would have just died that day they had the argument in the kitchen.

He had been about seventeen years old and needed the keys to her car that night. He had plans to ask Mary Lou to the senior prom. They were going to meet at the *Chilly Treats Soda Shop*. She loved the shiny, red T-bird with its purring engine and the speed of a cheetah. With the top down, she liked the feeling of the wind rustling through her long, blond curls.

He and Mary Lou had made out in the back seat of his mother's car on more than one occasion. Once she agreed to be his date to the final dance of the school year, the two would go from there. But that day, his mother, who he saw as an ornery cuss, refused him. What right did she have? He was her only child and the nephew of an archbishop in Rome. It was the least she could do for him.

Furthermore, she had won the car as a prize at the Church Bingo night. The Knights of Columbus had raffled off tickets for a month prior. Who would have guessed, he thought, that the homely, old bag widowed for years would have been the recipient? She never went anywhere just sat in her bedroom, watching the Fulton J. Sheen show or saying her rosary. He had every right to use the car whenever he felt, but mother didn't quite feel the same way.

On that night, she outright refused for no legitimate reason other than to be obstinate. The two got into a loud screaming match, neither hearing the other's voice. In a moment of heated anger, he grabbed his mother by the shoulders and shoved her down the basement steps. As she lay there on the dark concrete, crying for help, he found the keys in her purse and left. Later that night, in a much better mood, he returned home and called Doctor Ned Vincent. He told the doctor his mother had passed out, probably from a stroke, and tumbled down the stairs.

No one questioned him since that day. All in Winter Willows who knew him and his mother bought the story, and when he returned from the seminary, he let the caregiver go and said he would, from that day forward, take care of her himself. Of course, those in the small town saw this as an act of unconditional love, but Tanner saw it quite differently. His resentment grew with each day that passed. She was nothing more than an albatross around his neck: a sickening, decaying old woman who he secretly wished would die sooner rather than later.

"Tanner," the woman called out again, "My coffee...where's my coffee?"

The priest slammed the door and raced toward the Carmelite chapel.

*

Dana rang the bell to Father Merton's residence.

The priest gave her a hug. "Spoken to Tanner recently? I set him straight on how he should talk to a lady and, especially, one who is here to help." Continuing on, without waiting for Dana's reply, he said, "Adjusting to his life as a priest has been a challenge for him. Think he expected to rise higher in the ranks after the seminary and, especially, with the clout of his uncle being an archbishop in Rome. He's a bit disgruntled; that's all. Give him time, Dana."

"I hope you're right, Father. In the meantime, I was hoping to pay Doctor Vincent a visit. Might you know his address?"

Father's eyebrows rose. "Sorry about that, but the doctor is not part of the parish, Dana. He's an atheist and pretty much chooses to stay away from 'us' Catholics. I'll tell you who could help you, though."

"Who?"

"Dorothy Bennett, Father Tanner's mother, sees the doctor weekly. Or, should I say he sees Dorothy weekly. Ever since the accident resulting in her stroke, she landed in a wheelchair. Doctor checks in on her. Might ask her."

Interesting, Dana thought, Father Merton believes the story of the stroke. Wonder just how well he knows his associate, Father Tanner.

"Thank you, Father. I'll see Dorothy first thing tomorrow."

Chapter Seven

Dana put on a blue floral dress with capped sleeves. She left the convent by the side door and made her way toward the Tanner house, only blocks from the convent. The pastel homes, like candles on a birthday cake, lined the main street after all the touristy shops. Dana wished she had put on one of her long-sleeved sweaters. The wind blew hard as she held the soft folds of her dress from blowing upward. She passed a pink house, a lime-green, a soft yellow before she saw the peach-colored.

Dana walked up the twisting sidewalk lined with pebbled stones. For some reason, Dana felt uneasy meandering up to the peach-colored house. Maybe, she should have spoken with Father Tanner before arriving on the doorstep of his house. But his aloof attitude made her realize he was not interested in getting too close to her. He had, however, told her where he lived. She could hear the doorbell ring once, twice, three times. About ready to turn away, she heard some rumbles coming from inside. She waited a moment when the door opened a slight crack.

Mrs. Tanner peeked out. Her hair was set in bristly, red rollers partially covered by a pink cap with laced edges. She wore a rounded pair of glasses with faux diamond trim. "Yes?"

"Hello, Mrs. Tanner. The name's Dana Greer. I'm a private—."

"Yes, yes," she said. "I've heard about you from my son. Here to find out what happened to the pretty postulant Sister Mary Margaret."

"Right you are. Hope I'm not disturbing you."

"I'm always ready for company." By the sound of her voice, Dana sensed loneliness, isolation, despair. Wrapped in the folds of her hands were crystal rosary beads. "Can't make it to Church anymore unless someone takes me," she apologized, "so I do the best I can." She looked down at her fingers, stained yellow.

"Sorry if I interrupted your prayers."

"Not at all. I'd much rather speak to a real person than to God any day."

The two women laughed.

"What brings you by today, honey?"

Dana explained that as a private investigator, her job, for the most part, consisted of asking questions and piecing together the answers. By the look on the woman's face, Dana could tell she understood and was ready to help.

Mrs. Tanner explained how Doctor Vincent made a house call each week to check on her and to help her with her bed sores. "Doctor cleans and puts fresh dressings on them as needed. You know, it's no fun living your life in a chair."

Dana could feel the woman's sadness. "It must be difficult."

Dana's words must have served as a segue to the woman's inner thoughts. "Ever since I fell down the basement steps, my life's been a sacrifice offered for the sins of the world."

Dana had not heard that expression since she was in elementary school. The nuns had a way of shoving aside anything bad that happened. "Offer it for the souls of the sinner," they would encourage us.

"You say you fell down the basement stairs?"

Dorothy gazed ahead as if reliving that day in her mind. "Oh, that's when Tanner was still in high school. We got in a little squabble. One of those teenage disagreements, you know. Afraid I was too near the open door leading to the basement. I lost my balance and down I went."

The thought kept crossing Dana's mind. If that's what actually happened, why did Tanner say the woman had had a stroke...why not the truth? Dana had been in the business long enough to know something didn't smell right in Denmark. Could it be that Tanner had such a mean streak that he pushed his mother down the stairs? Something between mother and son's story didn't add up, and Dana knew it.

"It wasn't long after that my son went away to the seminary in Rome." Dorothy pulled a match and cigarette from the pocket of her housedress. "My weakness in life," she said. She lit a king-sized cigarette and continued, "Norman pulled that one off." She squinted and blew a string of smoke out of her mouth.

"Norman?"

She took another puff on her cigarette. "Norman wanted Tanner to attend the same seminary as he had. Norman's got connections with Rome...the Curia and all." Dorothy willingly spoke, filling Dana in on informative and interesting facts.

"Your son and his uncle's priestly studies sound impressive. I'd love to hear more, but I must run. I do have one question, though."

"Certainly, dear. I tend to get a bit long-winded."

Dana smiled. "By chance, do you happen to know Doctor Vincent's address?"

"Doctor Vincent, why of course. The man needed to move to the country. Seemed wherever he went around here, people bombarded him with medical questions. If it wasn't a gall bladder, then it was their backaches. Once someone even asked him a question about his private parts. Can you believe that?" She pressed what remained of her cigarette into an amber ashtray. "Doctor Vincent's address...he upped and took his wife Martha to Twin Pines."

"Twin Pines?"

"It's only a couple miles away, out in the country." In the same breath, she continued, "Martha is what you might call an *odd duck*. Keeps to herself, not interested in socializing. Well, I've never met the woman, but that's what I've been told."

"Their house in Twin Pines...?"

"Ah, yes, you won't need an address. I hear the doctor lives in a large, grey Victorian with purple trim...the only one like it in Twin Pines." Mrs. Tanner wheeled herself down the slate hall toward the back of the house. "Let me call you a cab."

"How kind of you. And, oh by the way, if there's anything I can do to help you please call for me at the convent. Please...I'm serious."

A small tear formed in the corner of the woman's eye. "I'll do that, dear. I will."

*

Dana felt silly after the cab left her off. It was a short drive. In front of One Hundred Evergreen Drive, a black wrought iron fence surrounded a three-story mansion surrounded by ruby red rhododendrons and blue lilacs. The front gate to the property open, Dana made her way up the slate stones to the front door, painted a shiny purple. About to turn away after ringing the bell three times, Dana stopped when a woman attired in a drop-waist dress with ruffled sleeves appeared.

"Yes?"

Dana introduced herself and asked whether the doctor was home. She could hear men's voices from the rear of the house. They were shouting and laughing.

The woman grabbed on the doorframe, her knuckles turning white. "My name's Gertrude…Armstrong. She invited Dana into the foyer where a tall grandfather clock chimed three o'clock with heavy gongs. "Please wait here while I call for the doctor."

A man who looked to be in his mid-forties with a lit cigar in his mouth came from the back of the house.

"Hey, Ned, hurry up. The game can't go on without you."

"Who have we here?" he asked.

Dana could smell a scent of whiskey from the man's breath.

He was dressed casually in a yellow sweater vest and pair of trousers with a sharp crease.

Dana offered her hand to the man. "Pleased to meet you, Doctor. My name's Dana Greer."

Without having to explain her role, he answered, "Ah, yes. I heard you've come to investigate the death of one of the sisters. Please, come in and meet my friends."

The two walked down a long hall and entered a smoky room with a large round game table in the center. Seated around it were three men...one, of whom, was Henry Gillion.

"Tonight's my poker night, Miss Greer. He introduced her to two of the men, and when he was about to introduce Henry, Dana said, "We've already met."

Henry clasped his chin and tapped his lips with his finger. "Let's all give a toast to Miss Greer, why don't we?" Henry went back to the table and picked up a glass of what looked to be gin. The men all raised their glasses and, in unison, said, "Welcome."

The heavy smoke of the men's cigarettes and cigars caused Dana to move toward the door. By their boisterous behavior, Dana could tell they were a bit intoxicated, and obviously, tonight would not be the night to question the doctor about Sister Mary Margaret's birth.

"I'd better be going. Nice meeting all of you," she said, at the same moment as Gertrude came to the door of the game room.

Dana's sixth sense told her something was wrong, definitely wrong, and she intended to find out what.

*

After the evening meal, Dana stopped to speak with Mother. "Might you have a

moment to talk, Mother?"

"Yes, my child, follow me."

Dana and the nun walked down the dimly lit hallway.

Mother motioned for Dana to be seated. She turned on a torchiere lamp in the corner and another lamp on her desk.

"I have some questions, personal ones, about Sister Mary Margaret. Father

Merton explained that the girl liked boys, and it sounds as if she was difficult to place with a family in the parish, correct?"

"Yes, Dana. You are right. After our sisters gained permission from Rome to let the girl enter our order at the young age of thirteen, I felt our problem was solved. Of course, that was not the case. Not until later did sister confess to being with child."

Dana ran her hand across her cheek, pushing her blond curls behind her ear. She bit down hard on her lip before she spoke, "The father? Does anyone have knowledge of who the father of the child was? Was he informed?"

"Good questions, Miss Greer, but you see, Sister Mary Margaret had many boyfriends. Your guess would be as good as ours, I'm afraid."

"I'm left wondering. Might it be possible that the father of the child is the one she was seeing the night of her death? Could it have been he who ended the young postulant's life?" Fiona Wharton had taught Dana to never rule out leads too soon.

Mother thought for a moment. "Possibly, except it is interesting that whoever killed sister waited until after she delivered her child. One would think if he were wanting to hide his deed that he would have done away with sister long before now."

"True, Mother."

"Is there anything else I can help you with?" Sister clasped her hands on her desk.

"Forgive me for my boldness, but it doesn't sound as if sister was living a cloistered life while here? I mean—."

"I know quite well what you mean. Hardly! Many nights Sister Agnus Dei would find her sneaking in the back door. Sister is in charge of the postulants and the novices. Her hands are quite full. But mind you, try her best, Sister Agnus Dei couldn't curtail the likes of Sister Mary Margaret. You'd think being with child and all might have slowed her down some, but no, she was a difficult one to pull the reins in on."

"May I speak with Sister Agnus Dei?"

"I believe you already have. She reprimanded you at breakfast the other day while she was doing her reading."

Of course, Dana thought, the masculine appearing nun with the broad shoulders. "Should I take that as a *no*?"

Mother straightened the edges of her veil. "I'm not saying you can't, but you must understand sister has a rather harsh demeanor. She still carries remorse at not being assigned as Mother Superior of the Carmelites. And, I can understand that; she has been a part of the order for at least fifty years."

"Commendable...her service, I mean."

"She has a good soul but comes across like a barbed wire sometimes."

"I see."

"Let me speak with her first and see how willing she might be to discuss the murder case."

Dana let her thoughts run away from her. A woman who had no fondness for Sister Mary Margaret entering the order, plus being resentful over being snubbed by her order, might she have it within her to do away with the nun? "That's all I can ask, Mother. Oh, there is one other thing.... Any idea, at all, who sister might have been going to see on that fateful night?"

"Where would I begin, Dana? You might want to speak with Jesse Carmichael, Betty's son. Rumors have it that he might have had something to do with sister's demise. Forgive me, Lord, for my gossip." Mother's face reddened, and she stood. "I must be going to chapel."

"Certainly," Dana said. As she stood in the hallway watching the sisters walk in single file, some to their private cells, some to chapel, she saw the two, young postulants who had been seated with her at breakfast the other day.

One looked directly at her with a forced smile. At her side, she twirled the wooden rosary as if it were a child's yo-yo. She tossed her veiled head backward, a lock of black hair landing on her forehead. She swung her shoulders from side-to-side.

The postulant behind her grinned, showing her perfectly lined teeth. Wisps of blond hair escaped the edges of her veil. Quickly, she cast her face downward in accordance with the cloistered rules.

Dana felt confident these two could give her an earful about Sister Mary Margaret.

Chapter Eight

The aromas of mixed bouquets filled the *Buds and Blossoms Floral Shop*. Twirling like a kaleidoscope, the colors of the bouquets swirled and blended one into another.

"My, so good to see you again, Dana," Betty said, while she wrapped some floral tape around a group of stems. "In the market for some flowers?"

Dana shook her head. No, what she had in mind was something that was rotten in Denmark, as the paraphrased Shakespearean line from *Hamlet* read. Betty had admitted that her son, Jesse, was under the suspicious eye of the island folks. Now, it would be Dana's job to determine if the boy was as innocent as his mother had said. A high school student, a black leather jacket, and a pack of Lucky Strikes were all she had to go on.

"I've wondered if I might speak with your son, Betty? Keep in mind, of course, that I am only gathering background information at this point, certainly, not making any accusations."

Betty set the flowers down and caught a crystal vase just as it was about to fall from the counter. She squinted, her brows lowering. "You first must know that there are those busy bodies who have nothing else to do with their time other than to fathom gossip and rumors. "Yes, I remember you telling me that."

Betty twisted the ties of her apron. "Well, then, if you can speak to my boy without any preconceived ideas, I guess, there's no reason to say no. Jesse is upstairs, listening to one of those worthless game shows.... 'What's My Line?' I think."

Dana could hear the blaring voices of Dorothy Kilgallen and Steve Allen as she made her way up the narrow steps of the flat above the floral shop. "Jesse?" she called.

A boy in jeans and a shirt picturing the planet Mars shut off the Philco radio. "Who are you?" he asked, his lips forming a snarl.

"Sorry. I should have introduced myself. Name's Dana Greer. I'm a private investigator living with the sisters while trying to solve Sister Mary Margaret's murder."

"Why are you here?" he asked. If sarcasm could throw a punch, Dana would have had a black eye.

"I'm planning on speaking to anyone who knew the young girl. May I have a seat?"

Jesse pointed toward a vinyl couch with cotton stuffing sticking out of several cracks. He continued to stand.

"I see you're an altar server."

"No choice of mine," he said. "Talk to my old lady about that decision. See, her favorite son, Jimmy, wants to become a priest one day. Before I knew it, she had signed us both up to serve Mass with Father Merton and now the new guy. He's a pretty cool cat."

"So, it seems," Dana answered, though remembering his previous shortness with her the other day.

"How well did you know Sister…Mary Margaret?"

The tough looking boy pulled out a cigarette from his jean pocket. He lit it from a book of matches he found on the scratched coffee table. "You mean Cindy?" He took a long drag on the Lucky Strike.

"I didn't know her name before entering the convent."

He smiled and cocked his chin upward. "Oh, my dear Cindy." When he lowered his jaw and looked into Dana's eyes, his twinkled. "She was the most popular girl in the eighth-grade class. There wasn't a boy dumb enough not to take her out. They went ape over her!"

"So, you were not her only friend?" Dana played the innocent perspective. "She liked to date?"

Jesse laughed and blew a ring of smoke. "You might say that, lady. Back seat bingo wasn't her only game."

"Promiscuous, then?"

"No, she wasn't a show-off."

"So, a hot number?" Dana asked, in Jesse's lingo to be sure he understood.

"Kidding me? With a sweet little ass like she had. And those jugs that shook like two ripe melons?" Jesse shoved his cigarette butt into a glass vase on the table.

Dana could feel her face flush. It was more than what Jesse was saying; it was the way he said it. She knew he was deliberately trying to make her uncomfortable. "But she entered the convent?"

"Yeah, man, such a shame! All because her old lady went to the looney bin."

"The St. Dymphna's home?"

"Some nut factory. With ten kids and no old man or lady, the Mother Superior and Father Merton went around asking who would want the job of raising one or two. Some say Father Bennett's connection with his archbishop uncle got the nun's permission to take Cindy. A sure shame, it was."

"Meaning?"

"Cindy got a bit too carried away one night and got herself a little bun in her oven."

"Sounds as if that wasn't planned."

"No, but once Cindy found out, she wanted nothing more than to be a mother."

"Did she know who the father of the child was?"His eyes focused on the brown shag carpeting. "She never did tell."

"Jesse, I don't know how better to say this, but was it you? Were you the father of Cindy's stillborn baby?"

Jesse pounded his fist into the palm of his hand. His voice loud enough to be a shout said, "God damn, you lady! You come here to accuse me. Guess, you've heard the rumors. Well, let me make something perfectly clear, private investigator. I didn't have anything to do with her murder. Why would I…I mean, I loved her."

"Sorry to sound accusatory, Jesse, but it is my job." Dana could feel her face tighten. "Do you think the person who murdered Cindy might have been the father? You know, wanting to do away with the evidence, so to speak?"

Jesse looked serious. "Why, that couldn't be? Her baby was born dead a week before the ol' grave digger found her body."

"Dead?" Dana pretended this was the first time she had heard this.

"Yeah, dead."

"A stillborn. How did you learn this?"

Jesse pulled a comb, missing some teeth, from his jeans and proceeded to run it through his greasy, black hair. "My old lady…she asked the sisters whether Cindy had a boy or a girl. Most everyone knew about her expectin' and all. Maw wanted to send flowers if you can believe. She's a good one for stickin' her nose where it doesn't belong."

"And?"

"Mother Superior told her the doctor said the baby was born dead."

"How awful."

"Guess, yeah."

Dana had learned so much about the young nun, but she still had an unanswered question. "Jesse? Where were you on the night Sister Mary Margaret died?"

"Me? Well, I was out with a bunch of the guys. We were burning rubber on Main Street like we do on every Saturday night."

Just as Jesse was about to light up another cigarette, Dana said, "I have one last question, Jesse. You said earlier there wasn't a boy who didn't want to take Cindy out. Might you have some names for me?"

"Don't get me in the middle of this shit. Why don't you talk to Brownell."

"Brownell?""The eighth-grade teacher."

"Thank you, Jesse, I'll do that." She headed toward the door of the boy's room as he turned on the radio to "Amos 'n' Andy," plopped down on one of the armchairs, propped up his legs on the coffee table, and stared at her with a chilling smile.

Chapter Nine

Dana found herself standing on the steps of Winter Willows's School. A bronze dedication cornerstone read 1893. The school looked every bit its age with a crumbling brick exterior, but its size was what impressed Dana. The building, a two story, looked to have no more than eight classrooms at most, but then again, Winter Willows, from what she had learned, had a mere population of 2,102.

The scents of lead pencils and loose-leaf paper greeted her as she opened the front door. The office door, immediately to her left, open, Dana stepped inside. "I'd like to see a Mr. Brownell," she said to a woman whose glasses slipped down her nose. She peered over them. "He is in room 106 down the hall on the right."

Dana found the man seated behind his desk, a stack of papers in front of him. "Dana Greer, right? The poker night…Ned introduced you." He stood.

Surprised, Dana said, "Ah, yes, you're right. We met the other night at Doctor Vincent's house."

"See you play with Henry Gillion, too."

"Oh, yeah, friends for years. Gene Willard is the other guy. He lives next door to me. But how do you know Henry and the doctor?"

Fiona had warned her not to answer unnecessary questions while the case was still under investigation, so that's how she responded. She said nothing.

"Of course, of course. Didn't mean to pry. Why don't you have a seat?" He invited her to sit in one of the student desks, an inkwell stained blue-green and the initials *BP loves* AK ground into the blond wood.

"'Bout time we ordered some new furniture." He sat on top of one of the student's desks. "You're here to learn more about Cindy Sullivan, I hear."

Dana dived in with her answer, "Yes, Sister Mary Margaret. Well, I've been told the girl was quite popular."

He laughed. "That's putting it mildly. You know eighth-grade boys. Their hormones work overtime, and Cindy didn't help matters."

"How so?" Dana figured she knew the answer, but Fiona had always warned her it was better to appear ignorant…at least from the start.

"The class is quite small…four girls and five boys. That's before her untimely death."

"Mr. Brownell, how well would you say these boys knew Cindy?"

"Well! Very well! Don't know how better to put this, Miss Greer, as to not offend you, but Cindy was a big-time player with all of them. She liked to play one boy against another, make them jealous."

"Was there any one boy in particular?"

He scratched his head. "No…I'm talking about all five. She dated a Jesse Carmichael for a time, but she refused to go steady with any one boy. Liked to play the field."

"Do you think any one of them might have wanted her dead?"

"Once he learned she was with child? Quite possibly. Every boy vied for her solo attention."

Dana was getting exhausted with the teacher's back-and-forth response. She would have to get him to be more direct. "Mr. Brownell, which of these boys do you think might be the father of the child?"

The man's face turned red. "Why, definitely Gordie Mansfield. All the girls liked Gordie. He and Cindy were an item for quite some time, but of course, Cindy two-timed. They went steady for at least five or six months."

"How might I arrange to speak with the boy?"

The man ran his fingers along his stiffly starched collar and loosened his paisley tie. "Afraid that won't be possible. The boy died in a motorcycle accident in Seattle two months ago."

"I see. Sorry to hear that." Dana could hear the defeat in her own voice. That left four boys, though, who might know something. "Could I have the names of the other boys in the eighth-grade class?"

"If it'll help any, I could arrange to have the boys meet you here after class tomorrow…if they'd be willing."

Finally, Dana's spirits picked up. Her work was cut out for her but maybe, just maybe, she might have found a lead.

*

Dana could smell the aroma of mashed potatoes and pot roast. Almost six o'clock, she entered the refectory and took a seat near the podium at the front of the room. Sister Agnus Dei had the Bible opened. She tapped her fingers along the gold-edged pages. Besides the clamoring of dishes, the room remained silent. Some of the sisters were fingering their rosary beads, obviously praying, while others sat with bowed heads. Such disciplined women, Dana thought.

Everyone directed their attention to Sister Agnus Dei. In a gruff voice, she said, "Sisters, let us begin." The elderly nun pounded on the lectern. "Let us begin." She said a short blessing for the meal then began to read from St. Paul's letter to the Philippians. When done, she closed her Bible with a thump and ambled toward where Dana sat. She lowered herself towards Dana's ear as if just passing by and whispered, "This is no place for you!" Before Dana could respond, the nun exited the dining hall.

The nun was telling her to leave but why? What was it that Sister Agnus Dei had against her? Was it a warning or a threat? And no matter what, Dana doubted Mother Superior would be able to arrange for her to have a conversation with the nun.

*

That night seated at her desk, Dana hoped to clear her mind by jotting down all the people she had met since coming to Winter Willows. Of these, she asked herself, who might have wanted Sister Mary Margaret dead? The only suspects so far were Sister Agnus Dei, who bore some agitation that Cindy Sullivan had even been admitted to the order, and Jesse Carmichael, the tough appearing guy on the surface who, obviously, had been hurt by Cindy's break-up with him. Not much to go on. Dana turned the lamp off and slipped into bed, only a sliver of light shone from under her door.

That's when she noticed a slip of paper being shoved into her room from the outer corridor. She jumped up and ran to the door, unlocking it. Shocked, her hand reached for her chest. The young postulant, the one with the black hair who treated her rosary as if it was a toy, stood in front of her.

In hardly an audible whisper, the girl said, "Sorry to have startled you. My name is Sister Magdalene." The woman bent down and placed the paper in Dana's hands. "This is a photograph of Sister Mary Margaret. The order does not allow such things, but this was taken on the first day she arrived."

Dana stared at the picture of the young girl, and for several moments could not take her eyes off it. Seated on a stone bench, near the cemetery grotto, the nun sat staring as if into the face of God himself. The glow from her white habit contrasted with her dark brows and eyes. Strands of black hair peeked out of her head covering. The look of an angel innocent and pure, yet in some way a resentful expression, maybe even that of bitter wrath. Dana glanced aside. "Might I ask why you've chosen to give me this?"

"Only if you come to understand who Sister Mary Margaret was will you be able to learn who might have wanted her dead." The nun bowed her veiled head, turned, and before Dana could reply, the sound of the postulant's habit swished along the marble floor, hurrying down the candle-lit hall.

The message kept ringing in Dana's ears, making it difficult to sleep. Who was Sister Mary Margaret, known as Cindy Sullivan, before her entrance into the cloister? And, who could possibly have wanted her dead?

Chapter Ten

An unusual chill pierced the afternoon air. The elm trees swayed. The dramatic change in temperature signaled a possible storm blowing in. Even the sound of the nearby bay roared loudly. Along the bank, in the tall grass, sat Henry, his arms around Gertrude, who shivered from the cold.

"Must you leave, darling, on the evening ferry? Seems we hardly see each other."

"We will one day, dear. I'll swoop you up and carry you away on my white horse."

Gertrude laughed like a silly schoolgirl. "Oh, Henry, that's what I most admire about you…your boy-like sense of humor. It's so endearing."

"Hmm, that's interesting. The poker guys say they most like my foul mouth."

The two laughed.

Henry squeezed Gertrude tightly and kissed her.

"If it weren't for Ned, we never would have met, my love. We owe him a bundle," Henry said.

"And likewise," Gertrude said.

The two laughed in unison.

Henry began to stand. "I'd better get over to the ferry, Gertrude, or I'll be forced to stay the night."

"And?" Gertrude looked up at Henry with her twinkling blue eyes. Her arms outstretched in an attempt to hold him back.

"I know what you're thinking....What's so bad about that?" Henry asked.

"You amazing mind reader. You have so many talents: coroner, poker player—."

Henry put up the palms of his hands. "Better stop there. I would'nt want anyone overhearing us."

"You're right, love. That's our little secret."

Henry helped Gertrude to her feet. "One of our secrets," he said.

The two embraced, smothering their faces in quick, little kisses.

Chapter Eleven

Dana climbed the concrete steps of Winter Willows's High, anxious to see what she could learn from the peers of Sister Mary Margaret.

Mr. Brownell met her outside of his office. "Pleased to see you again, Miss Greer. The boys are waiting in the secretary, Sharon's office. Feel free to take the boys one by one into the school office as you wish." He left before Dana could say anything.

She viewed the four students sitting in a line. They looked young and similar with buzzed haircuts; acned faces; and pressed school uniforms, complete with bow ties. "Hello, I'm Dana Greer."

"Michael, why don't you go with Miss Greer first," Sharon said, not looking at or addressing Dana. The woman continued typing, watching her hot-pink nails tap on her manual Royal.

The boy stepped into the room and slumped into a soft chair; many sizes too large for his small frame. His scowl spoke of his disgust at being there.

"Hello, Michael. I'm here to learn more about one of your former classmates Cindy Sullivan. Did you know her well?"

The boy nodded with a fed-up look on his face. "She was in my class. I didn't have much to do with her. She was pretty and all."

"Did you ever go out with her?"

Michael threw his hands up. "Oh, no! My parents wouldn't allow that, not until I'm sixteen and can drive."

Dana smiled at the boy's odd logic. "So, you never dated her?"

"Nope."

"What about the other boys in your class? Any of them have a special liking for the girl?"

"Andy Cohan liked her, but his uncle would beat his ass if he even looked at a girl."

"I take it his uncle is raising him?"

"Yeah. Andy's parents killed each other when he was in first grade. Ever hear of the word *hara-kiri*?" Before Dana answered, the boy continued. "I never heard of it until the thing with Andy's parents happened."

"Oh, how terrible."

"It's common knowledge. Andy's uncle is pretty cool, though."

"What about the other two boys in the class?"

"Better you talk to Charlie and Raymond. I don't want to speak for them."

Dana felt she had what she needed from Michael and thanked him for his help.

Next, Andy came in and sat down. He rubbed his hands along the arms of the grey chair, already worn from probably similar behavior over the years.

Dana introduced herself. "Andy, I'm here to learn more about Cindy Sullivan."

Andy chomped on a piece of gum. He cleared his throat, somewhere between that of a child and a man, and said, "If you think I got anything to do with her dying, I don't."

"No, of course not. I'm wondering how well you knew her."

Andy chewed down on the inside of his cheek. "Barely. Oh, all of us boys thought she had a classy chassis. We were all ape over her. She was out of my league. Wanted to French me, and I had no idea what to do." The boy's face lit up like a red Christmas bulb."My uncle would just as soon kill me in cold blood than to know I even looked at a girl. No, ma'am, I wouldn't take that chance."

"So, you would say Cindy was too fast for you?"

Andy didn't hesitate to answer, "For sure, lady, for sure."

For some reason, Dana could tell Andy was telling the truth.

Charlie came in next. His shoulders slumped. He looked at the floor. Charlie admitted to dating Cindy Sullivan a few times.

"How serious were you about her?"

"None of your bee's wax. lady. Can I go?"

"I'd prefer you give me an answer."

"If you're that nosey, Cindy and I went all the way on September fourth…when we started seventh grade. Still got it marked on my old calendar. When I found out she was interested in older men, I dropped her like a hot potato."

Last to come in was Raymond. He was the tallest of the boys, lanky and thin. He wore glasses and appeared more scholarly than the others. "Listen, lady, I ain't got nothin' to hide. If you're wondering who killed Cindy, I'd talk to that dude Tanner."

Dana stopped writing in her notebook and stared at the boy. "Wait a minute. Do you mean Father Bennett?"

"Hell yeah. That guy had the hots for her."

"Why do you say that?"

"Saw the two of them out one night. Cindy was wearing jeans and a T-shirt that read: *Ready for Action.*"

Dana sensed she might be onto something. "Do you remember where you saw them? Was this before Cindy entered the convent?"

Charlie scratched at the side of his head. His fingers slid down to his cheek and landed on a pimple. "Think they were headed to the cinema. When? Right after Tanner got out of the seminary and moved in with his Maw."

"About when would that have been?"

Scratching at the inflamed pustule, he said, "Geez, a year ago."

Perfect, Dana thought. The timing could possibly be right. According to Mother Anne Baptiste, Sister Mary Margaret entered the convent when she was already two months pregnant.

*

For now, Dana figured, if only she could get Dorothy to speak about her son's relationship with the young nun, she might have a lead to go on. She felt uneasy meandering up to the peach-colored house, knowing full well that she intended to learn more from the woman who loved to talk. Father Tanner was definitely an arrogant brat, but there might be more to his aloof attitude. Was he hiding his guilt for being in a relationship with Cindy Sullivan? Dorothy might be just the conduit she was looking for, she thought.

She heard some rumbles coming from inside after she rang the bell. She waited a moment when the door opened a slight crack. Dorothy, her gray hair held in place by a tortoise headband, looked up from her chair. "What a pleasure seeing you again, Dana. Open the screen if you will."

Dana followed the wheelchair into the living room, where paperback books lay straddled everywhere. On the coffee table was a green glass ashtray filled with cigarette butts. When the woman put the brakes on her chair, Dana took a seat next to her.

Dana got right to the point. "How lucky you are to have a priest for a son."

"Hmm. Suppose so. Been in this here wheelchair for almost six years now. Don't know what I'd do without my boy. His uncle is an archbishop in Rome."

"Believe I heard this."

"Because of Norman, Tanner got permission to live with me, not in a rectory."

"And, Norman is your brother?"

The woman nodded.

Dana knew what she was about to say was a bit bold, but she decided to take her chances. "Your brother…was he also influential in getting Sister Mary Margaret into the convent at such a young age?"

Without hesitating, Dorothy said, "Absolutely. The Carmelite order would have no ability to change their admission requirement. You see, Norman is close to the Roman Curia."

"That makes sense." Dana paused for a moment. "Dorothy, if I might ask, were you and your son close to Sister Mary Margaret before she entered the postulancy?"

The woman's eyes focused on the worn blue carpet. She pulled out a pack of Camels and a matchbook from the side pocket of her housedress. After lighting the cigarette, she blew the smoke into circles, rising upward toward the ceiling. "My only pleasure, you see," she said, taking another drag on the cigarette.

Dana rephrased her question. "Sister Mary Margaret…was she known to your family?"

"I knew about the Sullivan's but not personally."

"What about your son?"

Dorothy continued puffing on her cigarette, staring ahead as if gathering her thoughts. "That child was precocious. She pushed herself on anyone who wore trousers."

Dana swallowed head. "Does that include Tanner?"

"Oh, Lordy, I pray to God, no. Tanner is devoted to the priesthood, Dana."

Either Dorothy had no idea of her son's doing, or she was covering for him. Then, again, Raymond, the Winter Willows's boy, spoke of an older man Cindy had left him for.

Dorothy said, "You might have heard the disgusting jingle the boys used to sing about her."

Dana shook her head.

"'Nobody can find a man quicker than Sullivan can.' It was dreadful. Her poor mother lost complete control of the girl, not to mention her mind, as well. After the birth of her last child, the Kitsap County folks came in, and she was committed to some insane asylum in Seattle. That's when the sisters stepped in and suggested the Church find homes for all ten of her children."

"And, they were successful?"

Dorothy nodded her head several times. "Oh, yes, except for Cindy. The girl's reputation scared everyone off. Finally, with the help of Norman, the sisters were able to accept Cindy into the order, provided that she not even go so far as to make temporary vows until the age of eighteen."

That's when Dana recalled the night Sister Magdalene had come to her cell with the photograph of Sister Mary Margaret. She remembered the smug look on the girl's face...an expression that spoke to an insincere, spoiled child. Dana did not want to read into things too much, but it was almost as if the girl thought she was getting away with something, pulling a fast one on the very nuns who gave her a roof over her head.

Dorothy snuffed her cigarette into the ashtray and blew one long blast of smoke. "You're living with the nuns. Have you met Sister Agnus Dei?"

The elderly nun with the broad shoulders...the one that suggested Dana not stay.... "Yes, I have." Dana figured Dorothy was anxious to tell her some more gossip.

"That one's got a bug up her butt about not being made Mother Superior. But, let me tell you, Sister Anne Baptiste was the right choice. She's such a lovely, caring young woman."

Dana rested her elbow on the arm of the chair. She knew she would be here for a while. She tried to redirect the conversation. "I've heard Sister Agnus Dei was against the young girl entering the convent."

Dorothy resettled herself in her wheelchair. She rubbed the palms of her hands on its metal arms. "I don't mean to be the one to spread gossip, but from what I've heard, Sister Agnus Dei wasn't always the perfect angel she likes to pretend. Heard she had quite the background as a young girl."

"Do you mind explaining?"

Dorothy lit up another cigarette and let it hang from her lip as she spoke, "When the woman was quite young, she was involved romantically with a priest of all things. The man forced her to do away with the child." The woman inhaled on the cigarette and exhaled a long, hard puff.

Dana was stunned by what she was hearing.

"Her father paid a dowry and forced her to the nunnery. Been there ever since."

As if speaking to herself, Dana said, "My gosh, it sounds like Sister Mary Margaret's story." But Dana knew, full well from

Raymond, that Tanner and the young girl had been seen socializing together.

Dorothy snuffed out her cigarette before finishing it and added it to the over-flowing ashtray.

Dana felt restless, uncomfortable. Without anticipating it, Father Tanner's mother had given her an earful about the elderly nun. The similarities of the two stories could be a mere coincidence, or on the other hand, it could point a light of suspicion on Sister Agnus Dei or Dorothy's own son.

"I'll be getting on, Dorothy, but I'm still at a loss as to how well your son might have known the young sister."

"When Tanner left for the seminary, Cindy was a mere nine years old...a child. You can understand why when he returned to Winter Willows, he hardly recognized the girl. I might add she was quite developed for her age. But, if you're implying he had a personal interest in the girl...no, why of course not. Tanner is a devoted priest."

Just as she thought, more than likely, Dorothy was doing what mothers do...protecting her son. The only way Dana could get some straight answers would be to talk to Tanner directly, and if he refused, she might have to get Archbishop Boretti involved. If Raymond, the eighth-grade boy, was telling the truth, Tanner did more than recognize Cindy when he returned to the island.

"I've enjoyed speaking with you, Dorothy, but I'd better be going."

The woman unlocked her chair and slowly began to wheel herself toward the front door, the wheels squeaking.

*

Father Tanner looked through the brass metal grille that divided him from the group of cloistered sisters. He attempted to wrap up the last sermon of his retreat while four sisters dimmed the candle lights in the chapel. He stared out as if looking into the bars of a jail cell, yet before him were the most holy and innocent women gathered in one place. Tanner never approved of the cloistered lifestyle even before he became a priest. He questioned why the sisters were forced to live under such austere conditions, and further, why one would even want to.

When hearing the young nun's confessions, usually the postulant's, he came to understand the way the girls dealt with the stringent modus vivendi. Late in the evenings after the final prayer hour and when most of the other nuns slept, the girls managed to leave the convent walls. They changed into lay street clothes and roamed the darkened streets of Winter Willows usually to meet with boys, friends, and strangers alike. On one hand, he offered them the forgiveness of reconciliation; on the other, he understood their need for escape so well, in fact, that it was on those very streets he often found himself chatting with the sisters and, sometimes, even bringing them wine to drink from Grotto of Lourdes Church.

He closed the retreat with a blessing upon the women and a simple message to live their lives in the shadow of the cross.

Chapter Twelve

Dana awoke with a mild tension headache, not like her periodic migraines that forced her to stay in bed until they passed. She had more questions than answers, but that was not a bad thing. It meant she had follow-ups…many to make.

Something about her visit with Dorothy yesterday still troubled her. Although the woman freely offered to provide inside secrets, such as the one about Sister Agnus Dei having been forced to the convent by her father after the abortion of her child, Dorothy never did answer the question as to how well her son knew the murdered nun. No, she quickly diverted the question to speak about Sister Agnus Dei. Was she deliberately avoiding Dana's question? And if the reason behind her being in a wheelchair was an accident, then why did Father Tanner say it was a stroke? With each unanswered question, Dana rubbed at the nodes in the back of her neck.

Then, there was the Winter Willows's schoolboy, Raymond, who was more than willing to admit that he had personally seen the young priest with Sister Mary Margaret. Why would Father Tanner show interest in an eighth-grade girl? Of course, just seeing the two together did not mean the priest and the girl were dating. But, then again, Raymond did say they were headed toward the movie theater. Fiona Wharton, Dana's former mentor, had always cautioned Dana not to jump to conclusions. It was a hazard of the profession.

Even after Dana showered and readied for breakfast, she found herself still lost in a myriad of thoughts as she made her way down the corridor to the refectory. Under one of the small alcoves featuring a statue of St. Rita, there stood a bud vase with a pink rose.

Although only one in number, the scent was strong and forced Dana to take a whiff. She wondered if Mrs. Carmichael saw to it that at least one of the miniature shrines was adorned with a flower each day.

The thought of Mrs. Carmichael made Dana recall what the woman had said. Seemed there were those in Winter Willows who thought the woman's son Jesse might have had something to do with the murder of the nun. After speaking with him, Dana reserved her conclusions. For sure, he presented as a tough type of thug, but then again, being a thug didn't necessarily qualify one for being a murderer.

Dana recalled her visit with Father Merton and Henry Gillion. Gillion remained insistent that Sister Mary Margaret had fallen to her death. The broken piece of mausoleum covered in dry blood that Charles Filmore had found could potentially be the weapon that someone used to bludgeon the girl from behind. The muddy tracks leading to the open grave were possibly made when the murderer dragged the body to the open gravesite. Although her theory held some weight, there were other unanswered questions. Why was the young girl killed in the cemetery rather than somewhere else? Why was she murdered approximately one week after the birth of her child, rather than once someone was privy to the news that she bore a child? And as for her child, believed to be stillborn, Dana felt uneasy accepting that as fact.

She felt light-headed, almost nauseous, when she felt a tap from behind.

"Dana," a slight whisper called to her. The postulant who presented Dana with the photograph of Sister Mary Margaret, the one acting immature in the hall the other day, stood next to her. Her hands hidden in the folds of her large, drooping white sleeves. She quickly glanced around, her eyes almost hawk-like. "I need to speak with you privately. I have some information that might be of help."

Dana could sense the woman's anxiety by the tone of her voice; after all, the cloistered women were only allowed to speak one hour per day. Who was to say what would happen if the sister was caught conversing in the corridor? "Surely. Where?"

"Meet me after breakfast. Cell #32."

Dana nodded. A sudden chill embraced her. Who could she trust? What if she were being invited to her own death? No one other than the postulant and Dana knew of the arrangement. Dana tried to shrug off the thought. Her over-working mind was making her get carried away with preposterous ideas.

Most of the seats in the dining hall were full, but Dana found one between two professed nuns wearing the complete habit. She smiled at the women as she attempted to politely squeeze in between the two nuns. Sister Seraphim, the young postulant with the blond hair, was serving this morning with another nun Dana had never seen before. Without even looking into the small bowls situated in front of each woman, the snap, crackle, crunch gave the secret ingredient away. Dana, as a child, enjoyed collecting the box tops to send away for all sorts of trinkets...her favorite being the rubber faced image of Snap on an adjustable ring.

Once all the cereal bowls were filled, an elderly nun stood at the lectern and led the meal prayer. Then, she began to read from Ephesians...something about putting on a suit of armor and carrying a sword. The idea of being dressed as if for battle appealed to Dana. Not knowing who the enemy was, Dana felt she always had to be prepared. Even in the presence of these holy women, Dana kept on guard with an unsettling aura about her. If there was even a mere chance that Sister Mary Margaret's murderer lived behind the convent walls, Dana needed to be vigilant.

After breakfast, the sisters gathered in single file much the way Dana remembered having done in Catholic elementary school. The only difference was when Dana was a child the boys and girls lined up in two separate rows and always by height, the smallest in front. With that arrangement, Dana found herself at the start of the line.

Letting the nuns exit the dining hall, Dana waited until the last sister left. When the main corridor emptied, Dana slipped out of the refectory and turned down the second hallway to the left. Small wooden numbers were attached to each door...the odds on one side, the evens on the other. She tapped gently on the door numbered thirty-two.

Sister Magdalene opened the door and invited Dana into the small space. She asked Dana to have a seat as the young postulant pulled the chair out from under her desk. Before she said a word, the nun opened the desk drawer and took out a cigarette and a match. "Care for one?"

Dana tried to hold back her shocked expression at seeing a cloistered nun smoking. She covered her mouth with the palm of her hand. "No, no thank you."

Sister Magdalene continued to puff on the cigarette, filling the tiny room with white smoke.

Dana refrained from her need to cough.

The sister's arrogant mannerisms and self-assured attitude excused her from exhibiting any guilt due to her behavior. A luxury cigarette dangled from her lips.

Finally, Dana broke the oddity of the situation by saying, "Sister, why did you ask me to stop by?"

"It's this," she said, showing Dana an envelope with the name Cindy Sullivan on the front. Sister Magdalene pulled it back when Dana attempted to reach for it.

Dana could feel her eyebrows raise as she repositioned herself closer to the nun. "What is this?"

"Andrew Cohan, a freshman at Winter Willows…he's my cousin. His uncle is raising him."

"Andy?" Dana recalled him as one of the boys she had met at the school the other day. "I remember him. I interviewed the freshman class of boys to see how well they knew Sister Mary Margaret."

Sister Magdalene took one long, last puff on her cigarette and snuffed it into a makeshift ashtray formed from a cardboard box. "You mean Cindy Sullivan?"

"Why, yes."

Dana decided to feign ignorance. It was an investigator's way of gathering unknown details. "I'm afraid I don't understand. Why did you invite me here?""

The postulant lit up another cigarette. "After Cindy's mother got sent away to the mental asylum, all of her children were split up among the parishioners. No one, and I mean no one, offered to take Cindy. Mother Superior felt sorry for the girl."

"Are you saying Mother Baptiste took Cindy in as a last resort?" Dana feigned her ignorance.

Rapidly inhaling and exhaling, Sister Magdalene's eyes narrowed. Her face spoke of bitterness, anger. "Are you suggesting I'm making all of this up, Dana?" The woman pulled her shoulders back and glared at Dana. "Well, are you?"

"No, no, of course not. It's just why would Mother go through all that trouble. Could she not have left the girl be a boarder here in the convent? Why make her part of the order…a postulant? Why the pretense of the habit?"

The nun pressed her cigarette butt into the other one. "It's simple. Cindy was, to put it bluntly, a tramp. Mother thought that in due time if she took the girl in as a postulant, she might begin to act the part." The nun laughed. "As if that sure helped!"

Dana remembered being told that the young nun still stole out of the convent, so she knew Sister Magdalene's account was accurate.

The nun slapped the envelope into Dana's hand. "Here. This is all you need to know."

Dana tried to settle her shaking hands. "Mind if I open it?" In the same breath, Dana asked, "What has this to do with Andy?""You'll see. He's the one who found it."

Dana began to read the contents:

> *My dearest Cindy~*
> *I understand you're upset at learning you are with child.*
> *I will do whatever is necessary to take care of the matter. Let me speak with my friend Dr. Vincent."*
> *My love goes with you,*
> *Tim*

"Tim?"

"Tim Brownell, the eighth-grade teacher."

"Are you inferring Cindy and the Mr. Brownell were—?"

"Lovers? Dana. Certainly, you saw what he wrote. Why think otherwise?"

"But the man must be old enough to be the girl's father."

"I hear you. But, as I said, Cindy was known to leave her mark around town. Winter Willows is a small island."

Dana was speechless.

"I know what you plan to ask next. How did Andy get the letter? He found it one day on the teacher's desk, mixed among some graded exams. When Mr. Brownell left the room, Andy was scouring around, trying to find out how he did on the test. That's when he came across the letter."

"Sister, do you have any thoughts as to who the murderer of the girl might be?"

"Why, no doubt, it was Tim Brownell. He saw to it that Cindy was bludgeoned to death, but before that, he saw to it that Cindy's child was taken by Doctor Vincent."

Dana could not believe how freely Sister Magdalene relayed the information. Dana did not even have to ask any questions. It was almost as if sister was hoping to clear her conscience in some way. "Sister, how do you know all this?"

"Well, it makes sense, doesn't it? Mr. Brownell convinces the doctor to do away with the child, saying it was stillborn. Mr. Brownell thought it'd be easier that way. Tell Cindy the child was born dead. As for poor Cindy, well the rest is history."

"And you're positive about this?"

"Well,…."

Dana moistened her lips, shaking her head. "I'm aghast. I don't quite know what to say."

The nun opened a small box on her desk marked: hazel rose and lit the small stump of incense. In no time, the room smelled like a fresh garden. "You mean, the case is solved. You should be happy. You can get away from this place."

Something about the nun's quick attempt to tie up all the loose ends bothered Dana. She didn't know what, but something about the story didn't make complete sense. For one thing, why wouldn't Sister Magdalene have gone to the authorities long before now with this news if she felt it to be the truth? No, Dana was not going to buy it...not yet anyway. She thanked the nun and stood up to leave.

"Oh, there's one more thing, Dana. There's only one ferry a day to the mainland."

Dana turned on her way out. "Thanks for the tip. I'll keep that in mind when I'm *ready* to leave. Oh, and by the way, that stick of incense sure does cover the smell of Lucky Strikes."

The nun shut the door to her cell with a bang.

Dana needed to confront Mr. Brownell about the letter to Cindy, but first, she would visit with Mother.

*

In order to be as discreet as possible, Dana wrote a small note to Mother Anne Baptiste and handed it to her during the afternoon session in the parlor.

Sister looked surprised to read the message but nodded in agreement that she would meet Dana in her office at once.

"Thank you, Sister, for letting me disrupt your recreation time, but something has come up that I need to address at once.

"Surely, my child. Whatever is it?"

Dana appreciated the nun's calm demeanor as she felt terribly anxious, not quite sure how to put her complex thoughts into words.

"Do you intend to speak, dear?"

"Oh, I'm sorry, Mother. I was trying to figure out how best to say this."

"Just let the Spirit guide you."

Dana explained how she had met with Sister Magdalene and the letter she had shown her from Mr. Brownell. "Could it be true? I mean, could Sister Mary Margaret have been romantically involved with the schoolteacher?"

"Tell me again, Dana, what the note said."

Dana paraphrased it as best she could. "I can see sister confiding in Mr. Brownell as a father figure. You understand, the girl had no male adult role model in her life."

"But—."

"But as to Mr. Brownell being involved in an inappropriate way with the girl, hardly not. Mr. Brownell has a lovely wife and two sweet boys. They live out in the country."

"Near Doctor Vincent?"

"Why, yes, quite near as a matter of fact. The two men have been friends for a long time. I can totally understand why Mr. Brownell would seek out the doctor's advice."

Dana ran her hand over the small Bible in her bag. "Mother, do you think Mr. Brownell might have been suggesting the doctor abort the girl's child?"

Mother Superior clutched the crucifix on the front of her habit. "Jesus, Mary, the baby was dead…stillborn…dreadful! That is what the doctor told me. I have no reason to think otherwise."

As far as Dana concluded, much of what Sister Magdalene had told her was far from the truth. "The letter, though, the letter.... it plainly said that Mr. Brownell planned to speak to the doctor about the child Sister Mary Margaret was about to deliver."

"That might well be, Dana. It was common knowledge that the child was to be raised with the sisters. Doctor Vincent knew this. When news reached us that the baby was not alive, well...."

"Mother, are you saying that everything Sister Magdalene told me was a lie? That there was no truth in any of it?"

"All of us, dear, are born with our crosses. For sister, hers is compulsive lying. If there is a drama to be weaved, leave it to sister." She paused. The afternoon sun shone through the stained-glass window, casting a small rainbow on Mother Superior's face. "Does this help to explain things, Dana?"

"Yes, Mother, it does. It does."

Mother stood up and clasped Dana's hand in hers. "God be with you, dear." She brushed the edge of her veil to the side. "One more thing, Dana."

"Yes?"

"I'm not trying to tell you how to do your job, however, I'd be a bit more discerning as to whom you question."

Perfect segue, Dana thought. "Mother, might you have Mr. Brownell's address?"

Sister opened her desk drawer and took out a small billfold. "Why, here it is Dana. One-Hundred Thirty Evergreen Drive. The family lives in Twin Pines."

Dana thanked the nun and went back to her room. The headache she had awoken with had turned into one of her migraines. She decided to rest.

Chapter Thirteen

The next morning, Dana awoke to the Latin songs familiar to her own upbringing in the Church: "Attende Domine" and "Stabat Mater." The sisters loud yet angelic voices were coming from the corridor. Strong male voices sang the recant. She opened her door a crack and watched as the nuns walked in single file, each carrying a small lit candle, as they made their way toward the chapel. At the rear of the procession, she saw Fathers Merton and Tanner dressed in deep purple robes. Dana reminded herself that today was Good Friday, one of the most solemn days of the Church. She could not believe it had slipped her mind. Engrossed in the complexity of solving the mystery, she had completely forgotten. Rather than work on the case, she decided to follow the procession to the chapel. Tonight, she would confront Tim Brownell with the letter Sister Magdalene had given her.

*

Dana wandered down Evergreen Drive, looking for Mr. Brownell's address. A block away from the doctor's house, Dana saw the brown shingled house with two red rhododendrons out front. As far as the rest of the homes she had seen in Twin Pines, Mr. Brownell's appeared more like a house and, certainly, not like a mansion. She rang the bell.

"Good evening, Dana. What a surprise! Come in, come in." He immediately began to apologize. "I know you'd think you're in Twin Pines, yet our house is about a fourth of the size of those around here. My wife Nora wanted to raise the boys outside the tourist area, and this was the best we could find."

"No need to explain. It's lovely."

As if the man never heard her, he continued. "Have a seat. Nothing fancy here. The wife and I can hardly afford furniture after what we paid for this little place."

The home was sparsely furnished from what Dana could tell. From what little she had seen of the neighborhood, it looked to be an elite society for those who preferred living in the country. "Sorry if I'm barging in on you." Dana could hear children yelling from the back of the house.

"Not at all. What causes you to stop by?" In another breath, he shouted over his shoulder, "Keep it down, kids." He focused again on Dana, "Boys will be boys, eh?"

Dana smiled. She sat down on a metal card-table chair next to a floor-to-ceiling stone fireplace. Dana was not sure how best to broach the subject of the letter the postulant had shown her. "Cindy Sullivan…could you tell me more about her."

Mr. Brownell sat across from Dana and put his elbows on the rickety card table separating them. It wobbled as he spoke. "Sure. You know, she was well acquainted with the boys, a difficult teen for her mother to manage. Some girls are just that way."

Dana nodded.

"The sisters were good enough to take her in when her mother could no longer care for her or her siblings." He paused. "Well, I'm sure you've heard all of this by now."

"So, I know." Dana waited a moment. "I'm interested in learning what you can tell me about the girl that isn't common knowledge."

"That's an odd question, isn't it? She was a student at Winter Willows like any child her age."

"How well did you know her.... I mean beyond just being a student?"

"Wait a minute, Dana! You're not going where I think you are."

"I've heard rumors; that's all."

The man's eyes widened; his face reddened. He pounded his fists on the table almost causing it to tip over. "Then, let's put an end to those right now, shall we?"

"I'm confused, Mr. Brownell. You must have heard some gossip that makes you so defensive. What *have* people been saying?"

"Small town, island mentality. One of the reasons why Nora and I moved out here. I'm sure you can understand. Why, there were those who said the girl and I were romantically involved. Have no idea how such a horrible rumor got started. I've been teaching at Winter Willows School for twelve years. I sure don't need gossip destroying my career."

"Gossip, you say?"

The man stood up and put his hands on his hips. "Preposterous! An outright lie. Why the girl was more than half my age; furthermore, I'm happily married."

Dana took a deep breath. Sharing Sister Magdalene's news would not be easy. "Mr. Brownell, how well do you know Doctor Vincent?"

"Geez, we're like brothers. We go boating together, play poker once a week….Why'd you ask?"

"Do you recall writing this letter?" Dana asked.

He opened the envelope. His face began to twitch; his hands started to shake. He gave the paper back to Dana. "What in the hell is this all about? 'My dearest, Cindy, my love goes with you.' Who gave you this?"

"I'd rather not say, Mr. Brownell. You seem surprised."

"Surprised? I'm damn shocked. What makes you think this would be from me?"

"Are you saying it's not?"

"Why, of course, I'm saying it's not." He pounded his fist on the card table, and it almost collapsed. "Cindy was one of my students…plain and simple. Is someone trying to set me up? Why? Money?"

"I don't have those answers as of yet."

"Someone is trying to make me out to be some kind of pervert! I suggest you get rid of this trash at once!"

"Is there a way you can prove this note did not come from you?"

The man jumped up and stormed out of the room. Within minutes, he came back and handed a sheet of paper to Dana. "Read this."

Dear Mother,
I hope you are feeling better since last I
wrote. I hope to pay you a visit in the near
future once school is out.

Dana handed the letter back to the teacher. "Well, it confirms the handwriting is definitely different."

"What's that supposed to mean?"

"Did you have any idea that Cindy Sullivan was pregnant while in the convent?"

"Never! I was happy she had found a good home; that much is true, being with the nuns and all."

"Did you learn that she delivered a week before her murder?"

"Murder? Henry said the girl had a terrible fall...fell into an open grave or some such thing."

"And you believe him?"

"Why would I not? We're good friends. Why would he lie to me?"

"And Doctor Vincent...did he ever share any news with you about Cindy?"

He pounded his fist again on the table. "Of course not. He took an oath. He wouldn't share any medical news with me."

"Knowing the island is only so big, you must have heard that the girl delivered her child a week before her death."

"Gossip? Rumors? Yes, scuttlebutt gets around on Winter Willows. Eventually, I heard the whole story. Most say Cindy's child was stillborn, and Henry said he confirmed that. Anything else, I know nothing about. Now, I think, it's about time you left, Miss Greer. I've heard enough false accusations!"

"Just one minute, Mr. Brownell. "If Cindy told you directly that she was with child, wouldn't you send her to Doctor Vincent, saying he could take care of things?"

"That's a trick question if ever I heard one. Would you please leave, Miss Greer?"

"Would you have?"

"Why not? He's the only doctor on the island. Why wouldn't I? But that doesn't imply she came to me. I'm telling you I never wrote that note." The man stood abruptly and headed toward the front door.

Dana met the man at the door. "One last thing, where were you the night of March thirty-first?"

"My mother lives in Norway. She was involved in a horrible car accident, was near death, actually, and I took a leave of absence and spent a month with her. Ask Marian Torrino. She filled-in for me during my absence."

"Sorry to hear about your mother and sorry for my prodding."

Mr. Brownell wrung his hands together. Then, he swatted at a drip of sweat running down his temple.

More confused than ever, Dana trekked the couple of miles back to the convent.

Chapter Fourteen

Dana waited for recreation hour to approach Sister Agnus Dei. Although Dana saw the nun as a rather weak suspect in the case, there were some things she said that troubled Dana . "Sister Mary Margaret was not chosen for the order, I'll have you know! The Carmelite Convent was nothing more than a roof over her head," and to Dana, she had said, "This is no place for you!" Sister Agnus Dei's anger about Mother taking Cindy into the convent as a postulant was quite obvious. The nun felt the young girl had no vocation and might even being using the sisters for a place to stay. For Sister Agnus Dei to reiterate her frustration with Dana by pointing out that she, too, did not belong with the sisters either pointed to a bitter woman or to one that had reason for not wanting the case solved. It was the latter that troubled Dana. Could this be why a black shadow seemed to follow her at times? Was the elderly nun trying to scare Dana away? If this was true, Dana needed to find out her motive.

Nestled in the corner of the room on a large, floppy chair sat the nun. She rattled the newspaper as she placed missing letters into a crossword puzzle.

"Sister, might I have a word with you?"

The nun grunted and coughed up some phlegm into a large, white handkerchief. "What's that?" she said in a gruff voice.

"Might I sit next to you? I'd like to speak with you."

"Suit yourself," the nun said.

"See you like crossword puzzles."

"Isn't that obvious?"

Dana took a deep breath. The woman's obnoxious behavior would be a challenge. "Sister, I recall you saying that Sister Mary Margaret had no place in the convent. Could you tell me why you felt that way?"

"The Carmelite convent is not a dumping ground for the poor and needy. It's bad enough Mother occasionally leaves a basket of food by the front curb for those who have nothing to eat."

Just as Dana had expected, the woman bore a bitter attitude. "But where would the young girl have gone if Mother had not taken her in? Mother did, after all, have permission from Rome."

"Huh, it depends on whether or not you believe the archbishop there has the authority to make such ridiculous decisions."

"The girl was nothing but a thorn in Mother's side. Once she admitted she was with child, her moods gradually worsened."

"In what way?"

"Why, she fluctuated like a seesaw. She'd cry that she wanted her baby. Then, she'd cry that the child would never have a father."

"Did she say why she believed that?"

"Never did. I may be old, but I'm not stupid."

"Are you saying you suspect who the father of the child is?"

"No doubt in my mind: Father Tanner."

Dana swallowed hard. Two had reason to believe Cindy Sullivan and the priest were a couple, first Raymond and now sister. Dana swallowed again as her voice seemed lost in her throat. "Sister, if this is true, why would Father Tanner still be at the parish?"

Sister began to laugh in a sarcastic way. "The Church…perhaps you've not of the fold, but I've been around long enough to see it all. The Church would not want this scandal going public. Better to look the other way."

"Hiding it? Is that what you mean?" Dana immediately thought about Dorothy. Could it be that the Church chose to hide her son's abusive behavior toward her, as well?

"No one confronted him, and no one will."

Dana told herself to stay calm. Because someone had an opinion on something did not automatically make it fact. Calling Father Tanner the father was Sister Agnus Dei's opinion…just an opinion.

"But the age difference…wasn't Cindy a mere minor in the eyes of the law?"

"Cindy had the body of a woman, and the mind of a senseless child. Put the two together, and you have fire."

"Have you ever told Mother about your beliefs?"

"Mother? She is not a leader, Dana. She should never have been put in that position."

Speaking of fire, Dana felt as if she were in the middle of flames, touching some tender nerves, for sure.

Changing the subject, Dana asked, "Do you think the young priest might have done away with the girl to hide his deed?"

"Humph, that's a question for someone like yourself." She coughed some more into her handkerchief. "And quite possibly if he did, you can be sure that would be covered up, too."

"The coroner, Sister. He ruled the death as an accident. Said sister fell to her death."

"Pure nonsense. Someone wanted her out of the way."

Dana carefully watched the woman's expression to see if there might be any change. After all, if she was the one to have killed the nun, wouldn't her own question trouble her? But the nun acted unfazed by her own thoughts.

"Sister, after Cindy delivered her child, did she ever ask where the baby was? After all, the sisters planned to also take in the child and to raise it, at least, until Cindy turned eighteen."

"No, Doctor Vincent explained what had happened...told her the baby was dead. She never quite regained her composure. The week before her death, she sat alone in her cell crying. No one seemed able to console the girl."

The first thought that crossed Dana's mind was wouldn't Cindy have heard the baby's cry after birth? If not, why? Had the doctor drugged her, so she would not be aware the child was born alive?

The nun quickly changed the mood. "Now, let's see. A word for upset that begins with a *p*."

"Sister, one last question. You told me at one time that this place was not where I belonged. Why? Why did you say that?"

The nun's pencil fell to the floor. She glanced up from her crossword puzzle. Wiping the corners of her mouth in her hand, she breathed heavily. "You're in a hornet's nest, Miss Greer." The woman shook her head and pointed her index finger at Dana. "I'd get out before you get stung."

The words chilled Dana.

*

Dana asked Sharon, the Winter Willows's School secretary, if she might speak with the principal.

"Nancy Gleason…her office door is open. Go in."

The informality of the school seemed a bit odd, but it was a small school in terms of students.

"Oh, I've heard about you…Dana Greer, correct?"

"Yes, might I speak with you in confidence."

The woman got up and shut the door. She walked with a slight limp in her left leg.

"Have a seat."

"I wondered if you might have something Mr. Brownell wrote. I have a note in my possession that he claims is not his cursive. I'd like to compare two things, if I might."

"That's a first…a rather odd question, but you are an investigator. Let me see what I can find in his file." She opened the drawer to the cabinet and ran her cherry red nails through the stack. "Here, this might help. I asked each teacher to submit a request for new furniture in his classroom. Mr. Brownell gave me this:

Miss Nelson:
I need to order eight new desks for my
classroom. My desk and the files can wait
another year before being replaced.
Thank you.
Tim Brownell

There was no doubt in Dana's mind. The man's handwriting matched that of his note to his mother that she had seen only yesterday.

"Anything else I can help you with, Miss Greer?" Nancy asked.

"Might you have a record of teacher's absences?"

"Sure do. What dates were you considering?"

"Around March thirty-first."

The principal straightened herself back in her spindled chair. "Assume this is in regard to Mr. Brownell?"

"Yes, it is," Dana said.

"Looks here as if Marian Torrino subbed in his absence from March twenty-ninth through April third."

So far, the handwriting of Mr. Brownell's proved the letter Sister Magdalene had given her was not his writing. The dates that he had a substitute also matched that he might well have been in Norway visiting his mother. She only had to check with the airlines, and if that proved him on the plane, Dana could rule out Mr. Brownell as being the murderer.

*

She rang the bell of Doctor Vincent's house.

Gertrude answered and invited her in. The smell of sizzling steaks wafted from the back. "Doctor's out barbecuing," Gertrude said. "Why don't you join me in the yard?"

Dana followed the woman through the house as if walking through a furniture store. She lost count of the number of rooms they passed, each furnished in eighteenth century antiques.

"Doctor, Dana's surprised us with a visit."

He looked up from the barbecue, his face a scowl. His eyes were watering from the intense heat. He flipped the steaks and stepped over to a metal garden set in the middle of the yard. "Gertrude, why don't you take over for me while I have a chat with Dana?"

"Beautiful place you have. Your shrubs, the hedge, the vines—."

"Afraid I can't take credit for all that. We have a gardener who comes once a week."

"Not to take much of your time, Doctor, I'd like to ask you a few questions."

"Go ahead," he said, running his hand along his chin. "How are the steaks coming, Gertrude?"

She yelled back, "a few more minutes."

"Let's get to the point, Miss Greer. I need to get to my dinner."

"I'm questioning the death certificate of Cindy Sullivan."

"Ah, let the dead rest in peace. Isn't that what you Catholics say?"

Dana smiled. "Mr. Gillion insists the young girl died from an accidental fall, yet I was called to investigate the case. I don't see why the archbishop would have done so if he felt everything was above board."

The doctor clutched at his hands as if rolling a snowball. "Maybe, the archbishop wanted confirmation. Makes sense to me."

"Doctor, you signed the death certificate...a legal document."

"So, I did. I did."

"Do you still stand by the cause of death?"

The man leaned back crossing his arms over his chest. He stared at Dana and in a low, firm voice said, "Better leave this alone, Dana. There are some places you're better off not going."

In the same defensive voice, Dana asked, "Even if it leads to the truth?"

The doctor did not bother to answer her last questions; instead, he got up, went over to the barbecue, and put the steaks on a tray. "Be seeing you around, Dana. See yourself out, will you?"

As Dana found her way to the front door, she turned to see a woman on the staircase. The image jolted Dana. The woman, dressed in a dirty robe and slippers, her hair long and greasy, stood looking at Dana with a blank, hollow-eyed look.

"You must be Martha," Dana said, more a question than a statement.

The woman did not respond, only stared like a concrete statue.

Chapter Fifteen

Holy Saturday and the convent echoed a dead silence. No Mass in the chapel, no chanting by the sisters, no movement in the halls. Having listened to many stories, gotten many perspectives on who Cindy Sullivan the wayward girl was, Dana told herself she needed to regroup, to gather her thoughts, to try to make some sense out of the varied reports she had been given. The best place to start, she decided, would be at the beginning, at the grave site where she had met with Father Merton and the coroner. Who would have wanted the nun dead and why? The two questions played and replayed in her mind as she made her way over to the cemetery next to the convent.

Dana meandered through the wet grass, glad she had worn a pair of jeans and knee-high boots. She wove her way among the headstones as if following a maze. Several yards from where she had previously found the chunk of mausoleum concrete, she stopped short. A figure, dressed in black, knelt huddled over a fresh grave. She watched both in curiosity and fear while the person placed a white lily on the damp ground. As the person rose and turned in her direction, Dana recognized him...Jesse Carmichael. On a whim, she called out his name. The teen came over toward her, though reluctantly. "Nice to see you again, Jesse," she said.

Jesse fidgeted with the collar on his black, leather jacket and immediately searched for a cigarette in his pocket. "Hey, man. Cool."

Dana decided to be direct with the boy. "I saw you put a lily on that grave site over there." Dana pointed. "Sister Mary Margaret's?"

"Oh, shucks, lady. It was nothin' really." The boy pulled out some of his long hair caught from under his collar.

"Mind if I ask why? It certainly is a kind gesture."

The teen juggled his posture from one leg to the other. He bit down on his lower lip. He lit his cigarette and glanced away from Dana. "Gotta go, lady. I'm late. Gotta get over to the soda shop. My shift starts in ten minutes."

"I understand. I won't keep you. One question, though...."

He puffed on his cigarette nervously.

"Why? Why *were* you putting a flower on the nun's grave?"

"I've gotta beat feet out of here, or the old man down at the soda shop will have my—."

"Why?"

"She was my chick for a time, man. Now, I gotta go."

With that, Dana watched as Jesse ran out of the cemetery and down the street.

*

Anxious to get back to her cell, Dana took a shortcut through the small garden back of the convent. There she saw the two postulants sitting on a stone bench, deep in conversation. Must be recreation hour, she thought. "Hello, Sisters."

Sister Seraphim waved, and Sister Magdalene motioned for Dana to come over.

"Dana, I hope I didn't frighten you the other day. I didn't mean to."

"Frighten me? Hardly. I don't get swayed from my job that easily."

Sister Seraphim laughed quietly under her breath. Then, she excused herself. "We'd better hurry; we'll be late. Recreation hour is almost over." She rushed into the convent.

Dana sensed the girl's behavior was prompted by uneasiness.

"There is one thing I forgot to mention," Sister Magdalene said, standing now with her fingers running along the rosary beads at her side.

"Oh?""Doctor Vincent's wife…Martha. Did you know she is mentally unstable?"

Dana had just met the woman, not long enough to diagnose her, but she wasn't a psychologist either.

"She suffers from melancholy."

"Is that so?"

"Anyone who is around her for a short time could see that. She is not fit to be a mother. Can't even take care of herself. That's why Gertrude is there round-the-clock."

Rather than admitting she had gone to the doctor's house only yesterday, Dana asked, "I would think the doctor would get his wife help if that were the case." Dana started to walk away, tired of the nun's accusations.

"If I were her husband, I would never have brought her a child to care for."

"What? Whatever are you talking about? What child"

The nun pointed her chin downward, appearing like a child withholding a secret from an adult. "Cindy's child...I'm telling you the child was not stillborn as so many would have you believe."

Dana's jaw dropped. "But that's kidnapping? Why would Doctor Vincent dare take that chance?"

"Maybe, he would be the better one to answer that question, Dana."

"This sounds preposterous! The doctor kidnaps a child, gives it to his mentally ill wife, and the coroner writes it off as a stillborn?"

Sister Magdalene lightly tugged on Dana's sweater. "Do you know Gertrude?"

Dana pretended otherwise and shook her head.

"She's cares for the Vincent's baby. She's also been the doctor's nurse for as long as he's been in practice."

"How might you know this?"

"It was she who kidnapped Cindy's infant. Can't you see this?" Sister Magdalene smirked. "And now, she just happens to be the child's caretaker."

The couple of times Dana went to see the doctor, she never saw a child. Of course, there was the common explanation that the child was asleep. Dana could not rule out that what Magdalene was telling her *was* the truth. Yet, Dana questioned whether these were more of

Sister Magdalene's lies? Dana tucked her hair behind her ears. "How do you know all this?"

"How do I know Martha suffers from mental illness? Who doesn't? Winter Willows is small enough where word gets around. Doctor Vincent thought that maybe giving her a child would make her happy. Nothing else seemed to work."

In the rare event, the nun was telling the truth, Dana felt bound to do more investigating. She needed to find an excuse to return to Doctor Vincent's house.

Chapter Sixteen

Easter Sunday and Father Tanner pushed his mother's wheelchair toward the Church. "Can't understand why you can't find someone to do this, Mother! Do you think I have nothing better to do?"

"Honey, you know, I don't even go to Mass since the accident. It's nice to get out for a change." Dorothy looked up at the tree branches forming a shadowed arch over the sidewalk. "Such a beautiful day."

"Sure. Sure. Yeah."

The young priest rode his mother's chair up the ramp into the Church and positioned her in the side aisle. "Tanner, I'd light to light one of the vigil candles at Mary's altar."

"I need to get vested for Mass, Mother. Find someone else to help you." He genuflected and went into the sacristy. He peered out the entry and saw Betty, seated at the end of the pew, offering to help his mother. Betty unlocked Dorothy's chair and took her over to the row of red vigil candles. She lit a long stick with one of the flames and torched the wick of another. Tanner stared as his mother bowed her head before the Virgin Mary statue and prayed.

He wanted to pray, too, but his prayer was not one of praise and thanksgiving. If he had his way, his old lady would kick the bucket, and he could get on with his life. Then, he would at least have the opportunity to get off Winter Willows, perhaps move to Seattle, be in charge of a parish of his own. Yet none of this would be his as long as mother was around.

Tanner's uncle in Rome made it more than clear to him that he had arranged with the Archbishop of Seattle to see that he was placed on the island so as to care for his mother, even granting him the rare permission to live at home with her. But to Tanner, she was nothing more than an albatross around his neck. When she wasn't whining about this, she was whining about that. The only way he could keep her somewhat happy was to buy her cartons of cigarettes, which she devoured like a hungry vulture, sometimes as many as two and three packs a day.

If he had his way, he would put an end to her. There were nights when he stayed awake, pondering ways he might get rid of her yet make it look accidental. That day he was in his senior year of high school, that day they had argued at the top of the basement steps, he thought for sure the slight shove down the stairs would have been enough. He knew his face was covered in shock when the doctor told him that not only was she alive and had survived the fall, but given a life in a wheelchair, she might actually be able to live several more years. That was almost six years ago, and besides her occasional bedsores, she seemed strong as an ox.

Just then, Father Merton came into the sacristy. "Ready, my boy, to celebrate Mass together this fine Easter day?"

"Sure, Father. I was thinking the same thing," he lied. One more glance toward the now filled pews, he saw the cloistered sisters had filled the first three rows. Easter, the only day of the year, that the head of their order allowed them to actually come out of the convent and join the parishioners in prayer. Once Mass was done, the sisters were expected to immediately leave in single file and return to the convent. Tanner wondered how the women could hold themselves to such a strict lifestyle, one of continual prayer for the world and its sinners. He smiled to himself. In a way, he was pleased that he had someone praying for him, even though, they had no idea he was one of their sinners.

The altar boys, Jesse, chomping on a piece of gum, and Jimmy, led the procession down the main aisle of the Church, followed by the two priests. The congregation faced them as they made their way to the altar. Sister Seraphim, the more sensible of the two postulants, nodded and smiled as Father Tanner came closer. He hoped no one noticed as he returned the gesture and passed her by.

*

On Dana's way back to the convent, several people stopped her and introduced themselves. They were eager to ask her questions. She had heard stories of doctors at cocktail parties, speaking about gallbladders and acid reflux only because the guests felt entitled to get their questions answered for free. Now, she felt much the same being approached by nosey neighbors. One woman in a deep purple suit and matching hat with a white veil tapped her on the arm. "Ma'am, the name's Clorissa...Clorissa Mansfield. Might we speak for a moment. I think, I know something that might be of help to you."

"You do?" The name *Mansfield* sounded so familiar, but Dana couldn't recall where she had heard the name before. Dana and the woman stepped aside from the crowd leaving the Church behind them. "What is it?"

"My son," the woman stopped. Her face trembled, and tears fell onto her cheeks. "You see, my son...Gordie—.

"Immediately, Dana realized where she had heard the name. Gordie Mansfield was the student from Winter Willows School who died only recently in a motorcycle accident in Seattle.

"Gordie and Cindy Sullivan were going steady. I know, I know, it's a mortal sin, against the teaching of the Church, but Gordie refused to listen, and Cindy...well, Cindy was beyond reproach. They dated for six months. Couldn't get enough of each other." The woman reached for a handkerchief in her purse and dabbed at her face.

"Ma'am, might you like to talk elsewhere, a place we can sit down?" Dana noticed the woman's head shaking as well as her hands. It was clear what she was about to say provoked great anxiety. Dana did not wait for an answer but led the woman to the stone bench in the garden of the convent.

"But are we allowed here? This is a cloistered nunnery."

Dana smiled. "I happen to live here now while I'm working on the case. At this time of day, the sisters are more than likely engaged in the parlor."

"Okay, then, okay."

"Six months, you say? That's quite some time for two adolescents to be dating exclusively."

"I know; I agree. But if there's anything you should know, if you don't already, it's that Cindy was quite promiscuous. Actually, that was the only thing that broke the two of them up. Gordie found out she was seeing others on the side. Well, it near broke his heart. I still wonder if the accident would have even happened if it weren't for the break-up. That night, Gordie took his motorcycle on the ferry to Seattle. He was so upset. I'm sure he didn't even see that truck coming." The woman sobbed.

Dana patted the woman's hand. "I'm so sorry."

Clorissa sniffled and dabbed her face some more. "There's more, though, that you should know."

Dana nodded.

"Gordie told me one night that he suspected Cindy had been seeing an older man. She told my son that he was too immature for her, just a boy. Shortly afterwards, the two called it quits."

"Any idea who Cindy might have been referring to?"

"No, Gordie never said."

"Mrs. Mansfield, most know that Cindy was with child when she entered the convent."

"True. The two started going steady right after Cindy joined the order. It was around that time that the two started going steady. You have to understand, Cindy might have been a few months along, but she never showed, nor did she tell my son."

"So, are you trying to tell me that Gordie was not the father of the child?"

"Hardly. Without a doubt, the two were romantically involved, but Gordie took precautions."

"No offense, Mrs. Mansfield, but how can you be so sure?"

"His bedroom drawer was filled with rubbers. That's how I know. That's also how I know he was sexually involved with the girl."

"But then who——?"

"I must be going, dear. I wish I could be of more help."

As the woman rushed off, Dana heard herself whispering, "Oh, but you were. Trust me. You were."

Chapter Seventeen

The feeling of being enclosed, trapped, almost claustrophobic caused Dana to open the door to her cell just a crack. The day after Easter and the smell of lilies filled the walls of the convent. She sat at her desk letting her thoughts stray in many directions.

Mrs. Mansfield had mentioned Cindy Sullivan had been involved with an older man when she entered the convent already with child for two months. Although Gordie Mansfield had dated the girl for five or six months, it was after she had found out she was already pregnant. She barely showed, so who would know? The only older man Dana could think of was Mr. Brownell. But she had ruled out that he wrote the letter to Cindy. At this point, the only other older man Dana could think of was Father Tanner. Sister Agnus Dei thought the same.

Seemed only Sister Magdalene was confident enough to believe Cindy and the older man were the potential parents of the child and that there were plans in effect to rid Cindy of the child after its delivery. Dana needed to pay an unexpected visit to the doctor's house. Could this give the doctor a plausible reason to kill the mother of the child for fear she might tell Martha the truth? That's when the image of Jesse placing a lily on the grave of Sister Mary Margaret came to Dana's mind. He, too, was known to have a crush on the young woman. Even his mother, Betty had told Dana there were those in Winter Willows who believed Jesse did away with the young nun. But why? What motive would he have? True he found out the woman was seeing other men on the side, but why would he wait so long to murder the sister? Why wait until after she delivered her child?

Straining to think of who else might be a suspect or at least involved in some way with the death of Sister Mary Margaret, Dana recalled the conversation she had with Mother Anne Baptiste. Sister Agnus Dei's past was in a way similar to the postulant's in that she, too, had borne a child out of wedlock. Was there some lasting jealousy…anger even…that Sister Mary Margaret had a child out of wedlock and yet might very well find a way out of the cloister eventually whereas the older nun's life had already passed her by? She did not seem happy or even closely satisfied with her position in the convent, only being there on the authority of her father who banished her to the cloistered walls.

Or, could it be that there was someone…someone else who hadn't even surfaced as of yet that was responsible for the grisly deed? It was too early in the case to rule anyone out.

Late morning and Dana felt exhausted. She decided to pay a visit to Grotto of Lourdes Church. The walk there would get her outside for a while plus, hopefully, silence her over-wrought mind. She tossed her bag over her shoulder but not before reaching for the cover of her small Bible.

The front doors to the Church were open. Dana genuflected and entered a pew in the back. The dark setting lit only by the sun's rays through the stained-glass windows helped to immediately relax Dana. She closed her eyes and breathed in and then out. She began to count the seconds, trying each time to extend the amount of time she held in or let go of her breath. She could hear her heartbeat with each rise and fall of her chest.

Deep in meditation, Dana jumped at the sound of the front doors of the Church slamming. She opened her eyes expecting to see one of the parishioners or one of the priests. She looked behind her to the vestibule. She looked from side-to-side. And strange as it seemed, no one was ahead of her or at the altar.

A sixth sense, she thought, but something did not feel right. She knew what she had heard. Someone had closed the doors of the Church. Of that, she was positive, yet she had not seen anyone when she entered. Maybe it was Father Merton coming up from his apartment and leaving through the Church. Odd, though, that he had not attempted to acknowledge her. Then again, perhaps, he did not want to disturb her. The uneasiness prompted Dana to rise.

As she did, she noticed a on the pew next to her white envelope that she had not seen when she first entered. Her name was scrawled on the front. She ripped it open and swallowed hard. A postcard of Grotto of the Lourdes Church, complete with a partial view of the cemetery off to the side. Scrawled in red, scratchy letters were the words: *Rest in Peace, Cindy.*

Beneath the black-and-white picture, she read a message, pieced together with newspaper print. It read:

Do not disturb the dead.
Let them rest in peace,
For it has been said
If you do,
Death will do away
…with you.

A chill covered Dana's bare arms. She glanced about as if half expecting to see the bearer of the news peering over her. The silence of the Church walls closed round about her almost to the point of suffocation. She hurried out, letting the heavy wooden door slam shut and ran down the sidewalk toward the convent. No sooner had she stepped inside, then, she ran into Mother Superior. Sister Anne Baptiste was coming out of the parlor, where Betty Carmichael busied herself with one of her floral arrangements.

A slight blush covered the nun's face as if she had been caught with her finger in the cookie jar. She looked downward and quickly left.

Dana noticed Betty sniffling. "Are you coming down with something?"

The woman turned her face toward Dana. "My son…Jesse…someone is out to get him."

"What are you talking about?"

"Mother told me someone is spreading gossip about the boy yet again."

"You mean in connection with Sister Mary Margaret?"

Betty nodded and tried to busy herself arranging some of the dahlia buds. "Why can't he be left alone? He's innocent."

"If you don't mind me asking, what exactly was said?"

"Someone reported seeing Jesse placing a flower on the girl's grave. Someone told mother."

Dana remembered speaking with Jesse after seeing him at the grave site, but there was no one else around…at least that she noticed. Was someone trying to set her up…to say that she was the one to go to mother? That she was the one to squeal to her? Is that why mother abruptly left when she saw her? But, why?" Then, Dana remembered what Sister Agnus Dei had said to her soon after she arrived on Winter Willows. "This is no place for you." Even Sister Magdalene had inferred she leave on the next ferry. And, now the secret message, telling her to let the dead rest in peace.

Betty held a spray bottle and misted the plants sitting in the front window. "The rumors still remain that Jesse murdered the girl. I don't know why he is suspected of such a horrendous deed. Why, my Jesse wouldn't hurt a fly."

"I'm sorry to hear this, Mrs. Carmichael. Did Mother tell you who she spoke with?"

Betty turned and looked at Dana directly. "No, mother wouldn't do that. She said she refused to commit the sin of gossip, but she did want me to be aware."

"It sure would help knowing; at least, you could confront the person."

"If that would do any good," Betty said, wiping her hands in a pink floral apron.

Chapter Eighteen

Dana had to find an excuse for why she was returning to the Vincent's house. After the way the doctor had treated her the last time she visited, she wondered whether she might even be allowed inside again. Then, it came to her. She would tell Gertrude she had some questions about the doctor's wife, Martha."

"Hello, Miss Greer, nice to see you again." The woman invited her into the foyer where a tall grandfather clock chimed three o'clock with heavy gongs. "What brings you by?" Gertrude invited Dana into the parlor of the house, where a gold cat lay on the fireplace hearth. Dana sat down on a celery-green striped chair that looked as if it came out of a museum showcase…an authentic antique.

"Gertrude, when I left the last time I was here, I believe it was Martha I saw standing on the staircase. Maybe, I should have introduced myself, but the woman looked somewhat frightened."

Gertrude bit down on the inside of her cheek. "Ah, yes, I'm sure she was. Martha doesn't see that many people. She's somewhat of an introvert, I'd say."

Dana reached into her bag for her small Bible and took a deep breath. The miniature book had a way of instantly calming her, especially, when she found herself in difficult situations. "Could you tell me anything else about her?"

Gertrude rubbed her hand along the arm of the loveseat that matched the Louis XVI chair. "What do you care to know?"

Dana knew her question would be answered with one. It was a perfect technique to avoid the topic at hand. Another technique was the one Dorothy used…changing the subject abruptly.

"I've learned that rumors are common on such a small island. That's all. I want to be sure I learn the truth."

Gertrude's fingers, meticulously manicured, scratched at the arm of the couch. The gold cat leapt from the fireplace into her lap. "Ginger, no, no!" she said, pushing the animal onto the Oriental Rug at his feet. The cat screeched and ran out of the room.

"Martha suffers from schizophrenia. Her symptoms began showing shortly after the doctor and she married…oh, I'd say, maybe a few years later. Martha was in her middle twenties. Coupled with that diagnosis, she suffers from melancholia."

"I'm sorry to hear that. I suppose that is the reason why the doctor has you here, correct? I mean, to look after Martha."

At that moment as if on cue, a woman with shoulder length auburn hair that appeared as if it hadn't been washed in days appeared. Her face white as snow with large dark eyes, she bit down on her lips which appeared dry and indented from too many bites. She carried an infant in a pink flannel cloth. The baby wailed. "Gertrude, I'm sorry to interrupt, but I can't seem to get Jewel to settle down."

"Martha, please, can't you see I'm busy? Go ask Ned…yes, of course, ask Ned."

The woman slightly bowed her head. No sooner had she stepped into the foyer than Ned appeared. "Here, Ned, get her to stop her crying." Her husband, who looked as if he were about to say, 'Why can't Gertrude?' noticed Dana sitting across from the woman. Martha's husband took the infant, who by now was screaming, her face red, and rocked the baby in his arms. He walked toward the back of the house.

Gertrude stood up and made her way to one of the long, narrow windows next to the fireplace. She stared out while she tugged on the cuff of her blouse. Her hand rubbed against the back of her neck.

An aura of tension filled the room. Dana waited in the silence.

When the woman finally turned, Dana saw deep creases around her eyes…her face stiff almost like a mannequin in a store window. "Quite the shame. Cindy claimed to have felt her child move only a day before she delivered. The cord, unfortunately, was wrapped around the child's neck, not once but twice."

Dana said nothing.

"The sisters had hoped to take in the child, to raise her as their own. Poor Ned had to relay the sad news to them and to Cindy. It's not an easy job telling a mother that her child was born dead."

Although Dana knew that was the explanation she would hear from the doctor and Gertrude, that the infant was stillborn, something troubled her about the story. "So…the baby…Martha's?"

"Yes, yes. Quite a joy…baby Jewel."

"Martha wasn't supposed to have children. You know, her being on meds and all."

"How old is the baby if I might ask?"

"Jewel? She's three months. How quickly time goes."

Dana could not help herself, so prodded further. "She sure looks tiny…for three months, I mean." Not having been around children much and never having had one of her own, Dana hoped her comments didn't allude to what she was actually thinking. Could it be the doctor's child was Sister Mary Margaret's, or was she letting her imagination get carried away again? Fiona Wharton, her past mentor, had warned her more than once about filling in the blanks too quickly, about skipping steps in an investigation, all in an effort to solve a case.

"The child was born premature, I'm afraid. We almost lost her," Gertrude said, her eyes blinking rapidly until tears formed. "Martha's just lucky the baby is perfectly normal, her pregnancy occurring while on her schizophrenia medications."

Dana assumed the woman was telling her the truth; at least, what she said made sense. Dana felt badly for jumping to her earlier conclusion. Furthermore, why would the doctor risk being accused of kidnapping? His career would be at stake, his marriage. That's when the image of Sister Magdalene came to mind. The postulant was adamant that the baby Doctor Vincent's wife cared for was indeed Sister Mary Margaret's. Then again, Mother Superior indicated that Sister Magdalene was a compulsive liar. Someone was not telling the truth, and Dana had to find a way to get to the bottom of this.

"Is there anything else I can help you with, Miss Greer?"

By the tone of her voice, Dana understood she was being asked to leave.

*

Dana went back to her cell and peered at the message found on the Church pew. Sister Agnus Dei told her it would only be a matter of time before she got stung in the convent beehive, and Sister Magdalene told Dana there was one evening ferry to the mainland. Other than these two, Dana couldn't think of anyone that might want her out of the picture. A frightening message for sure, but she wasn't about to leave until the mystery was solved.

Chapter Nineteen

Gertrude threw her hair into a ponytail and sipped on her strawberry milkshake. Her rosy-pink sweater matched her drink.

The customers in the *Chilly Treats Soda Shop* were mostly teenagers. Once they reached drinking age and, sometimes even before, they headed to the Red Barn Tavern, where their IDs were never checked.

"Hard day at work today?" Henry asked. Dark circles under her eyes and deep creases at the corners spoke to her worn out look. There were times when Henry regretted the choice he had made. Thirty-nine years old and caring for a baby appeared to be too much for the woman.

She fingered her straw. "Let's say it's nice to have a night off. Jewel has been a bit ornery the last few days, and Martha has been beside herself. There are times when she is completely incompetent and reaches out for help. The basic mothering jobs often overwhelm her."

"How well I can imagine. That woman has enough of her own issues. A baby is the last thing she needs. And with her being on all those medications for her depression and mental condition, I find she often appears as if she is in her own world. Of course, don't tell Ned that."

"It was his idea. He thought a child could lift Martha's spirits. Gertrude reached across the Formica tabletop and held Henry's hands in hers. "Let's not talk about Martha, Henry. Let's talk about you…us."

"Ah, let's see what's interesting with me. The sheriff is still on a kick about the tourism slowdown on the island. There are those who are riding his back and holding him accountable. Something about it affecting the economy, which then affects his job or, at least, could affect him getting re-elected to his position. Bunch of politics…."

"Could it affect you, Henry, your job? I mean your position is under the sheriff."

"Listen, love, I don't want you worrying your pretty little mind over this. Though it's part of the reason why I try to keep things simple. A murder becomes a mere accident, for example. I try not to add to the sheriff's grief."

"You're such a good man, dear."

"What do you say you let me prove how good a man I am?"

"Oh, Henry," she said. She loved to drag out the letters in his name when she was feeling amorous.

"You've got the night off. Why not put it to good use?"

"But people will talk." Gertrude's studio apartment was located above the soda shop. On her nights off, she had a Murphy bed that pulled out of the wall and a tiny bathroom. Not only was it all she could afford, but since the baby's arrival, she found herself spending most nights at the Vincent's and less time at boarding room.

He smiled. "They haven't so far. Furthermore, there's so much gossip around here already, who's to say what's true or not."

Henry put twenty-five cents on the table, and the two of them walked out of the Chilly Treats Soda Shop and up the narrow wooden steps on the backside of the building.

Chapter Twenty

Ned kissed his wife on the forehead. Martha rocked baby Jewel. The slits of sunlight shone through the closed blinds.

"You know you can put her down, honey. She won't disappear."

Martha looked at her husband strangely. She did not see the humor in his response. She had waited so long for a baby, was told she should never bear a child. Martha looked down at the baby wrapped in a light-yellow blanket with pink bears on it. She felt convinced she would not leave the house with the baby. No one would take Jewel from her. No one need even know that she was a mother, a title she still had trouble believing. She watched Ned give her a loving smile. He stooped to touch the baby's black hair.

"I'm so glad, you're happy, Martha. Nothing brings me greater delight." In the same breath, he said, "When do you think you'll take her for a buggy ride? You know, the weather is getting pleasant. You might enjoy going out for a bit."

Martha glared at her husband. She got up with a huff and stood at the bottom of the staircase. "Getting out? I have no such intention. Neither the baby nor I will leave this house." Martha could feel her shoulders stiffen, her breasts heave outward toward the child she cradled. "Do you understand me?"

Ned tried to kiss her on the cheek, but Martha pulled away. "If you want to keep me happy, I suggest you leave us alone," she said, as she looked down at the tiny infant who had by now fallen asleep in her arms. Martha tiptoed up the carpeted stairs, staring at the pattern of red rose bouquets at her feet. She entered the nursery at the end of the hall, the wallpaper swirls of brown teddy bears on a yellow background, the curtains white eyelet. She lay the baby in her white wicker bassinet.

Martha stepped toward the window and glanced at the bay. A freighter pulling a tugboat filled with large pieces of metal slowly passed by. A Chevrolet Bel Air honked its horn at three small fawns who meandered to the other side of the street. On the sidewalk below, two elderly women walked by, one of whom glanced up at Martha and pointed her finger. Martha quickly let the curtain slide through her fingers and wrapped her arms around herself.

She shivered. She knew there were those who talked behind her back. She knew the gossip they spread. Some said Doctor Vincent's wife had gone mad, and that's why he had bought her the large estate in the country. There were those who said she had some terminal illness, and her husband wanted her to lay low and rest. And there were even those who said a witch lived in the grey Victorian house with violet trim.

Little did any of them know that here lived a mother with her new daughter, and never did she intend that they would find out. She brushed the greasy strands of hair behind her ears, making her way to her master suite. She refused to look at herself in the mirror. She often wondered why the doctor had ever agreed to marry her…an ugly hag.

*

It had been awhile since Dana joined the nuns in the refectory. An elderly sister whom Dana did not remember seeing before placed a piece of white bread into the bowl of water before each nun. Dana watched in disgust as the bread, like a sponge, absorbed the liquid. She wondered how she would down the breakfast when one of the sisters at the end of the table passed a small container of cinnamon. Dana told herself she would imagine she was eating a piece of French toast.

Mother Anne Baptiste stood at the lectern ready to begin the morning's prayer and reading. She offered a thanksgiving meditation for the food they were about to eat. Then, she opened the Bible. A card fell onto the floor from the gold-gilded pages. She bent down, picked up the picture, and stared at it for several seconds before she spoke. She turned the photograph over. Mother looked out at her congregation. Silence passed. She walked away from the podium and strolled up-and-down the aisles of the refectory, holding the picture for each to see. Then in the stillness of the room, Mother questioned, "Who does this holy card belong to?"

Dana glanced around the room, waiting for someone to reply.

"Mother, it's mine." Sister Seraphim braced herself against the dining table.

Hushed whispers filled the room.

"Sisters, please! This is our hour of silence. Must you sin against the order's rules?"

Immediately, the room went still.

"Sister Seraphim, please speak."

The young nun placed her hands under her scapula, the typical standing posture for the sisters. "It was in my missal, Mother."

Mother's eyes narrowed. She bit down on her lower lip.

Dana had never seen Mother's otherwise beautiful face look so stern, so perplexed.

Mother's face reddened. "How do you explain this, Sister?" She turned the card over in front of the postulant. "Read it! Read it out loud!"

Sister in a shaky voice did as she was told. "Keep your hands off him, Cindy! Elaine."

Sister Agnus Dei stood. "Mother, I found it on the floor in the kitchen. I hoped by placing it in your Bible, you might find the rightful owner."

Dana wondered why the elderly nun could not have given her finding to Mother at another time…why now in front of the whole community. She watched as Sister Agnus Dei snubbed the young nun.

"I see, Sister Agnus Dei. You may be seated. We will not be dismissed this morning until we resolve this. Sister Seraphim, will you tell the congregation your baptismal name?"

The postulant stood again. Her face a deep rose. Her arms trembled. "But, Mother, could we discuss this in your office or during the speaking of our faults later tonight?"

"No, Sister. I will make the decision."

Mother Superior's demeanor stern…her body rigid as a rod waited for the woman to speak.

"Mother, my baptismal name is Elaine Reed."

Like a wave rushing to shore, the room filled with oohs and aahs.

"Please, I will not ask for silence again!" Mother said. "Sister, does this holy card of the Archangel Seraphim belong to you?"

"Yes, Mother. It was given to me by my brother on the day I left for the convent."

"The message on the back of the card…is it your writing."

As if waiting for a loud bang of thunder, the room filled with a restless anticipation.

"No, Mother."

"Then who, Sister? I'm assuming this refers to our departed soul Sister Mary Margaret known by the baptismal name of Cindy Sullivan. Would you agree?"

"Yes, Mother."

"Then who do you suppose is the him in the message applies to?"

The nun hung her head. Her shoulders slouched. "Why, I have no idea, Mother."

Dana knew the answer or at least partially. Was someone trying to set-up the postulant to make it appear as if she were threatening Sister Mary Margaret? Or, was it to be assumed that Sister Seraphim and Sister Mary Margaret were vying for the same man? And, if so, what man was the message referring to?

A sound like bees in a hive swarmed over the refectory.

"Please, I ask that you abide by the order of silence!"

Sister Agnus Dei stood up abruptly. "Mother, isn't this prying into the privacy of Sister Seraphim? What business do we have sharing this?"

"You may be seated, Sister." The Mother thought for a moment. "Sister Seraphim, you are to confess this at the speaking of faults tomorrow evening. Now, let us read from Luke Chapter Three."

While Mother read, Dana could not believe the incident that had just played out before her. For once, she agreed with Sister Agnus Dei. Had it been necessary to delve into the postulant's past life in front of the entire order of nuns? It seemed like a breach of confidence. Did Sister Agnus Dei know that the photo belonged to Sister Seraphim, and if so, why would she want to set the postulant up? Why not return the picture to its rightful owner in private? Why involve Mother? Then, again, it could just be an innocent act…a way to find the owner. But was Sister Seraphim lying? Might she have written the message to Cindy? Dana thought she had a possible list of suspects in mind who might have had a motive to kill Sister Mary Margaret when she realized she had one more to add to the list.

*

Dana waited in her cell until it was time for the socialization hour in the parlor. She casually walked up to Mother, sitting in the corner, in her lap lay a skein of light blue yarn. Sister manipulated two knitting needles, mindlessly creating something from scratch…no book of directions to be seen.

"Knit one, purl one." Mother looked up. "Dana, how are you, my dear."

Mother, I do not want to disturb you, but I'd like to speak with you in private, if possible."

The mother superior gathered her work and placed it into a tapestry bag. "Yes, my child. Follow me."

Dana and the nun walked down the dimly lit hallway. "You look to be quite the knitter, Mother. What were you working on?"

"A sweater...for the baby."

"The baby?"

The nun's face went from bubbly to a somber look. "Started it for Sister Mary Margaret's child. For some reason, I can't put it down. I believe, God will show me a purpose for it one day."

Dana tried to smile, but the thought of knitting a sweater for a so-called deceased baby seemed too morbid to consider.

"You look well, Dana. How's your investigation going?"

"I'm afraid I'm not close to finding the suspect I've come looking for. There's a reason this job is described as solving a mystery."

"You will, dear." The woman placed her hand on Dana's sleeve. "The Spirit always comes through if we only can trust."

"I hope so." Without being able to find a segue to her thought, Dana said, "Not to change the subject, Mother, but I'm curious. What is the speaking of faults?"

"Oh, my dear. It is a tradition as old as the order. It's a weekly ceremony. Each of our sisters confesses out loud their shortcomings for that week. It's a great lesson in humility."

Dana smiled. "I wouldn't think these good women would have anything to say."

"Oh, but you're wrong. The younger girls are usually guilty of giggling at inappropriate times. The older sisters are forever dropping or spilling something."

"Sins?"

"Faults, Dana. We all strive for perfection here."

Dana realized how happy she was that she had not decided to join the convent. Her speaking of faults might just take up the entire evening.

"That is why it became imperative that I address the photograph I found in my Bible. No sister should be interested in the past." Mother breathed heavily. "When will these young girls learn?"

"But, Mother, the message on the back of the holy card might very well have something to do with the person who murdered Sister Mary Margaret. Sounds to me as if Sister Seraphim is trying to warn Sister Mary Margaret. This is where I need to step in, to find out who the *him* on the back of the card refers to."

Mother's eyebrows raised like two *Vs*. "Have it your way then, Dana, but sister will still address the matter at the speaking of faults."

Dana walked back to her cell determined to speak with the postulant about her past. It might be frowned upon by the order of nuns, but as an investigator, it was what she needed to know.

Chapter Twenty-One

The following morning, Dana awoke with tension rising in the back of her neck. It felt stiff and sore to the touch. How typical, she thought. At about this time in past investigations, she had the same symptoms…soon to appear as a migraine. She hoped to go back to sleep for a bit when someone knocked on the door to her cell.

There stood Sister Seraphim. The young woman bit down on her lower lip, her right eye twitching. She fumbled with her hands as if not sure where they belonged.

"Sister, come in." Dana pulled the chair out from her desk and sat on the corner of her bed.

"Sorry to bother you at this hour, but I am not required to do chanting in the chapel today."

"I'm glad you came. I was hoping to speak with you anyway."

"About the holy card?"

Dana nodded. "Yes."

"Please understand. I was put on the spot in the refectory yesterday. I ask God's forgiveness, but I could not tell the whole truth." Sister rolled her thumb and index finger over the rosary beads at her side.

"You are speaking about the message?"

The nun nodded. "You see, I did write the message to Cindy, but I never gave it to her. My soul bears great guilt. If I had given it to her in time, she might…."

Even after being in the investigative business for twelve years, Dana still found it difficult to conceal her demeanor when she received shocking news. "I see." Hoping to calm the nun, Dana asked, "Could I get you a glass of water?"

The postulant swallowed hard. "No," she said, her eye continuing to twitch, "thank you, though." She brushed a wisp of her blond hair, shoving it under the edge of her veil. "I think, what I'm about to say might help you in your investigation."

"I see. Go on."

"Sister Mary Margaret, Sister Magdalene, and I were friends. Sister Mary Margaret joined the convent shortly after Sister Magdalene and me. I'm not trying to excuse my sinfulness, Dana, but the three of us often would leave our cells, change out of our habits, and meet in town some nights. I don't know why I went. I want to give my life to God, but I went anyway. I let temptation overtake me."

"God is forgiving."

"I know, but there is no excuse for my sin."

"Where in town did you girls go?"

"Usually the Red Barn Tavern. Joe Mikowski knew we were underage and that we were sisters, but we could trust him not to tell anyone. He would laugh that we were too beautiful for God. He would give us whiskey, beer, wine."

Dana listened intently. She was pleased the young woman felt comfortable revealing all this to her.

"And, Sister Agnus Dei never knew?"

"She caught us sometimes. Made us say the rosary on our knees in front of her. Other times, she would take out a stiff rod and slap it on our backs."

"Why the message to Cindy? You say you wrote it?"

"I did." The nun looked at the floor. "I was afraid."

"Afraid?"

"That Sister Mary Margaret would get...well, you know."

"Pregnant?"

The young postulant nodded.

"But I heard Sister was two months along when she entered."

"Few knew then."

Dana stood up and put her hand on the girl's shoulder. She could only imagine how difficult this must be for the sister. The girl felt stiff to the touch.

"Sister Mary Margaret appeared mature for her age. No one would guess she was only thirteen. I did not want to get her in trouble...only to warn her for her own good."

"But why couldn't you just tell her face-to-face?"

Sister Seraphim's face became blotchy, and small beads of sweat dripped from under her veil. "I didn't...I didn't want Sister Magdalene to know. Both of them were fond of the same man."

"Who might that be?"

Sister coughed into her hand and cleared her throat. "An older man from the parish."

"His name…I need to know his name."

Sister shook her head several times. "I can't do that"

"But it could be a possible lead in the investigation. You must."

She shook her head again…her eye twitching out of control. "I tried to tell Cindy to stay away from…from Father Tanner. Little did I know that it was too late for that."

"You mean Cindy was pregnant by then?"

Sister Seraphim nodded.

"You're telling me Sister Magdalene is also fond of the young priest?"

"Yes, but Father was in love with Cindy.

Dana sat on the side of her bed, stunned. Then, again, wasn't this what Sister Agnus Dei had told her?

*

During the social hour, Dana decided to go out to the garden, rather than to the parlor. She sat on the stone bench. Low, dark clouds formed overhead as the billowing mass moved quickly over the horizon. Until she felt the splatter of raindrops, this would be a perfect spot to gather her thoughts and try to make sense of all that had happened since she arrived on Winter Willows. She pulled a pencil and notebook out of her bag when she sensed someone behind her. "Oh, hello, Sister."

"Mind if I join you?" Sister Magdalene asked. Without waiting for an answer, she sat down beside Dana. "There's something I think you should know."

After Mother's warning that Sister Magdalene was a compulsive liar, Dana was not sure she wanted to hear from the postulant. Dana had enough to sort out without adding sister's drama to the story.

Again, without waiting for Dana's acknowledgment, Sister Magdalene began. "The other day during breakfast...the card that fell out of Mother's Bible...."

Dana, tired of sister's ability to unduly elaborate, remarked, "I think, that issue has been more than resolved." Dana felt quite the contrary, but she tried to do whatever it took to get the postulant to go away.

Sister cringed; her eyes blinked rapidly. "Are you calling me a liar, Dana? Are you inferring that I don't know what I'm talking about? I can't believe you'd discount me in this way!"

"Sister, you are over-reacting, aren't you? I never made any accusations against you." Dana sensed the woman's anger was more than mere irritation.

The nun bolted up and stared at Dana. "I only thought you might want to know who the older man is."

Dana wondered if, perhaps, the nun's quick change of temperament meant she was serious in what she wanted to share and decided to listen to what the nun had to say. "Go ahead, then."

The woman peered down at Dana. Her eyes narrowed in contempt. Her arms wrapped in the folds of her habit sleeves, she blurted out, "Joe Mikowski."

Dana repeated the name.

"Right, the owner of the Red Barn Tavern, where us girls like to go some nights. Elaine, I mean Sister Seraphim, tried to caution Cindy not to get involved in the older man's advances."

"Did she pay heed?"

"Cindy was far beyond being told anything. Cindy did things her way." The nun reached into a deep pocket of her habit and brought out a cigarette and match. She proceeded to light it. Turning her head slightly to the left, away from Dana, she inhaled and exhaled.

"So, are you saying the answer is a 'no'?"

The woman picked at a loose piece of tobacco on her tongue and continued puffing on the king-sized cigarette. "Why do you think I held such contempt for Cindy? She tried, believe me, to take Joe away right from under my nose. That's when Joe told her he didn't go for any two-timing bitch!"

Dana stood up, feeling herself a bit unsteady by the choice of the nun's words.

"Sister Seraphim's got loose lips. Joe told her if she ever leaked a word of this to anyone that he would kill her. Joe's a big talker."

"Do you think he might have killed Sister Mary Margaret?"

She continued to puff on her cigarette, squinting her eyes as the smoke blew in her direction. "Heavens, no. He wouldn't be that stupid. He's got a reputation to uphold.'

"Oh?" "Joe's a huge contributor to the parish. Father Merton knows that. Ask him if you don't believe me. Nobody, but nobody, would want to cross Joe. His pockets are worth far more than his idle threats." Sister Magdalene snuffed out her cigarette under her round-toed black sandal. "I'd better go. I'm due in chapel."

No sooner had the nun spoken than a bright streak of silver lightning lit the sky followed shortly afterwards with a deafening bang of thunder.

Dana watched the woman rush off, her long habit swishing along the pavement as she made her way into the convent. She could not help but stare long after the nun closed the door behind her. "Liar," Dana called out in a soft voice.

Chapter Twenty-Two

Gertrude, wearing a blue-flowered dress with pink bolero, entered the parlor, where Doctor Vincent was smoking a cigar, the scent of sweet cherry. She twisted one of her brunette curls around her finger. "Doctor, seems there's something wrong with Martha. I'm not quite sure what to do. She has been in her bedroom most of the day, refusing to come out. I tried several times knocking on her door, but she said she wanted to be left alone."

"What about Jewel? Has she been taken care of?"

"I've given her, her morning bottle and rocked her. She is napping peacefully in the nursery, Doctor."

The doctor inhaled on his cigar and breathed out circles of smoke that rose toward the ceiling. "Ah, yes. She is such a good baby, is she not?"

"Why, yes, she is."

With his right hand loose and his palm up, he said, "With Jewel asleep, I think, I might take an afternoon walk to check on Dorothy Bennett."

Gertrude stepped aside from the doctor. "I'm troubled."

"How might that be? You just said Jewel is a good baby."

"It's not that. It's not Jewel I'm speaking about." Gertrude covered her lips and coughed from the strong scent of the cigar.

"Ah, might this be bothering you?" He snuffed out his cigar in an amber ashtray on the corner table and straightened his pale blue sweater vest.

Gertrude raised her voice, "Ned, it's not Jewel that concerns me; it's Martha."

He had heard enough. In a stilted voice, he asked, "What are you talking about? Martha's a big girl. You were hired to look after the baby, not my wife."

"But…Martha…she seems to be drawing more-and-more inward. I can't get her to even speak with me now."

Ned put his arm around Gertrude's shoulder. "Oh, you know Martha. She's a major introvert. Why, I'd go so far as to call her an agoraphobic. She much prefers staying in. This is nothing new. Always has been that way."

"What you say may be true, Ned, but I think, it's getting worse."

The doctor began to leave the room, obviously finished with the conversation.

Gertrude grabbed the man by his sleeve. She took a deep breath. "Won't you please check on her for me? See if you can get her to respond?"

The doctor sighed heavily. "Gertrude, if you insist—."

Gertrude followed the doctor up the long set of stairs carpeted in the deep red rose pattern.

He tapped on the door to Martha's bedroom several times and then opened it. "Martha?" The woman was not in her bed nor in the adjoining bathroom. "That's odd," the doctor said. "You checked the nursery?"

Gertrude nodded. "Only minutes ago."

He opened the door to the large, walk-in closet and gasped.

Gertrude screamed in an ear-piercing ring. "My God, no!"

There hanging from a large noose in the ceiling, her eyes bulging, her purple tongue bulbous, her face a greyish blue, was Martha.

"Quick, get me my surgical bag...there on the chair in the corner!"

Gertrude did as told and watched the doctor remove a small scalpel with which he began to saw back-and-forth against the rope.

With a loud thud, the body of Martha fell onto the carpet below.

The doctor cradled his wife in his arms, sobbing and calling out her name over-and-over as Gertrude rushed to call Doctor Henry Gillion, the coroner.

Chapter Twenty-Three

Mid-morning, Dana hurried over to the Church of Lourdes intent on finding Father Merton in the **rectory** after the ten a.m. Mass. The storm from last night left a chill in the air, and the darkened Church smelled damp. Dana rang the bell when a grey-haired woman struggled to make it up the stairs. She held the railing and studied each stair. Father Merton waited at the bottom.

"Sorry, Father, to disturb you. I don't have an appointment."

"I didn't either, Miss. Father is good like that," the woman said, hobbling beside Dana.

"Lillian's right, Miss Greer. Please come down."

Father invited her into his parlor, where Francine lay covered in a plaid blanket. The dog did not seem disturbed by her entry. Father asked Dana to have a seat but not before offering her the purple afghan he had given her before. "You look a bit worried...concerned, my daughter, in the Lord. Are you here to confess?"

"Oh, no, Father. I'd like to speak with you some more regarding the investigation."

"Sister Mary Margaret, may her soul rest in peace," the priest prayed.

"Amen."

A line of wrinkles covered the priest's forehead. "How can I help, Dana?"

"Father, I've learned of a parishioner...a Joe Mikowski, the owner of the Red Barn Tavern."

"Good ol' Joe," Father said.

"That's what I need to speak with you about. What can you tell me about the man?"

Without pondering the question, Father said, "Joe's been a parishioner here for at least forty years and has owned the tavern for about the same amount of time."

"Without being a gossip, Father, I hear the man has quite the reputation."

"Don't most owners of beer gardens?" Father put Francine on his lap and rubbed his fingers over her ears. The dog settled back to sleep.

"More than alcohol, Father, what is his interest in women?"

"Joe likes his ladies, all right, young, old…Joe likes 'em all."

"So, I've learned." Dana guarded her words so as not to release the source of her information. "Not sure how best to say this, but what was his relationship with Sister Mary Margaret?"

"Oh, come on, dear. You're not telling me a sixty-year-old man had an interest in a thirteen-year-old girl. That's preposterous!"

Dana tried to soften her tactic. "What about his relationship with the Carmelite sisters?"

"He's generously supported them over the years. Their garden, the Stations of the Cross, the labyrinth, the benches…all found out back of the convent were possible due to his financial contributions to the good sisters."

"I see. Any reason for his outpouring of contributions to them?"

"He would give willingly no matter what, but his aunt was a Carmelite until her death at ninety-four."

"So, he respects their mission, their work."

"Goes without saying. Joe is one of those Catholics who sees the dollar bill as his way of helping, of doing what he can for the Church and for the convent."

"He donates to the Church then?"

"Without question. My golden chalice and paten, my vestments, the altar candelabras…all thanks to Joe."

Dana restlessly moved in her chair. Her frustration with the man's answers were beginning to show in her movements. "It's quite clear, Father, that you respect the man highly, but is there anything about Joe that I should know that might not paint such a pretty picture?"

"Hmm." Father continued to pet Francine. "The man likes to gamble on some sports, but c'mon, aren't most men interested in football?"

"Gambling? That's illegal. Are you saying Joe is a bookie?"

Father pulled the lapels of his green cardigan across his chest. Francine sighed. "Now, now, let's not go that far! To be honest, I don't know what he does in his spare time, nor do I want to know. The man's entitled to his privacy, Dana."

The deeper Dana tried to pry, the less likely Father wanted to divulge. Without a doubt, Father Merton covered for the man. Whether it was because Joe's aunt had given her life to the Church,

Joe's elaborate Church contributions, or merely Father Merton's fondness for the man, he felt obligated to protect Joe.

Dana felt a pang of discouragement. Why did Father not feel comfortable saying anything against Mikowski? Why the need for a cover-up? Could it be that Father did not know what was being said about the man? Could it be he knew but could not bring himself to face the truth? She thanked father for his time and went back to her cell.

*

Puddles of muddy water lined the curbs. Neighboring birdbaths overflowed from last night's rain. No boats were in the bay. The month of May more like an evening on a fall night as Dana found her way to the Red Barn Tavern. The establishment matched its name in appearance. The bar stood out on the dreary landscape with its bright, red glossy color, it's *A*-shaped roof, and double doors with white *X*s. A sign in bold, black lettering read: Red Barn Tavern. It hung from a rusted chain above the doors.

The scent of freshly brewed beer greeted Dana as she entered. A long bar ran the length of the tavern with walled shelves filled with every type of liquor one could imagine. Red vinyl stools provided seating for those desiring a drink at the bar, and round white-painted tables and chairs filled the room. Country tunes played in the background creating a casual mood. Servers dressed in denim overalls and yellow T-shirts mingled among the tables taking orders. Dana squinted through the dense smoke-filled room. A man who wore a cowboy bandana around his neck approached her. "You new to these parts, pretty lady? Been sometime since I done seen a blondie like you around." A string of saliva slipped over his lower lip. "Care to dance?"

That's when Dana saw the small wooden dance floor near the back. Four or five couples moved to the lyrics of "A Bushel and a Peck." Dana could not recall the artist, but the singer belted out his words in a southern drawl.

"Afraid I'm not here to dance; I'm here to speak with Mr. Mikowski."

His voice gruff, he answered, "You've just met him, Now, how 'bout that dance, dolly?"

Dana pretended she did not hear the man's comment. "I'm here to ask you are few questions in regard to the murder of Cindy Sullivan."

"Oh, that kid."

"A postulant from the Carmelite order of cloistered nuns named Sister Mary Margaret."

Joe laughed and reached out to slap Dana on the back.

She stepped back just in time. "What's so funny?" she asked.

"Those wanna-be sisters, right! They're out for more than a drink or two if you know what I mean."

Dana knew exactly what the man hinted at, but said, "Afraid not."

"Come around here in their short skirts and shorts with halter tops…don't play dumb, lady. What in God's name do you think they want?"

Dana asked if there was a place where they could talk, instead of trying to scream over the country singer's lyrics.

"C'mon round back. We can talk there…outside my office."

Dana wondered why they couldn't talk in his office. Was he trying to hide something from her?

"I kinda run the tavern pretty much single-handedly, so I don't got much time to waste, lady."

"Dana's my name."

"Let's get right to the point, Dana. I run the tavern. What people decide to do when they come and go is their own bee's wax."

"That's not exactly what I've heard. Were you personally involved with any of these girls?"

"Hey," he said, revealing his front tooth missing. I ain't gonna say I never gave one of them a little hickey on the neck or a pat on the butt, but trust me, nothin' went any further than that."

"Did you ever…well, play one against the other? You know, for her affection."

"Shit, lady! What kind of man would do such a thing? I've got morals."

In the shadows, coming from the back of the building, two men's voices began to escalate.

"I gotta tend to this here little brawl if you don't mind. Also, wear the hat of a bouncer."

Without him realizing it, Dana followed the man around back. Two men were shoving and pushing each other, saying something about one stepped ahead of his place in line. Joe Mikowski settled things by pulling both men to the ground. "Get the hell outta here!"

The two men brushed themselves off and stood up. That's when Dana noticed the words scrawled on the back of the building above a small hole, not much larger than an eyeball:

Peep Show – Get Your Thrills!

The whole matter disgusted Dana to see a line of about ten men waiting for their turn to view through the small opening. She turned abruptly around the building when she bumped headlong into, of all people, Father Tanner Bennett. "Father?"

"Deidra?"

"Name's Dana…Dana Greer."

"Yes, so it is. Got a little spiritual work to do here."

"Right, Father, right. Some sins to forgive, I take it?"

"Why don't you do your job, and I'll do mine, *Da-a-na*."

"Sure thing, *Fa-a-ther.*"

The night was cold and dark. Dana shivered as she made her way back to the convent. She could not wait to get to bed to warm up. Hours passed, though, as she tossed and turned. Her thoughts whizzed like a film strip slipping on its reels.

Chapter Twenty-Four

Dana awoke with a stiff neck and a slight headache. She grabbed a paperback out of her bag and went to the parlor to read. If only she could get her mind off the case even for an hour, it would be a blessing. She hadn't counted on running into anyone, but Betty Carmichael busied herself, humming, "Now thank we all our God" while she snipped some stems off a bouquet of yellow roses.

"Did you hear the news?" Betty asked Dana.

Almost afraid to inquire after Dana already felt her mind was bogged down with enough unanswered questions, she looked at Betty and in a quiet voice, said, "Depends."

"I mean about Martha…the doctor's wife?"

"No." Dana ran her hand against her throat, expecting the incredulous.

Betty put down her clippers. "She committed suicide."

Dana threw her hands to her face and gasped. "What? I just saw them only days ago."

"Gertrude found Martha…hanging from a beam in her closet."

Trying to make some sense of it, Dana said, "Maybe a baby blues. She recently had a child."

"You didn't know?" Betty had her hands on her hips.

"Guess not."

"No one told you?"

Dana's irritation at the cat-and-mouse game became apparent. "Told me what?"

There's gossip going around that the baby was Sister Mary Margaret's"

Dana plopped down on the chair beside her. "But I was told the baby was stillborn."

"Uh-huh. That's what they'd have you believe. From the rumors circling, the doctor led the poor nun to think so, but instead, he gave the child to Martha to raise. Martha was never supposed to bear a child…something to do with medications she takes."

"That can't be…the doctor taking the child. That's illegal."

"So, it is, but getting him to admit the truth is another story."

Dana stood in shock. She hadn't realized that Betty was still rambling on.

"Of course, there was no funeral. You know the Vincents weren't Church goers. I still say those people who don't profess to believe in God are capable of most anything."

That's it. Henry Gillion, the coroner. Dana dug through her bag until she found the man's business card. She needed the truth. Something about the two recent deaths and his reporting of them made no sense. Charles Filmore had found the murder weapon, yet the coroner listed the death as accidental. The doctor stole a baby recorded as stillborn.

Filling the last vase with three roses and some baby's breath, Betty went on. "Martha…it was common knowledge…had some type of mental condition. Near as I could make out, the doctor thought having a child of her own would pull her out of the doldrums."

Dana excused herself and left to use the phone in Mother Superior's office. Luckily, the door was open, but Sister Anne Baptiste was nowhere to be seen. Dana dialed the coroner's number. "Mr. Gillion? It's Dana Greer, the investigator on Sister Mary Margaret's case."

"Ah, yes. How do you do?""Fine, thank you, but I do have a concern that involves this case."

"Surely, how can I help?"

Dana wasted no time. "I recently heard the rumor that Martha Vincent did away with her life."

"Tragic, yes. It was the doctor's wish that she be interred in Seattle."

"Mr. Gillion, I've also heard that Jewel, the Vincent's baby—.'

The man drew his breath and released it before speaking. "Now, now. Don't tell me you're going to fall for nasty rumors."

"What do you mean?"

"Gossip, ah, yes. It spreads thicker than butter. Bet you're going to tell me the baby was not the biological child of Martha's."

"That *is* what I was about to say. I've been told the child *was* Sister Mary Margaret's."

The coroner laughed. "Doesn't that take the cake?"

"What do you mean?"

Gillion sighed. "Sister Mary Margaret's child was stillborn, Miss Greer. I signed the death certificate myself. I ought to know."

"I've been told Martha was not supposed to have children."

"Stranger things have happened." He laughed. "Gotcha on that one too, didn't they? It's hogwash, Miss Greer. Pure hogwash." He paused. "If I could give you a bit of advice, dear, I'd say beware of what you hear."

Was the coroner covering for the doctor? Dana said good-bye and hung up the receiver. She reached into her bag and fingered her miniature Bible. She wished there were someone she could trust…someone she could talk to about the case.

At that moment, Mother stepped into her office.

"Sorry, Sister, I needed to use your phone, but—."

"That's fine, my child, but my, you look as if you're ready to burst into tears."

"Feeling a bit overwhelmed, Mother. That's all."

"Pray to the Spirit, dear, for guidance. He won't fail you."

"Perhaps that's who I should be speaking to. Someone who knows the truth." Dana excused herself and headed toward her cell. The Gregorian chanting from the chapel, echoing off the walls of the cloister, soothed her frayed nerves. The flickering hall candles beneath the statues of each saint cast shadows on the marble floor. She entered her room with plans to get a good night's sleep, perhaps, even say a prayer, and begin her investigation anew in the morning.

Chapter Twenty-Five

"Son, weren't you on call the night before last?"

"What business is that of yours, Mother?"

"Father Merton has been trying to reach you for the past two days. You know, if you lived in the rectory, you wouldn't be able to be so foot loose and fancy free."

Tanner planted a false kiss on his mother's head and said, "That's why I choose to live here with you, *mother.*"

"Well, no matter, but Father Merton told me one of the parishioners needed the sacrament of Extreme Unction, and you were nowhere to be had."

"Merton is more than capable," Tanner said.

"Son, I did not bring you up to be so disrespectful, did I?"

You brought me up to be the son of a bitch that I am, Tanner thought. Changing the subject, Tanner inquired as to where Doctor Vincent was. "Thought he was stopping by to check on you today."

"You didn't hear?"

"I pay no heed to gossip, Mother. You ought to know that."

"This isn't gossip, dear. I heard it directly from Betty. She stopped by yesterday to bring me some daisies."

Tanner hated it when his mother let her thoughts get diverted from the point she was trying to make. "Great, she brought you some damn flowers."

Dorothy wheeled over closer to the vase and whiffed the bouquet. "The doctor's wife…Martha…she hung herself."

Tanner took a step back. "God, no!"

"According to Betty, Martha had some mental issues. I'd heard that before, as well. The new baby might have been too much for her."

"New baby?"

"A little girl…Jewel."

"Had the doctor told you Martha was pregnant? I mean, he sees you every week. Why wouldn't he have said something?"

"No, now that you mention it, he never said a word. Well, whatever, I'm sure doctor is overwhelmed with grief. He's such a kind-hearted man."

The young priest watched his mother wheel herself toward the kitchen. Under his breath, he mumbled, "…a little girl, huh?"

Chapter Twenty-Six

Dana sat at her desk. She tapped her pencil on the notebook in front of her. So far, Sister Magdalene and Betty were the only ones who claimed Doctor Vincent delivered a live baby that night. As for the others, they were either believing what they were told, or else they were lying to cover the real truth. On the sheet of paper, she began to write down the older men who Sister Mary Margaret might have been involved with:

- *Tim Brownell*
- *Doctor Ned Vincent*
- *Joe Mikowski*
- *Jesse Carmichael*
- *Father Tanner*

If the teacher or the doctor had been romantically involved with the young girl, each of them would have motive for wanting the nun dead. Both Mr. Brownell and Doctor Vincent would stand to lose their professional positions in the community. Looked to her that Mr. Brownell was not as likely a suspect since she found the letter to the doctor to be bogus. But, as for Joe Mikowski, Dana did not put much weight on him having a guilty conscience nor fearing his reputation on the island. The wheeler-dealer man, according to Sister Magdalene, had a big bark but little bite.

The question remained did Doctor Vincent and Henry Gillion work in cahoots to start a rumor the baby had been stillborn when, in reality, the two men knew the baby was born alive and would be given to Martha to raise?

As far as Dana was concerned, the doctor was not out of the woods yet. Did he know all along that his intention was to give Sister Mary Margaret's baby to his wife? Did he pay off the coroner, Henry Gillion, to put *stillborn* on the death certificate? Was the nun better off dead than to take the chance she might find out the truth about her child?

That still left Jesse Carmichael and Sister Agnus Dei as having possible motives, though not nearly as strong as the two others. Breaking up was never easy for adolescents, but would the teenager kill the girl merely out of feeling rejection? Plus, why would he be seen putting a flower on the girl's grave if he bore such hatred toward her? Or, could he be feeling guilt, thinking he was the father of the baby? Sister Agnus Dei, on the other hand, never felt the convent should have welcomed the nun into the order to begin with. Again, not the strongest of motives for murder.

There were some facts of which Dana was sure. Sister Mary Margaret and the two postulants were known to leave the convent some nights and to visit the Red Barn Tavern. Everyone she spoke to agreed Sister Mary Margaret had been pregnant and did deliver a child at the hands of Doctor Vincent. Dana saw what appeared to be a newborn in the arms of Martha Vincent.

And as for alibis, Jesse claimed he was drag racing in town. For sure, Dana wanted to confirm this story. Additionally, something still bothered her about the lifestyle the postulants and, for that matter, the young priest, Father Tanner, were living. Something did not add up, and she knew for a fact the priest had lied to her about his mother's disability. Dana wondered if Father Merton knew about his associate's behavior. Even if he did, would he cover for the young man in the same way he had covered for Joe Mikowski's illegal dealings?

Like being caught in a spider's web, Dana felt trapped. There were those who wanted her gone. Sisters Magdalene and Agnus Dei had basically told her that, and then, there was the note Dana found in the Church pew, telling her not to get involved with the dead. But as a private investigator, Dana knew she had no choice but to move ahead until the case was solved. She took Mother Baptiste's advice and whispered a prayer for guidance to the Spirit.

Chapter Twenty-Seven

Dana rang the doorbell several times. From within, she heard, "I'm coming. I'm coming." The door opened, and the woman who opened it took a step back, her mouth open in surprise. "Oh, it's *you*."

The only thing that would bring on such a reception is that the doctor must have been talking to Gertrude. It was clear Dana was not one of his favorites. Dana edged closer to the entry. "May I speak with you a moment?"

"May I ask what this is about?"

Dana knew the truth would only cause the woman to slam the door in her face, so, instead, she said, "I've heard about the doctor's misfortune."

"Please, come in." Gertrude led the way into the dining room, furnished with a banquet-size mahogany table with twelve chairs upholstered in gold velvet. The overhead chandelier provided a dim light. Along the shadowed wall were replicas of famous paintings, such as Girl with a Pearl Earring, Arrangement in Grey and Black, and Head of a Woman. "Have a seat."

"How is doctor doing?" Dana asked.

"Processing might be the word. He's trying to understand the *why* of it all. He thought Martha's depression might be cured after the baby, but it might have been the nudge she needed to…." Gertrude cried.

Dana folded her hands together and set them on the table. "No note then, explaining her actions?"

Gertrude stared down at her empty hands. "Nothing. Makes it that much more difficult on the living." She glanced at her watch. "I'm keeping the baby on a Doctor Spock feeding schedule, so I don't have much time…that is to discuss Martha's tragic demise." She frowned, squinted at Dana, and then began to fumble with her wristwatch. Her left foot began to tap uncontrollably as she peered through a long strand of her hair that partially covered her face. She pulled a tissue from her pocket and blew her nose.

Dana observed Gertrude's expressions, her body movements. Not what she said but her inauthentic behavior puzzled Dana. Gertrude was, obviously, not comfortable discussing Martha's suicide, but it was more than that. Was she fearful where the discussion might take her? Was she trying to cover up a lie? The empathy Dana expected to see was met with a cold indifference, a troubling façade.

Gertrude changed the tone of the visit offering Dana a cup of tea. "It's peppermint"

Dana thanked the woman as she stepped into the kitchen. Water running, soon a whistling teapot, and Gertrude set a pewter tray with teapot, creamer, and sugar bowl on the table. She returned to the kitchen with two China saucers and cups, each finely detailed in a white lace pattern.

The women sipped on their tea in quiet when Dana noticed a studio portrait of the doctor and his wife placed on a teacart in the corner. "Beautiful picture," Dana commented.

"Ah, yes. Century Photographers out of Seattle came to the home and took several poses of the couple." In a whispered voice, Gertrude said, "Afraid that was the last time Martha washed her hair."

Staring at the photo, Dana could read the uneasiness in the woman's posture. Her face bore a pasted-on smile. "She fought with depression?"

"Chronic."

Dana studied the portrait longer. Of particular interest, Dana noted Martha had long, auburn hair done in an updo, and the doctor was completely bald. "Any pictures of the new baby?" she asked.

"Here, let me get the family album. The photographers put together an entire book." Gertrude reached into the cabinet beneath the hutch and laid it in Dana's lap.

Dana paged through the book until she came upon some photos of baby Jewel. "My she certainly has a head of hair for a newborn."

"Yes, black curls and the biggest brown eyes," Gertrude added. "Look here. Look at this one," Gertrude said, as she pointed at the next photo, where Jewel was lying on a pink blanket, a matching pacifier in her mouth. "She's so alert."

"I can see that. She sure is adorable, her dark features...sure doesn't resemble the doctor or his deceased wife," Dana said. "Was she adopted, by chance?"

"Adopted? How presumptuous of you! No, the child was Martha's." Gertrude tried to soften her tone with, "Hard to tell in newborns, isn't it? They change so much the first year."

"Oh, but doctor told me on my last visit that Jewel was a few months old, born premature."

Gertrude tapped her fingers against the China saucer and diverted her attention toward the window. "Oh, there's that pesky pigeon again. Think he must have a nest around here." Gertrude focused on her wristwatch again. "I don't mean to rush you off, Dana, but I need to care for the baby. I'm providing motherly love 'round the clock ever since Martha's passing."

"I understand." Dana picked up her cup and saucer.

Gertrude raised her hand as if to say, stop. "Just leave those. The maid will be here in the morning."

"Of course," Dana said. Trying to catch Gertrude off guard, she said, "Gertrude, the night Mary Margaret was murdered, where did the doctor happen to be?"

Gertrude cocked her head to the side. "That's a question out of the blue, isn't it?"

"Suppose you're right, Gertrude, but as an investigator, I ask questions as they come to my mind, no matter how random they might seem."

Gertrude continued to look at Dana as if her lipstick were crooked. "Let's see. That was a Wednesday night...the last Wednesday of the month. Doctor has his local AMA meeting in Olympia." She laughed softly. "I know that well because beside being doctor's nurse, I also keep his calendar. You know, some of these doctors are like absent-minded professors."

"I see," was all Dana said. She couldn't wait to get back to the convent to look at the photo of Sister Mary Margaret. No matter what, the photograph of Jewel did not resemble the doctor or his auburn-haired wife. She also planned to double-check the date of the last AMA meeting.

*

Dana opened her desk drawer and slipped out the photograph of Sister Mary Margaret. Whether it was the white habit or not, the nun's dark features were prominent…her chocolate-brown eyes, her black brows, and the black wisps of hair that escaped her veil and coif. Jewel had a remarkable resemblance to the nun, not to Martha. The comparison between the infant and the nun, although striking, was not enough to go on to confirm the child was definitely Sister Mary Margaret's, but it was more likely than not.

Next, Dana needed to find the baby's father. Could it be that he was the one to do away with the nun, rather than admit his role in the pregnancy? Again, not a definite but, certainly, a possibility. She might as well take one more look at Tim Brownell as a possible suspect. Where had he been the night of the murder? To be sure, he was in no way involved in the murder of the nun, she decided tomorrow she would pay the family a visit. That still did not rule out Father Tanner. Sister Seraphim said he was the older man she had hoped to warn Cindy about, but it was far too late for that. Dana headed to Mother's office to call the AMA.

*

"American Medical Association, how may I assist?"

"My name is Dana Greer. I am a private investigator, working under contract for the Catholic Church. Presently, I am on Winter Willows working on a case involving the death of a nun. I need to verify the whereabouts of some residents on the night of March thirty-first. I understand that a Doctor Ned Vincent was present at the meeting. Could you verify that for me?"

Dana was surprised when the woman said, "Surely, Doctor Ned Vincent was at the meeting that night. The doctors always meet on the last Wednesday of the month unless, of course, it falls on a holiday."

"Was his name on a sign-up sheet?"

The woman laughed nervously. "He was the keynote speaker that night."

"I'll make a note of that. Thank you." Dana put the receiver down. She had her answer.

Chapter Twenty-Eight

Two o'clock…too early for the recreation hour, Dana decided to take a short walk on the grounds of the convent. When she stepped out of her room, she noticed Betty in the hall replacing the small roses in the alcove vases. Her delicate fingers tossed the dead bloom of a red rose into a small trash bag hung over her wrist. She replaced it with a white one.

"So good seeing you again, Dana. Headed to the grotto?"

"The grotto?"

"Yes, it's May…the May crowning celebration. The sisters process to the cemetery grotto to crown the Virgin Mary statue. Other than Easter Mass, it is the only time the whole congregation leaves the cloistered walls to assemble. I'm heading that way if you care to join me," Betty said.

"Yes, I'd like that. Let me grab my coat. Looks mighty nasty out there."

*

The two women stepped out of the convent when a strong gust of wind whirled around them. The pines marking the pathway swayed mercilessly, several branches already broken. A haze of rain mixed with snow fell from the darkened clouds.

Making their way to the grotto, Dana paused for a moment.

"Is everything okay?" Betty asked.

"Yes, but why don't you go on ahead?" Dana sidestepped closer to the tombstones, some over a century old. That's when she noticed the mausoleum with the chipped corner of concrete…the possible murder weapon of Sister Mary Margaret. She refused to believe Henry Gillion. He was lying, and she needed to find out why. Dana wondered whether sister had even been aware of her impending death or if the murderer had come from behind and hit the young girl in the head. She hoped that had been the case…a horrible way to die but at least not being aware of one's demise.

She braced herself against the wind and continued along the dirt path. Faint Latin chanting followed behind her as the sisters bundled in black, woolen shawls attempted to hold onto their red leather-covered song books while the blustering gusts did their best to drown out their singing.

Ahead Dana could see the grotto, where a multitude of parishioners had already gathered. Father Tanner, in the center of the crowd, held a floral wreath made into a small crown for the statue of Mary, standing in the center of the shrine. Next to the priest were the altar boys Jimmy and Jesse.

Dana walked toward Betty. The sisters, led by the two postulants, processed toward Father, where he handed the crown to Sisters Magdalene and Seraphim. Once the ritual was complete, Father Tanner bowed to the postulants. The two nuns genuflected in front of the statue and returned to the rest of the sisters, who formed a semi-circle on the pathway. They sang "Ave Maria."

Father asked the group to sit down on the wooden benches in front of the altar. "I welcome you all during this crowning of Mary, difficult as it is to believe this is the month of May. Spring is a season of birth and renewal." Father Tanner continued with his sermon, cutting it short as the weather began to worsen. The wet flakes accumulated on the moist ground, the bustling wind sounded like a pack of howling wolves. When done, Father Tanner led the procession away from the grotto while at the same time Jesse motioned with his index finger for Sister Magdalene to step aside. The order of Carmelites followed father out of the cemetery, all singing "Holy Mary, Mother of God."

Dana stayed seated while the rest of the people began to leave. Dana pulled up the collar on her lightweight jacket, and Betty shivered as she found a pair of mittens in her coat pocket.

Jesse and Sister Magdalene were motioning with their hands as if in some type of argument. Jesse wore a scowl, and the postulant's face turned a bright tomato shade.

"Wonder what's going on over there?" Dana asked.

"I expected you to ask that," Betty said, "being a private investigator and all."

"Do you have any idea?" Dana continued.

"Those two? Jesse not only dated Sister Mary Margaret, but he also went with Sister Magdalene for a while. I know. I know. He's only sixteen, and what business would he have getting involved with an older woman...and a nun at that? Trust me, Dana. There are some things that are out of a mother's control." Betty trembled, her eyes watering from the cold. "All a mother can do is support her children."

Dana shivered as the temperature seemed to drop several more degrees. She stuffed her hands into the pockets of her jacket. "To further what you said, Betty, I could see Sister Mary Margaret…Cindy Sullivan, dating Jesse but the other? Well, she is a religious in the Carmelite order."

Betty shook her head. "Do you think that matters? When a young boy's hormones get boiling, it don't matter none what the girl wears."

Betty's comment made Dana cringe. "Are you serious?"

"Hate to say it, Dana, but the young nuns are known to sneak out some nights. They meet over at the tavern to dance, drink, and meet men. Jesse tells me he's even seen Father Tanner down there a number of times."

Dana remembered bumping into the priest near the peep show at the back of the tavern. "So, I've learned." Dana did not explain that she had visited the tavern and witnessed Father Tanner's behavior for herself.

"Humph. Some think the owner of the Red Barn Tavern may have had something to do with the nun's murder, just the same way people think my Jesse might be a suspect."

"I see. Where was Jesse the night of the murder? Certainly, that would clear him of any accusations."

"Down on the main street of town, drag racing with those other silly boys. Jimmy told me he saw him and feared he would lose control of his jalopy…the speed he was going. Mothers and sons…always worries."

Confirmation of Jesse's alibi, Dana thought. One small step closer to solving the crime.

"What do you think about Joe Mikowski?"

"There's rumors that he's been with some of the young girls. I'm not saying he might not be the one to impregnate Sister Mary Margaret but murder? I don't think so." Betty paused and blew her warm breath into her mittened hands. "That's just Joe. He's thicker than thieves with Father Merton, though, so I hardly think he'd risk murdering a nun."

"Does Father Tanner know about this…Father's friendship with Joe?"

"He's a mere kid. I doubt Father would confide such information to him."

Dana tried to process all that Betty had said.

"Joe is a big contributor to Grotto of Lourdes Church. Known to have purchased vestments, chalices, and even cherry-wood pews for the church."

"Does Father Merton know about the young people going to the tavern?"

"I doubt it. And if he did, he'd never make a deal of it with Joe. Father has too much to risk, as well." Betty rubbed her hands together. "What do you say, we get going before we turn into snowmen?"

Dana looked back. Sister and Jesse were gone.

*

As soon as Dana returned to the convent, she asked to borrow Mother's phone and dialed the sheriff's office.

"Brady Olsen, speaking."

"Sheriff?"

"Yes, Ma'am."

"Could I speak with Henry Gillion, please."

"Out of the office. May I help?"

"You might," Dana said, and explained who she was and why she was called to the island.

"Miss Greer, you're questioning our coroner's ruling of death? Is that correct?"

"Yes, Sir. You see the groundskeeper of the cemetery found a broken piece of concrete covered in blood. Archbishop Boretti assigned me to the case because he has strong speculation that this was the item used to murder the young nun…not an accidental fall as Mr. Gillion reported."

The sheriff cleared his throat. "Guess you don't have much experience working these cases that are overseen by large cities, such as Seattle. You see, Winter Willows is an unincorporated area of King County."

"Meaning?"

"We serve the people, Ma'am. We run for office, and we're elected to our positions."

"I understand that, but what has that got to——?"

"It means a clean slate is better than too many dirty ones. You see, about nine years ago, there was a long drawn out case about a woman who was said to be murdered on Winter Willows. It almost closed down the place. Businesses suffered. Tourism dropped incredibly low. Henry and I almost lost our jobs mid-term."

"Wait one minute, Mr. Olsen. Are you trying to tell me that Henry Gillion deliberately lied about the nun's death, so as not to make waves? Is that what you're saying?"

The sheriff breathed heavily. "I wouldn't quite put it that way. I'm sure Henry does believe the girl fell to her death, but why would he want to believe otherwise?"

"Are you telling me it's about job security? Better to have a clean record of no deaths, rather than to record the truth on a death certificate?"

The sheriff chuckled softly under his breath…a nervous laugh. "It's in everyone's best interests, don't you see? The young nun is put to rest, and Winter Willows moves on as the prosperous, little tourist spot people love."

"And it's ultimately your responsibility to agree to this?"

"Let's just say I'm going on almost ten years here in Seattle. That's something to be pretty proud of."

"Proud of? That the city re-elects you to your position because you keep business as usual? Is that what you're saying?"

"I'm saying the people of Winter Willows have job security, and it's known as a safe place to live, to visit, and to shop."

The explanation shocked Dana. She dropped the receiver to the floor.

"Miss Greer?" she could hear the man calling.

Chapter Twenty-Nine

After a good night's sleep, the first since Martha's funeral, Ned Vincent felt refreshed. He positioned himself on the striped wing-backed chair by the window and let his thoughts drift as he sipped on a hot cup of coffee.

A tiny gurgling sound interrupted his quiet. Gertrude entered carrying baby Jewel, dressed in a lime green sweater with booties to match.

"How's my little jewel doing this morning?" Ned asked.

Gertrude kissed the baby's head. "She couldn't be more beautiful. If only Martha could be here to see her daily changes."

Ned stood and in a gruff voice said, "Well, she's not, and that was her choice, not mine."

"I agree, Doctor. I wasn't trying to insinuate blame."

Ned turned toward Gertrude and the baby, and his expression immediately changed. "Of course, you weren't. Sorry to be so snappy this morning."

"Does it have something to do with that investigator?"

"Probably does. I mean, what right does she have offering condolences for my wife? She never even met the woman."

Gertrude set the baby in a small cradle in the corner of the room. "Myself? I thought it was a kind gesture. She made it a special point to offer her sympathy."

. "True, but what's with snooping around in our family album? You had the gall to show it to her. What were you thinking, Gertrude?"

"Sorry, Ned, it's just that she expressed interest."

"She can stay out of Jewel's life. I say there's some sinister reason for coming over here."

"Like what?"

"Oh, forget it. Maybe I am looking for something to fret about."

"Maybe, you are."

*

Henry hugged Gertrude and kissed her on the lips. "How is my little rosebud tonight?"

"Doctor seems to be a bit on edge, but other than that, things are fine."

"Something to do with Martha's passing?"

"He indicated he was upset that the detective stopped over to offer her condolences."

Henry brushed a piece of lint off his sport coat. "Sounds like a kind gesture to me."

Gertrude bit down on her lip. She tossed her hair away from her face. "Got angry with me for showing the Greer woman the family album."

"Trying to make comparisons, is she?"

"Well, if she knows anything about babies, it's that they change so much day-to-day in the first year."

"I hope you told her that."

"I did."

"Let's find something more interesting to talk about, shall we? Your place or mine?"

"I'd love to see where you live, Ned. I've heard it's quite the place. On Lake Washington, correct? Ten bedrooms, four baths? A gazebo in the rear yard? Should I go on?"

"Someday, I hope it'll be yours to share." He kissed the woman again.

"I know. I know as soon as things settle down here."

"Patience, my love, patience. This will all be behind us once the Greer woman gets her ass out of here. Olsen tells me she—."

"Wait a minute. Are you saying Greer contacted the sheriff?"

She's still on the kick that Jewel's birth certificate and Cindy Sullivan's death certificate were feigned."

"Well?"

"Olsen made up some shit about the importance of the coroner keeping a clean slate."

"Did she accept his explanation?"

"Who knows? She's a pretty smart cookie."

Chapter Thirty

Ten o'clock and the Busy Bristles were keeping the dance floor full at the Red Barn Tavern. Guitars, banjos, and violins kept the beat. Dana sat at a corner table, deep in the shadow, a glass of Coke-Cola in front of her. She hoped the two postulants might show-up tonight, so she could watch Joe Mikowski in action.

She watched as the side door opened. She placed her elbow on the table and peered out from the side of her arm. Father Tanner, dressed in jeans and a Navy pullover sweater, went up to one of the girls standing alone along the wall of the tavern. Before Dana could swallow, she watched the priest and a girl in white boots, a red-checkered skirt, and a tight-fitting Angora sweater proceed to the dance floor. Several danced in a line, then one couple formed an arch as the others ducked under it and came out the other side. Tanner and the girl curtsied to each other and walked his own way. The band took a ten-minute break and put Brenda Lee's record "I'm sorry" on the turntable.

Dana was mesmerized by what she saw. Still at the bar stood Sister Magdalene...alone with a cocktail in her hand, sulking. Dana pretended to play with her blond curls, looking through some thin strands to hide her face. Joe Mikowski came up to Sister Magdalene. The two chatted for about five minutes with Joe pointing in the direction of Father Tanner. Joe nodded, scowled, and tapped Sister Seraphim on the shoulder as was the custom when one wished to change dance partners. Sister Magdalene kept her place at the bar when Father Tanner came over. He ordered a drink, swallowed the alcohol in three quick gulps and turned to the girl in the white boots.

Dana watched in disbelief as Sister Magdalene removed her coat from the hook and in a haste left the tavern. As the drama played itself out, Dana concluded that father was a womanizer, for sure, and that he did not exhibit any interest in the dark-haired beauty who went by the name of Sister Magdalene.

On her walk back to the convent, Dana wondered whether jealousy might have played some part in the death of Sister Mary Margaret. Trying to enter the convent by the entrance adjacent to the garden, Dana jumped back as the door seemed to open by itself.

Standing in front of her stood Sister Agnus Dei. "Sister, you frightened me."

"Is that so?" the elderly nun donned in a white flannel nightgown with matching cap and swaddled in a black shawl, asked. "What might be keeping you out so late?"

Quickly thinking, Dana replied, "I was doing some research, Sister."

"Research?"

"On the case…."

"At this hour? It's half-passed one."

"And yourself, Sister, isn't it a bit late for you to be awake?"

"As Mother may have told you, Dana, I am in charge of postulants. Sisters Magdalene and Seraphim report to me. When they did not show up at ten p.m., I readied myself, saying my rosary, right here by the back door."

"I see, Sister. Seems a bit inconsiderate of them to keep you awake."

Sister Agnus Dei let the beads drop to the side of her habit. "A job for an old woman," she said.

Dana sat down on the narrow wooden bench as Sister squeezed her heavy body next to her. "This Carmelite order, it is a cloistered one, is it not?"

"In my day, yes, that was the case. Today, the young ones are given too much freedom, but as Mother says, "We must give them some latitude, or they might not stay for final vows."

"I can understand Mother's concern, but isn't postulancy the time where the young women learn to acclimate to convent life?"

"Ah, yes, Dana, this is true. The two girls we have, though, are live wires. So, too, was Sister Mary Margaret when she was here."

"But she was considerably younger than Sisters Magdalene and Seraphim." Dana said, more as a question.

"If you had seen the girl, you might think otherwise. Part of her ability to be so promiscuous was due to a womanly figure and a mature attitude. You know, until her mother was hospitalized, sister ran the household, played the part of a mother. If someone did not know better, they would have thought she was at least seventeen or eighteen years old…the same age as the two postulants."

Dana could not believe that sister was speaking, let alone so freely about the nuns. After she had seen for herself how the priest and Sister Seraphim got along and the way Sister Magdalene had angrily stormed out of the tavern, Dana could only speculate that Sister Magdalene was angry at not being given the attention she probably came looking for. Dana turned toward the nun and realizing her forthrightness, said, "Sister, about Mary Margaret?"

"Yes?"

"Were there any hard feelings between the three nuns?"

Sister stood up abruptly and excused herself.

Dana assumed the answer might very well be a *yes*.

Chapter Thirty-One

Tanner wrote up his notes for Sunday's sermon. He scratched out some words, then a full line, and finally rolled the paper into a ball. He attempted to throw it in the wastebasket but missed. His nerves were on edge and had been ever since that snoopy came to Winter Willows, he told himself. He hoped the note he had left for her in the Church pew might have scared her off but no such luck. He didn't need his reputation being destroyed by some woman. If he needed to occasionally visit the tavern's peep show, so be it. Father Merton had no knowledge of it, and Tanner didn't need Dana squealing on him. Tanner could hear his mother bellowing in the next room. He chose to ignore her. Most of the time, she only wanted to know where he was and had nothing substantial to say. Furthermore, he had his sermon to write. The Sunday's theme focused on the importance of serving others. It actually was a plea to parishioners to volunteer for one of the non-paying jobs at the church. He laughed. He could sure use a writer to free him up from the task of composing sermons. Since coming to Grotto of Lourdes Church, he could tell his did not go over well. Not a Sunday went by when he did not spot at least a handful of yawns and at least as many Church goers fast asleep. The reaction sure did not inspire his motivation to write. Things were different when he said Mass at the convent. Tanner assumed the young women were too engaged looking at a young, good-looking man to fall asleep. At least, that's what his mother often told him. She tended to be his number one supporter, even though he despised her. If it hadn't been for her being in that damn wheelchair, who knew where he might be. He might have landed in Hawaii or some other tropical island. Rome decided his mother deserved his attention, and so, he was stuck. Until she kicked the bucket, he had a feeling he'd be stuck on the island of Winter Willows. He wondered if this wasn't God's punishment for what he had intentionally done to his mother.

The door to his study rattled. "Tanner, Tanner, I need you."

"Yes, Mother," he said, opening the door. "What in the hell do you want? I'm trying to work."

"There's someone on the phone for you, honey."

Tanner shoved Dorothy's chair into the wall and made his way to the phone in the kitchen. "Father Tanner Bennett speaking." He repeated his salutation three times before a voice spoke.

"This is Grace Newman."

"Who?"

"Sister Magdalene.

"Sorry, surely, Sister, what is the reason for your call?"

"Last night…at the tavern…I wondered if you saw me at the bar."

"Excuse me, Sister," Father said, more a question than a comment.

"I mean did you purposely avoid me?"

Tanner felt his back stiffen. Who was she to interrogate him like this? "No, of course not. I'm sure I don't know what you're talking about."

Are you telling me I'm overreacting, Tanner? C'mon. Isn't it obvious?"

Tanner bit down hard on his lower lip. He hated when woman fawned after him. It was a problem he faced ever since junior high. Some nights his mother had to take the receiver off the hook as girl after girl tried to speak with him. He knew the only way he could get rid of Sister Magdalene was to lie. "Actually, I looked around for you, but you must have left suddenly." Silence filled the other side of the line. Tanner could tell this was not the response the nun was looking for.

"Oh, well, maybe we'll get to dance the next time we see ourselves. I have to get back for my evening obligatory prayers in the chapel. No harm done."

This time Tanner knew the woman was outright lying. She could care less about praying.

Chapter Thirty-Two

Dana sat at her desk the following morning, questioning just how many times she would go over her list of possible older men, connected in some way with the case.

So far, she wrote down Tim Brownell. Although he adamantly refused to take credit for the note written to Cindy, Dana needed to confirm whether or not he was in Norway on the night of the murder as he had told her.

Then, there was Joe Mikowski. He claimed he had no intimate relationship with any of the nuns. Sister Magdalene tried to say that he was indeed dating both herself and Sister Mary Margaret. Could it be the two women were impressed with the man's riches and would do whatever was necessary to win his affection? From what the pastor, Father Merton, said there was no doubt Mikowski was a wealthy man.

Then, there was Doctor Vincent. She could not rule him out as the father of the nun's child. He certainly had an alibi for the night of the murder as he was a speaker at his AMA meeting. According to the coroner, though, the young nun's baby was stillborn, and the doctor insisted baby Jewel was the biological child of his past wife, Martha. On the other hand, if the doctor was the father of the child, it might give him good motive for wanting his child.

The only other older man, if you could call twenty-three being older, was Father Tanner. After all, he was observed at the Red Barn Tavern, and he had also lied about his mother, Dorothy, having a stroke when his mother stated her son had pushed her down the stairs. Without a doubt, he was untrustworthy, as well.

Betty's son Jesse could still be considered a suspect but hardly fit the image of an older man, though he was three years older than the murdered nun.

Dana heard a light knock on her door. She put her pencil down and found Mother Anne Baptiste in the corridor.

"Sorry to bother you, Dana, but we have received an immediate request for prayers. I assume you're Catholic, working for the Church and all."

"Yes, Mother, I am."

"A petition was called in asking the sisters to pray for Doctor Vincent's child. She's missing!"

Dana threw her hand over her mouth. "Oh, my God, Mother, no! When did this happen?"

Tears streamed down Mother's face. "The doctor stopped by late last evening and asked for our prayers. He said Gertrude had taken the child for a buggy ride into town. Jesus, Mary, Joseph…you know how many tourists there are in the shops, walking the main street?"

"She couldn't have left the child unattended. I know she wouldn't be that careless."

Mother shook her head. "No, according to Gertrude, she had stopped to look at a ring in the McFrankle Jewelry Store. While the clerk reached into the glass cabinet and Gertrude tried the piece on, the child was taken…straight out of her carriage!"

"Dreadful…it's terrible. I'd be glad to pray for the child's safe return."

The nun dabbed at her cheeks. "First, Martha's untimely death and now this. God be with them, I pray." Mother turned away…her head bowed low. Under her breath, she mumbled, "Jesus, Mary, Joseph, no."

The news shocked Dana to her knees as she began to pray.

*

During recreation hour in the parlor, the tone was somber. The only voices heard were those of the whispering sisters as they moved their fingers over the wooden rosary beads at their sides. Although the environment impressed Dana as the holy women emphasized prayer over their usual conversation, for the first time since arriving at the cloistered convent, she felt out-of-place.

In the corridor, she saw a man polishing the marbled floors. She had not seen the man before, but she assumed he probably was a hired janitor for the Church and convent. She turned in the opposite direction and stepped out of the convent. The air so fresh with the scent of blue creeping phlox, pink thyme, and purple horned violets that covered the ground like a carpet.

A woman with her hair pinned into a bun and snuggled beneath a long coat, much too heavy for the day, came down the steps of the church. She hurried her pace toward Dana. "Excuse me, lady. Aren't you that policewoman?"

"I'm a private investigator, yes. Who might you be?"

The woman slightly out of breath began to cough into her gloved hand. "The name's Darla. I'm a member here at the Grotto. Try to get to Mass on days when Father Merton's here."

"Not a fan of Father Tanner?"

The woman frowned. "Not really. Maybe you don't know," the woman said, sucking in her lips. She waited until Dana continued the conversation.

"Is there something I should know?" The woman came across as a busy body type who anxiously wanted to share her news.

"Father Tanner is a young man…too young to have committed himself to the priesthood."

Following some advice Fiona Wharton had taught her about white lies, Dana said, "What makes you say that? He seems dedicated and all."

"I've gotta be going but let me tell you one thing you obviously don't know."

Dana waited.

The woman wasted no time in replying, "He had no regard for the fact that Sister Mary Margaret was only a child."

Dana listened intently.

"While father was gone to Rome studying the priesthood, Cindy Sullivan turned into quite a woman, hardly looking like a thirteen-year old. I knew the family quite well…the Sullivans. Poor Mrs. She never was quite stable, and Cindy stepped up to the position of mother. It made her age well beyond her years, not to mention that she had the shape of a twenty-year old. Why, Father Tanner sure had eyes for the girl."

Dana hoped to hear more. "Is that so?"

"Listen, I'd better be running. Looks like rain, don't you think?"

Before Dana could further the conversation, the woman left as suddenly as she had appeared.

Chapter Thirty-Three

Doctor Vincent held Gertrude in his arms as the woman sobbed uncontrollably.

"My fault…it's all my fault. I should never have taken my eyes off her."

"Dearest Gertrude, as much as I love and miss baby Jewel, you can't keep blaming yourself for what's happened. We should be concerning ourselves on finding where Jewel is, rather than on how she was stolen."

She slumped away from the doctor, her shoulders slouching. She braced herself against the wall. "The last time there was a kidnapping on Winter Willows was back in the eighteen-hundreds. A small boat docked at the shore, and a man yanked a sleeping newborn from his mother's arms. The baby and the kidnapper were never seen again. Things like this aren't supposed to happen here."

The doctor wiped the tears off Gertrude's cheeks. "We'll get to the bottom of this. The island isn't that large. Whoever took Jewel won't be able to get away with this. I promise you."

"But who?" Gertrude asked. "Who would do such a thing? It's not like you or Martha had any enemies."

"Enemies? Of course not, dear. We kept to ourselves. Live out in the country. Unless…."

The doctor straightened his tie. "Unless…."

Chapter Thirty-Four

D ana could see why Winter Willows attracted tourists from Seattle and the suburban areas south of the city. Tiny shops lined the streets for blocks…a woman's clothing store with fashions from the Gatsby era; a man's tailor shop with styles replicating Dean Martin and Perry Como; a trinket store with souvenirs from the Pacific Northwest; and, of course, the soda shop and floral store among at least more than a dozen other quaint places.

The crowds wandered the sidewalks, making it difficult to get by. Finally, she found the McFrankle Jewelry Store sandwiched among the other shops. A forest green awning hung from the roof and a wooden door painted a bright gold bore a wreath of purple flowers. Something about the way each store had its own unique painted theme made the street unusual and intriguing.

A tingling bell rang as she entered, and a man came through a lace curtain from the back of the shop. No customers were in the store although looking at some of the prices in the showcase, Dana could see why.

"Hello, Miss, looking for anything particular today. Our precious stones are half-off." He was about to unlock one of the glass cases.

"Actually, I'm not here to purchase anything." Dana removed her ID card from her bag, something she was gifted with after solving her first case.

"Private detective, hmm. Isn't that a dangerous job for someone like yourself?" He took his reading glasses from off the twine around his neck and propped them on the tip of his nose. He peered over them. "I mean, a woman and all…."

The comment irked Dana. Being a woman and a young woman at that had nothing to do with her abilities. "I've been in the business for twelve years, and I'm still alive."

"So, I see. Work for Henning?" The man laughed as most people did hearing the man's name. From what Dana had heard, Henning was the local and only police officer on the island but, supposedly, in name only.

"No, I work for the Catholic Church."

"Hmm, maybe that has something to do with you still being alive."

Dana was not quite sure what the man meant but decided to get to the point of her visit. "Sir, I understand a woman was in your shop a couple days ago when her child was stolen from its carriage. Were you in the store that day?"

"With the sales going and all, you can imagine I don't have much time to take in my surroundings. I do remember we were very busy that afternoon."

"Do you remember the woman with the baby buggy?"

"Can't say that I do. It's a darn shame, though. Winter Willows don't need that kind of PR. It hurts business for all of us."

"What about the parents? I would think you'd find the disappearance of a baby most shocking instead of worrying about the reputation of your shop."

"Of course, of course. I didn't mean it the way it sounded."

"Here's my card should you remember anything from that day."

*

Betty's son, Jimmy, opened the screen door. "Yeah?"

"We haven't had the pleasure of meeting. My name is Dana Greer, and I'm working on the murder case of the young postulant."

"Suppose you wanna come in?"

"That would be nice." Dana followed the young boy up the stairs to the living quarters. A stench of smoke lingered.

In the darkened shadows of the living room sat Jesse, smoking a cigarette, his legs propped up on a coffee table in the center of the room. "So, we meet again, huh?"

Jimmy left the two alone.

"Hello, Jesse."

"My Maw ain't home."

"That's fine. I came to see you," Dana said.

"Me? What the hell for?"

"Mind if I sit down?"

"Suit yourself," Jesse said, spiraling cigarette smoke to the ceiling.

Dana sat across from Jesse. "I'd like to ask you a couple of questions, Jesse."

"Everyone around here is getting fed up with this Cindy Sullivan story. Maybe you should be giving up instead of going ape shit over this."

"You're not the first to tell me that, but I am not about to leave until the case is solved."

"Well, if I wuz you, I'd beat feet outta here."

"Back to Sister Mary Margaret…where did you say you were the night she was murdered?"

"Clever chick, aren't you? Tryin' to trip me up and all. Like I said before, I was out drag racing with some buddies. We were out cruisin,'lookin' for some action."

"Any idea who Sister Mary Margaret might have been with that night?"

"I found out the hard way, lady. Cindy wasn't the type to settle for too long with any one guy."

"You assume she was with a guy that night?"

"Knowing Cindy, the way I did? More than likely, she was."

Dana deliberately changed her mode of questioning. "Jesse, how well do you know Sister Magdalene?"

The boy took his feet off the table, snubbed out his cigarette, and lit another. His fingers trembled.

"Why'd you ask?"

"The day at the grotto—."

"Or, so you were casting an eyeball my way?"

"As a matter of fact, I did see you with the nun after the devotion."

"Sister Magdalene...I used to think she was hep until I found out she was lighting up the tilt sign."

"Excuse me."

"She's a liar, lady, plain and simple."

Dana ran her hand along the doily covering the armrest. "What makes you say that?"

"Caught her red-handed one too many times. She's trouble."

Dana decided to be forthright. "Did that have something to do with her arguing with you the other day?"

"Lady, I don't want to get into that shit. Let's just say she wanted me to do some dirty work for her."

Bingo, Dana thought. She wondered if the disagreement had something to do with the kidnapping of baby Jewel. "Such as? Dirty work?"

"Let's just say I told her to go fly the coop. She wasn't none too happy with me."

"Any idea who she might have gone to next to do her so-called dirty work?"

Jesse shook his head and began to cough. He crushed his cigarette butt into the edge of the table, where there were several other burnt stains, and stood up. "No idea. Some fool she'll try to put the moves on."

Ah hah, Dana thought. So that was the payoff. She'd try to come on to a man as payment for what she had in mind.

"One last question, Jesse. What exactly was she asking you to do?"

Jesse looked at his watch. "Boy, oh boy, it's after two. I'm supposed to be at the soda shop. Better get goin.'" He brushed past Dana and slammed the door behind him, leaving Dana alone in the dark room.

Chapter Thirty-Five

A perfect Saturday for a spring walk, Dana strolled toward Twin Pines. From the Sound, she heard the ferry's horn, making its way back to Seattle after dropping off its morning tourists. After briefly visiting with Mr. Brownell, she planned to stop by the doctor's to see how he and Gertrude were handling the recent loss of the baby.

The closer she got to the secluded neighborhood, she smelled freshly cut grass and watched as two robins basked in a garden hose. Slightly less than two miles away from the downtown section, the atmosphere spoke of peacefulness and relaxation. The white pines shadowed the narrow streets while the sun tried to peek through its branches.

There out front of his home, Mr. Brownell pushed his grass cutter near the curb as a brunette-haired woman trimmed a small shrub near the porch.

"Mr. Brownell," Dana called out.

He stopped short and wiped a steam of sweat trickling from his brow. "I thought I made it clear to you, Miss Greer, that I had no more to say to you."

"Perhaps, you did, but I have one more thing to say to you.

The man's face reddened. He removed a handkerchief from his back pocket and swatted at his face.

"The Norway trip...by chance, do you still happen to have your boarding pass?"

"Why, no. Why would I keep that?"

"What about your family? They must have known you were leaving."

"My wife and two sons went to Seattle. Nora's parents live there. Nora took me to the airport the morning I left."

Although Dana felt awkward not being introduced to the man's wife, she continued just the same. "Nora...I've not met her yet."

Brownell stepped closer toward Dana. "Nor will you. I understand you have a job to do, but I will not let you drag my family into this."

"Mr. Brownell, is there anyone who could confirm your trip?"

"I'm sorry, but you'll have to leave."

The brunette woman stopped snipping at the bushes and stood with her mouth open.

*

Gertrude answered the door, holding a flannel blue blanket in her arms.

"Gertrude, you have Jewel?" Dana could not believe her eyes.

"Come in. Please have a seat."

"I'd like that. Thank you."

"So, you heard...about Jewel's disappearance? The doctor and I did our best not to make public news of the event, particularly, if the suspect happened to be someone on the island."

"Yes, Mother Anne Baptiste told me the doctor had asked for the sister's prayers in the hopes of finding the child."

Gertrude rocked the baby, and she made soft gurgling noises. "It was quite a scare. I feared we'd never see Jewel again."

"It must have been terrifying for you."

"…especially since it was my fault. I only took my eyes off her carriage for a minute at most, but that's all it took." She planted a kiss on the baby's forehead.

"I'm assuming there wasn't enough time to see the person lift Jewel from her carriage."

Gertrude shook her head. "Afraid not."

Dana crossed her legs and folded her arms across her chest. "Could you explain how she was found?"

"Thank God, whoever stole her from me had placed her in a trash receptacle in the alley behind one of the shops. A garbage man on his weekly run heard Jewel's wailing. The thought of what might have happened had the man not checked is frightening. I mean, Jewel would be left for dead."

"Sounds as if that is what the kidnapper must have wanted. Can you think of anyone who would be cruel enough to do such a thing and with that consequence in mind?"

Gertrude stood up and looked out the large bay window, her back to Dana. In a muffled voice, stumbling over some of her words, she said, "Why, n-n-no. What makes you thi-i-nk I'd know?"

"Anyone who might be jealous of the baby? Maybe, it was someone who wanted a child."

"That doesn't ring a bell with me. Ned and Martha are private people. It isn't as if they took Jewel out in public, even." The woman returned to the loveseat and sat down. Her face pale and creased with worry lines.

"I know this must be hard for you, Gertrude, but I'm trying to see if there might be any connections here."

"I understand. You are doing what you need to do."

"What about Martha? Might she have had anyone who envied her?"

"Dana, you must keep in mind Martha was a recluse. She never socialized. It was one of the reasons doctor bought her this house in Twin Pines. On an island, you know, it's easy to get to know most of your community. Martha wanted no part of that." Gertrude began to hum a lullaby to the baby. I'm afraid Jewel has fallen asleep. I should be putting her down."

"I do have one question."

"Yes?"

"Just out of curiosity, why were you in the jewelry store that day?"

Gertrude's face started to turn pink, then rose, like a heavy rogue. "Perhaps, you hadn't heard."

Dana turned her head to the side.

"Henry and I are getting married. I was picking out my dream ring."

Dana hoped her expression did not give away what she was thinking. For sure, Gertrude knew Henry after the baby's birth, the death of the nun, and lastly the death of Martha, but the two of them being involved in a relationship left Dana speechless. That did not stop her mind, however, from running away with questions.

Chapter Thirty-Six

Mother Anne Baptiste invited Dana into her office. Mother was singing "O Thank We All Our God."

"You seem to be in a happy mood."

"Did you hear the news, Dana? Doctor called last night, thanking us for our prayers. The baby was found."

"Yes, so I heard. It has to be such a relief."

Dana wondered if the Mother Superior knew that Gertrude and the coroner were planning on marrying but decided not to be the harbinger of gossip. Instead, she asked if she could use the office phone.

"Help yourself, dear. How is the investigation going?"

"I'd like to say it's going well, but I'd rather say it's going slowly...more slowly than I'd like."

"Really? You should ask Sister Agnus Dei to pray for you. Something about her prayers get immediate results. The sisters and I joke about it during recreation hour."

"At this point, I'd like to employ anyone who might help."

Sister said, "Count me in, as well. Is there anything else I might do to help?"

Dana smiled, "A phone book would. I need to call an airline...one that travels to Norway."

Mother's eyebrows rose. "Norway? Who's going to Norway if I might ask? Not you, I hope."

Dana smiled. No, no such luck."

"You have yourself a seat and take as long as you like, Dana. I'm off to chapel."

Dana nodded and opened the pages to the letter *A*. When she finished going through the list, she came up with Trans World. "March thirty-first," she said to herself. This was the date on which Sister Mary Margaret was murdered. Trans World had a two-fifteen p.m. flight. Dana dialed the number.

"Good afternoon, Trans World Airlines. How might I assist?"

Dana introduced herself and briefly explained her reason for the call. "I'm wondering if there might have been a Mr. Tim Brownell on your flight to Norway on March thirty-first? " Dana could hear papers being ruffled and piles being stacked.

"Could he have checked in under another name by chance?" the airline receptionist asked.

"I don't think so," Dana said, but the woman had a point.

After more paper shuffling, the woman said, "I'm afraid there was no passenger under that name on our flight."

"Hmm," Dana said, feeling as if she had hit another dead end. She was far from bringing the case to a closure, she reminded herself. The names Sister Agnus Dei and Sister Magdalene came to mind. What were their reasons for trying to get her to go, to leave Winter Willows? What or who were they trying to hide? That's when she recalled the poem she had found in the Church pew. That still left Father Tanner who she had not investigated or spoken to at length.

He had a natural inclination to brush her off, but maybe it was time she confronted him again.

*

Dana could hear the rubber wheels of Dorothy's wheelchair on the wood floor.

"Oh, hello, dear. Good to see you again. Please step in."

"Good to see you, too, Dorothy. By chance, is your son at home?" Dana figured if she chose an off time in the afternoon, she might be more likely to find the man in.

"Tan, Tan, Tanner," she screamed.

Dana could understand how the young man might find it irritating to be an adult and to be living in his mother's home. The woman's shrill voice would be enough to drive Dana crazy.

"Yeah, Mother, what is it?" Tanner's hair was scuffed up and his face had a five-o'clock shadow. He looked as if he might have just gotten up. When he saw Dana, he stepped back. "Did you tell us you planned to pay us a visit?" He spoke to her in a gruff, irritated voice that spoke of discontent.

"Happened to be in the neighborhood," Dana said, and smiled.

"Tanner, could you be more respectful of the investigator. Thought I brought you up better than that!" She turned her focus toward Dana.

"Okay, what might be our pleasure to see you, Miss Greer?"

Dana quickly was getting fed up with the sarcasm that poured out of the man's mouth.

"Let's all sit down, shall we?" Dorothy asked.

"Why don't you get the hell out of here, Mother. Sounds as if Miss Greer is interested in speaking to me…not you."

"Maybe, Tanner is right, Dorothy. This is rather personal," Dana said.

"Why!" Dorothy carelessly wheeled her chair around the corner.

Tanner sat on the sofa while Dana sat across from him on an old, wooden piano bench without a cushion. She was glad Dorothy didn't join them as Dana wondered how she might approach some uncomfortable, awkward questions if the man's mother was present.

"I won't take much of your time."

Tanner's eyes darkened. He bit down on the inside of his cheek.

"I'm left wondering, Father, how well you might know Sister Magdalene?"

"As well as any of the other nuns," he flippantly replied.

"Father, I don't mean to negate your answer, but certainly, that couldn't possibly be the case. The order of cloistered sisters is rather large. Would you say you are more personable around the younger sisters?"

"Why don't you quit beating around the bush, Dana. Are you asking whether I am friends with the postulants? Yes, I am."

Dana thought the priest might well have backed himself into a corner. "Sisters Seraphim and Magdalene?"

"They're the only two."

"Ever socialize with them?"

Dana could feel the sense of discomfort in the room; a dead silence lingered.

"If you're asking if I've gone out with either of them, of course, not. I have taken a vow of chastity, after all."

"Come, Father, don't even priests get tempted to sin?" Dana knew her words were sharp as thorns on a rose bush, but she wanted to get Tanner to admit what he knew and to speak the truth.

"If you're asking if I am infallible," he laughed uproariously, "I would be free to say no."

"Tanner, let's get to the point. You're playing a cat-and-mouse game, and we're wasting our time. Are we not?"

The man's face turned the color of beets, and his hands shook in his lap.

"Okay, okay, so you saw me at the Red Barn Tavern once or twice. Does that make me a criminal?"

"Seems a rather odd place for a priest to be, wouldn't you say?"

"This is the fifties, Dana. Some things have changed. If you're saying a priest is not entitled to a night out to get a glass of beer, you're quite off the mark."

"I'm asking if it is acceptable for a priest to buy a drink for a nun? Is it proper for a priest to dance with a nun?"

"I see. In your spare time, you stalk my whereabouts?"

"Not only yours, I interview and visit others, as well."

"Why not leave me alone then? Sounds as if you've got plenty to keep yourself busy. Let's end this ridiculous talk, shall we?" Tanner stood up to leave the room.

"There is one more thing I'd like to ask if I may," Dana said.

Tanner turned back. He looked over his shoulder.

"How well did you know Sister Mary Margaret?"

"I conducted her funeral Mass and saw her put to rest in the grotto cemetery, if that's where you're going with this."

"That's interesting," Dana said. "I've spoken to at least two sources who say they had seen you with the young girl."

"I'd suggest you question the authority of your sources, Dana. Winter Willows is known for its vicious gossip. I hear it confessed more than you'd like to know."

"Gossip, rumors, lies…I've heard all of it. I'm tired of listening to excuses, rather than the truth, Father. Maybe, it best I begin with you. What is the truth?"

"Listen to me, lady. You're not the one I confess my sins to and until then, I don't owe you an iota of anything."

"Wonder if Archbishop Boretti would agree with that. I report to him."

The priest pounded his fist into the palm of his hand. His eyes narrowed as he bit down on the inside of his lip. "Damn it to hell, after all! Okay, okay, so Cindy and I dated before Mother took her into the convent."

"And, we all know Cindy was two months pregnant at that time. Could it be that you're the father of that child?"

With his two fists balled until his knuckles turned white, he said, "Try to pin that one on me, why don't you?" With his upper lip curled, he said, "You have no proof, nor will anyone else. Cindy was a wild card!"

Dana had to agree that the priest had a point. Other than speculation, who could say positively he was the father of Cindy's child? The only thing further Dana could ask was where was the young priest on the night of the nun's murder.

"March thirty-first? I was home with mother. Why not ask her yourself?"

This time he did leave, headed to the back of the house. "Mother? I believe our guest is leaving."

From around the corner came Dorothy. "My, my, Dana, it does seem, as though, Tanner is none too happy with you interrogating him."

"That was not my intent, Dorothy. I am only trying to get at the truth, but rather, it seems that everyone around here is covering for someone else. It's difficult to solve a case when this is the pattern."

"Dear, maybe you're working overtime. You might need to get some rest."

Dana chose to ignore the woman's remark. "By the way, Dorothy, I do have a question for you. What do you remember about the night Sister Mary Margaret was killed?"

"Why Tanner and I were shocked to learn the news the next day. Here we were only the night before listening to the Lone Ranger with Brace Beemer." She paused and glanced at her Philco radio hidden in the corner of the room under a stack of newspapers. "It was the last show for the season. I remember because a major storm was passing through, and Tan and I were hoping our Philco reception wouldn't quit on us."

"I see," Dana felt comfortable believing what Dorothy had told her. She was a woman who spoke her mind. And as for the weather, Dana recalled Charles Filmore telling her about the storm that swept through the Sound March thirty-first. He had found the young nun's body in an open grave filled with inches of rainwater. "I'll see myself out, Dorothy."

"I can tell you one thing for sure. My son is a loving man who loves his God and loves me. He has made a fine, young priest who I am more than proud of."

"I can see that, Dorothy. Thank you for your time." Dana found her way to the door.

Chapter Thirty-Seven

The next day at recreation hour Sister Anne Baptiste approached Dana. The nun held a bundle of blue yarn in her hands. "I've completed the sweater." She unfolded her work and showed Dana the project she had been working on for weeks. The tiny sweater boasted mother-of-pearl buttons in the shape of hearts."

"Oh, Sister, it came out beautifully."

"Might I trouble you to take it to the doctor's place? It could be a nice welcoming home gift for the little one."

Dana reached for the sweater, feeling the soft yarn in her hands. "I'd be happy to do that for you, Sister."

"Bless your heart, and thanks be to God. The sisters are I are so grateful the child was found. I overheard someone say the baby was wailing inside a trash can. God, in his mercy, must have put the garbage collector there at the right time."

Dana remembered a time when her faith was that strong, but ever since she had left the Church years ago, she felt a hollowness in her soul. She kept hoping one day it would return in the same way a lost item often finds its rightful owner. "I spoke with Gertrude the other day, and she expressed her excitement and gratitude for Jewel's return."

Mother Superior grabbed at the large crucifix resting on the starched cloth around her shoulders. "Oh, dear, I keep forgetting to tell you, Dana. Someone from the jewelry store has been trying to get in touch with you."

"I did leave my card with the owner. Mind if I go to your office to return the call?"

Mother smiled. "Go in God's peace, my dear."

*

The man who answered the phone sounded the same as the owner had the other day. "Don't know if this means much to you, Miss Greer, as I heard the kidnapped child was found, but the week of the sale, a woman…damn, what was her name?" The man stopped and Dana waited to hear more. "Deidre, Donna, Dottie, um…Darla…yes, that was her name. She came into the shop and told me she saw someone in a black leather jacket carrying a screaming child out the back door of the shop. Said he smelled like a carton of cigarettes."

Darla, the woman who had approached Dana the other day…the one who had a disliking for Father Tanner. "Did she happen to leave her number?"

"Never thought to ask. You might try the church."

"That a great idea, Sir. And your name?"

"Harry Mansfield."

Must be the father of the young boy who dated Cindy Sullivan until she broke up with him, and he crashed his motorcycle in Seattle. She questioned, "Mr. Mansfield, are you related to Gordie?"

"My son…died in Seattle."

"Sorry for your loss." She hung up the phone.

*

Weeks ago, when Dana spoke to Tim Brownell, she remembered him saying, "Gordie Mansfield. All the girls liked Gordie. He and Cindy were an item for quite some time, but of course, Cindy two-timed. They went steady for at least five or six months." The pieces of a puzzle were coming together but not necessarily in the places Dana hoped. Winter Willows was a small island, and it would only be natural that soon names would start to overlap, she told herself.

*

Dana rang the bell to Father Merton's residence.

"Good to see you, my child. How are things going with you and the case?"

"Afraid not too well, Father. I find myself spinning in circles."

"Sorry, Dana. I'll pray for you. Such a difficult job you have, I'll say."

"Thank you, Father, but you might be able to help me."

Father stroked Francine's head. The dog licked father's hand. "How's that?"

"I'm wondering if the name Darla means anything to you?"

Before she asked anything further, father's face brightened. "My, my, Darla Wheeler. She attends Mass every week. Sweet woman…she was good friends with Mrs. Sullivan before she was sent away. You did know she was committed to an institution in Seattle, did you not?"

"So, I heard." Dana recalled Charles Filmore telling her the same.

"I need to speak with Darla, Father."

"She'll be at Mass tomorrow morning...guaranteed."

"I'll be there." About ready to leave, Dana stopped. "Father, do you know why the woman has a dislike for Father Tanner?"

Father scratched his head. "Doesn't surprise me any. Darla has her opinions."

"Such as?" Dana asked.

"Story has it she claims she saw Father with Sister Mary Margaret shortly before the girl joined the Carmelites. It was one of the reasons why we had such a difficult time finding someone from the parish to take in the girl."

"Father, when you say she saw father with—?"

"Yes, Miss Greer, in an inappropriate way."

"But Sister Mary Margaret was only thirteen-years old, Father, and Father Tanner is twenty-three, correct?"

"Besides being newly ordained and the age difference...well, it troubled Darla. I had no idea of this, but I trusted Darla. I spoke with Father Tanner as Darla did to the young girl. As far as we knew, that was the end of it. The girl joined the convent, and as for Father Tanner, he never has been a favorite of Darla's."

"That's understandable."

"Please don't take what I've said any further. We don't need the higher ups calling me now, do we? I'm only trying to help."

"Father, I need all the help I can get." Dana hesitated before asking the priest what was on her mind but posed her question anyway. "You say the parish had a difficult time finding a home for Cindy because of her reputation."

"True."

"And Cindy was two months pregnant when the good sisters took her into the convent."

"Not to their knowledge, though. The sisters found this out a bit later."

"Mother Superior told me they hoped once the girl delivered her child that the baby would be raised by them in the convent."

"This is fact," father said.

Dana tapped her fingers on the arm of the chair. "By chance, do you think they felt obligated to the girl for any reason?"

Father Merton put Francine on the floor. "Care for a cup of tea?"

Dana needed an honest answer. She repeated her question.

"I see where you're going with this, Dana."

"Do you?"

"Most certainly. You're asking me if the sisters felt they needed to cover-up a scandal between Father Tanner and the girl?"

"Exactly. Could that be?"

"Only if Cindy admitted Father Tanner was the father, I suppose."

"Well, what do you think?"

"What do I think? I think, you'd better run that question past Mother. Surely, she is the only one who could truthfully answer that question."

For once, Dana finally thought she might be getting somewhere.

*

After the eight o-clock evening vespers, Dana waited for Mother to come out of the chapel before she approached her. "Mother, sorry to disturb you at this hour, but could I speak with you?"

Mother agreed and said she would come to Dana's cell.

Mother sat down on the chair. "You look terribly worried, my child."

"Perplexed, yes."

Dana sat on the edge of the bed.

"Mother, how best might I say this?" Dana stood and chewed down on her index finger.

"Understand, Dana, I know why you've come here and that you need honesty and answers to do your job. I will help in whatever way I can."

Dana felt as if a concrete block fell off her shoulders. She told the nun about meeting Darla and what her thoughts were on Father

Tanner. She also relayed that she had come from seeing Father Merton, and his story collaborated with Darla's.

Mother cupped her cheeks in the palms of her hand. She let out a loud sigh. "As much as I'd like to say this isn't so, Dana, Sister Mary Margaret, months after her arrival here, confessed to me that the child she was carrying was that of Father Tanner. We offered to take her child, to raise it here in the confines of the convent. Promised her no one need know. That's when weeks later we received the news the child was stillborn. Sister was devastated as were we all."

"Do you think Father Tanner knew?"

"I would assume Mary Margaret told him, but I can't be positive of that."

"My questions must be difficult, Mother, but I must ask, "Do you think Father Tanner had any idea you knew he was the father?"

"Can't say for sure."

"Did you feel obligated to go public with what you knew?"

"Why, Dana, and ruin a young man's vocation? What was done, was done, I'm afraid."

In her heart, Dana believed the priest's secret should have been confessed to the bishop, if not by Tanner, then by the sisters. From what she was learning about the young priest, Dana felt convinced he had no right to be in the ministry.

Chapter Thirty-Eight

The next morning, a heavy rain pounded the pavement, and the wind thrashed against the branches of the rose bushes and rhododendrons leading to Grotto of Lourdes Church. Dana hoped Darla had made it to Mass despite the weather conditions. From the look of the sky, the storm had no plans to end anytime soon.

Dana waited in the rear vestibule as the parishioners sang the closing hymn. A handful of people exited. Dana peered inside, and there was Darla still in her pew. She wore a plastic see-through raincoat and a fringed scarf on her head.

"Excuse me, Darla, Mr. Mansfield at the jewelry story told me you wanted to speak with me. When might be a good time?"

"Now is as good as any, I suppose." The woman rolled up the rose-colored beads of her rosary and stuffed it into a black, velvet pouch and moved down the pew, making room for Dana. The vigil candles were the only light in the darkened church.

"The day you were coming into the store, what did you see?"

"I didn't actually see the person pick-up the child, but I did see someone carrying the child. His elbow brushed past me in his effort to hurry out of the store. This was the back door leading into the alley."

"Did you notice what was he wearing?"

"I did look back as I found him to be quite rude, never even saying, 'Excuse me.' He was wearing a black, leather jacket and was carrying a screaming baby. That's all I know, but when I heard an infant had been kidnapped that day from the store, it got me thinking. Has the child been found? There was nothing about it in the papers."

"Thank God, the baby was found almost as quickly as she was stolen. The baby was found by a local garbage collector. Seems the child was thrown into a trash bin."

"Lordy, no, who would do such a thing?"

"That's what I'm wondering, too."

Something about the argument Jesse had had with Sister Magdalene at the Grotto and the black leather jacket gave Dana reason to pause. Could the postulant have convinced Jesse to do her dirty work as Jesse referred to it? Might it be she was trying to get back at Father Tanner for having conceived a child with Sister Mary Margaret? People were known to do strange things in the name of love. With sister out of the way and the hopes of doing away with her child, Sister Magdalene would have no physical memories left of the relationship Father Tanner once had.

Chapter Thirty-Nine

"I told you before, Mother. You're not to open the door to that bitch! Do you hear me?"

"Tanner, Dana Greer is a wonderful woman who is only doing her job."

Tanner's eyes squinted.

Dorothy cowered in her chair.

"You call doing her job trying to convict people of crimes they didn't commit? Is that what you're saying, Mother?"

"Tanner, please, don't raise your voice like that to me. I told the woman that you were a kind man and a good priest. Didn't you hear me?"

"Uh huh, and did you tell her I was the one to push you down the stairs? That you hit your head on the concrete floor? That you injured your spine? Huh, did you tell you that, too?"

Dorothy pulled her body to the side of her wheelchair, snuggled deep into its corner. "Must you raise your voice like that to me?"

"Maybe it's because that's the only way you understand that I'm fed up, mad."

In a quivering voice, she said, "I'll try, son. I'll try to avoid Miss Greer as best I can."

Tanner laughed, showing all of his teeth. "You'll what? Try to avoid the bitch?"

Dorothy only nodded.

"Not enough, Mother. Did you not hear me? I said to never let her in this house again…to stay away from her…to keep your big mouth shut, do you hear me?"

Dorothy started to cry. She tried to suck in her gasps, so her son would not notice.

"Mother, I hate when you act so pitiful, so helpless." Tanner stood before his mother and grabbed her by her shoulders. He shook her until her chair wobbled. He jiggled it some more. It teetered until it tipped over on its side. Tanner left the woman, crying on the living room floor.

Dorothy dragged her weakened body to the kitchen, using her elbows to navigate. In what seemed like an hour later, finally making her way to the phone on the wall. She pulled on the cord, and with her index finger, she dialed zero. "Please connect me with Doctor Ned Vincent."

Chapter Forty

Dana felt content that she finally had some solid leads. She went to the refectory for lunch, planning afterwards to deliver the baby sweater to Jewel. Scents of meatloaf came from the kitchen. Dana took a seat next to Sister Agnus Dei. The two sisters serving the food slid one portion per each dish and smothered it with brown gravy. Dana was not impressed with the menu choices but had to admit meatloaf sure beat bread and water.

Mother stood at the podium to lead the blessing of the meal. When done, she waited for the room to silence from the clicking of the silverware and the banging of the coffee cups. "Before I begin this afternoon's reading, I have an announcement to make." Mother waited until all attention was on her. "I recently received news that Dorothy Bennett, Father Tanner's mother, has suffered an injury."

Like a swarm of bees whizzing through the room, the sisters whispered among themselves.

"Please, this is mandatory silence time, sisters. I would like to add that she is resting and doing okay after she took quite a tumble from her wheelchair. I know, we will be offering our work, our play, and our prayers for her comfort."

Sister Agnus Dei raised her arm.

"You know, Sister, that we do not speak at this time. Please save your words for recreational hour."

Dana could hear the elderly nun make a snorting sound in response.

Mother opened the large Bible that always stayed on the podium and began to read a psalm.

All Dana could think about was Dorothy. In her heart, she knew Tanner had to be involved in the accident.

*

On the way out of the dining hall, Sister Agnus Dei grabbed Dana's sleeve and pulled her to the side. "Did you hear what really happened to poor Dorothy?"

By this time the corridor had cleared, some sisters going to chapel, and the others to their cells. The sun shone through the stained-glass windows making rainbows on the tiled floor.

"This is the first I've heard."

"The poor dear's elbows are raw as she attempted to crawl along the floor to the phone."

"How did the accident occur?"

"From what I heard, she fell out of her wheelchair."

"That sounds a bit difficult to understand. How could her chair tip over, I wonder."

"That's just it. Could it? Unless…."

"Are you insinuating that someone may have pushed or shoved her?"

"…the only thing that makes sense to me." The nun pulled out a large, linen handkerchief from the side pocket of her habit and blew her nose, making a loud honking sound.

"Besides the doctor who looks in on her, does she get visitors? I mean, someone had to have—."

"Knocked the chair over, Dana, is that what you're trying to say?"

Something about the elderly nun's masculine, gruff voice made Dana believe she was obligated to agree, even though, she did. "But who?"

"I'm saying it had to be her son, Father Tanner. Never have cared for him much. He's quite the arrogant one. Think it has something to do with his uncle being an archbishop. Why, Father, thinks he has some special clout."

"I'd like to say, I hope you're wrong, Sister, but I can't think of anyone who might have done this."

"Agreed." Sister glanced around the corridor. Mother Superior came toward them. Sister Agnus Dei pretended to be saying the rosary on the beads at her side while walking ahead, leaving Dana standing alone.

*

Dana climbed the stairs to the peach house. She did not plan to knock as Dorothy probably was in bed. She peered through the screen door and became startled when Doctor Vincent met her. He opened the door and told her to come in.

"I heard from Mother Superior that Dorothy took a tumble."

"She's actually been asking for you." The doctor led Dana to Dorothy's room where she lay in a large canopy bed. Behind her shoulders, four pillows propped her in a semi-sitting position. On her night table lay a pack of cigarettes.

"I'll be back to check on you tomorrow, Dorothy," the doctor said, and left the room.

Dana put her hand on the woman's shoulder. "Dorothy, I'm sorry to hear the news. Mother Superior asked for prayers."

"How kind of her. I'm doing okay…just some bruises and floor burns on my arms."

"What happened?"

"Stupid me, I was doing some dusting and tried to reach up to the window ledge. My chair tipped sideways, and I couldn't prevent myself from falling." Dorothy lifted her bare arms out from her blankets to show Dana the backside. "See, some scuffs; that's all."

"Ouch! Looks painful. Were you home alone at the time?"

Dorothy nodded. "Tanner wasn't here."

Dana thought better to not say anything, but she did note some purple bruising on the woman's upper arms, near her shoulders…both shoulders, not something that could have occurred if the chair tipped to one side as Dorothy had said.

Dorothy was about to continue when the two women jumped simultaneously at the bang of the side door.

"Tanner is that you? Honey, are you home?"

"I'll go check for you, Dorothy."

"No, Dana, go out the front door. Hurry!"

Dana deliberately chose to confront the man. As she made her way to the side door, she thought she heard Dorothy say, "No, stay here."

Dressed in his black cassock with Roman collar stood the young priest. His eyebrows lowered. His right hand held his Bible and his left was balled into a fist. "What in the hell are you doing here? Didn't mother tell you to stay away from us?"

"As a matter-of-fact, I stopped by to check on her after her sudden fall."

"That's no business of yours. Mother is fine…just fine."

"Hmm, interesting that you should say that, Father. She didn't look that *fine* to me. I found it hard to believe both of her shoulders were bruised when her chair tipped sideways."

"I'd leave the diagnosis to Doctor Vincent; after all, you're only an investigator."

"Precisely and that was the purpose of my visit…to see exactly how your mother was doing."

"And now you've seen, so I suggest you get out." Father tossed his Bible on the side chair. With his balled fist, he pounded into the palm of his right hand. He began to step toward her when the phone rang. He turned toward the kitchen.

"Why are you calling me? Why are you bothering me?"

Dana left before he returned. Something about his mannerisms and his facial expression left her filled with fright. From what she had observed, she wasn't sure what he might be capable of.

*

A cool breeze blew in from the Sound as Dana trekked toward the doctor's house. She could hear her heart throbbing after her encounter with the priest. She tried to breathe deeply and take in the Pacific Northwest scenery to get her mind off things. A two-mile walk would calm her, she told herself.

When she approached the doctor's house, she rang the bell, and Gertrude opened the door.

"Is Jewel up? I'd love to see her. I have a gift from Mother Superior."

"She's right here. Come on in."

Jewel lay on a pink blanket on the floor, kicking her legs and arms and cooing softly. Her black hair and dark, round eyes against her pale complexion made her look almost doll-like.

Dana took out the sweater from her bag. "Could we try it on her?"

"Yes, let's." Gertrude lifted the infant and delicately put her arms in the soft sleeves.

"She looks precious. Might I hold her?"

The woman handed the baby to Dana. Jewel gurgled and cooed and reached for a strand of Dana's hair. She tugged on it and tried to put it in her mouth. "She's adorable."

For a moment, Dana wondered what it might have been like if her marriage to Nate had worked out. Would they have had a child of their own by now? Once she suspected he was involved with a prostitute, any thought of the marriage continuing ended.

The infant smelled of baby powder and fresh laundry detergent. Dana braced the baby's head in both hands and held her at arm's length. "So sweet. So happy she was found."

Gertrude took the baby and propped her over her shoulder. "The doctor is grateful for her return."

"No further word on who took her?"

"Nothing. You can be sure, though, I'll never take my eyes off her." Gertrude patted the baby on the back. She swallowed hard, her eyes blinking rapidly. "Dana, this sweater is so cute. I don't know Mother, but could you pass along my thanks."

Gertrude's words caused Dana to ponder. Under normal circumstances, one would question why a stranger would have taken the time to knit a sweater for the child. The fact that Gertrude did not address this convinced Dana, even more so, that Jewel was not the biological infant of Martha and the doctor. "I'll be sure to do that, Gertrude," Dana said.

By this time, the woman was showing Dana to the door.

Chapter Forty-One

Betty replaced the carnations in the small vase under the alcove of Saint Peter.

Dana could hear the woman sniffling. "Are you not feeling well? Betty."

When the woman turned around, her face was red, her eyes swollen. "Oh, Dana," she cried, and reached out to hug her. "My boy, my Jesse, no."

"Is he okay?"

Betty let go of her hold and set the vase down. She wiped her nose in a handkerchief embroidered with a purple *B*. "He's fine. But the island people are saying such wretched things about him, making accusations."

"Such as what?"

"They say he murdered Sister Mary Margaret, that her baby is alive, and that Jesse tried to kidnap her from her carriage. Lies, they're all lies."

"Why would they say these things? And who?"

"A woman from church...Darla Wheeler. Do you know her?"

"Yes, I've met her...once." Dana bit down on her lip before she said anymore. Her white lies weren't easy for her. According to what Father Merton had told her, Darla did have her opinions. But the problem with opinions is they aren't necessarily facts, Dana thought.

Betty dabbed at her eyes, almost closed now. "I don't know what to do. It's sheer gossip, and my Jesse is innocent."

"From what you've told me Betty, you, too, believe that Sister Mary Margaret's child was not stillborn. People have been insinuating that Jesse might have murdered the nun. That's nothing new. The only part of this gossip that's new is that Jesse had something to do with the kidnapping. How do you feel about that?"

"That my boy might have taken a newborn? I can't fathom it. I just can't."

"What if it wasn't his idea? What if he was put up to it?"

Betty's face hardened. Her eyebrows hovered over her eyes. "I'm not sure I understand where you're going with this, Dana."

"I met with Jesse the other day. He mentioned doing some dirty work for Sister Magdalene."

Betty screamed, "No, my boy wouldn't be talked into anything like this. You don't know Jesse." The woman ran her hand over her left cheek and fingered her lips.

"You're correct. I don't know him that well, but I have had the chance to get to know Sister Magdalene quite well during my stay at the convent. The argument at the Grotto, the two had. Did Jesse ever tell you what that was about?"

"No, no, he didn't. I know *that* woman can be emotional, and I figured they might have had a spat over dating or something."

"That might be a question you need to raise with your son, Betty? But from what I know, that nun could be capable of most anything."

Betty's eyes filled with tears, she continued to sniffle. "…even convincing someone to commit a crime for her? That's outlandish!"

"Even that." Dana kept thinking about the black leather jacket Darla had mentioned. It didn't convict Jesse of the crime, but it didn't exclude him either. "By chance, can you think of what sister might have over your son…a 'Do as I say, or else'?"

"You mean if he refused, she'd…? Well, I don't know." Betty shook her head from side-to-side.

"I don't know either, Betty. All I do know is Jesse had no desire to explain what he and Sister Magdalene were arguing about. Maybe he'll be more willing to share that with you, and if he does, I'd appreciate it if you told me. If he's not involved in the kidnapping, it's time we find that out anyway."

Betty forced herself to smile.

Dana patted the woman's hand. She was not one to fall for gossip, but she had to admit she worried that some of what Darla had said was true. When Jesse told her he was not about to do Sister Magdalene's dirty work, Dana believed the boy lied to her. All she had to go on was a motive and a black leather jacket, but it seemed enough to convince Dana. If Sister Magdalene was in love with Father Tanner, she might very well wish to do away with any memory of his time with the deceased nun. The baby may have been too much for her to bear. For some reason, Sister Magdalene had Jesse wrapped right around her finger.

*

Dana wished she could turn off her former mentor, Fiona Wharton's, voice. The didactic words kept repeating themselves, "Don't be fooled. A strong motive does not necessarily make a strong suspect." Taking the message to heart, Dana went through her list. Convinced now that Father Tanner was the father of Sister Mary Margaret's child, certainly, moved him up a rung on the ladder of suspects. Why he waited until the baby was born before the murder remained a mystery, though.

Betty's son, Jesse, sure appeared to be taking orders from Sister Magdalene for an unknown reason. The thought of the pretty postulant being a compulsive liar, as Mother said, made it most difficult to put any weight on what she said. Darla spoke her mind, and Father Merton respected her. Sister Seraphim spoke from her heart, and Dana trusted her. Based on things she had told Dana, she ruled out Joe Mikowski from her list. That only left Tim Brownell, who was not on the plane to Norway as he had said.

Chapter Forty-Two

Dana left her cell and headed to the chapel. The soft, melodic lyrics of the nuns drew her in as if she glided on wings. She sat in a back pew, impressed by the group of sisters before her. Most never looked at their hymnals but sang from memory. Something about the music, the prayers, and the overall community spirit reminded her of her childhood and her desire to be a nun.

Unfortunate as it was, her intention was sharply dashed ever since the night on her uncle's boat. A mere child, yet her image of herself as unworthy, unholy, to commit her life to God lingered with her into adulthood.

After her failed marriage to Nate, once she learned of his dreadful affair with a prostitute, Dana knew the closest she would ever come to a religious vocation would be her contract with the Catholic Church, working as a private investigator to solve crimes within the institution. No matter how she felt, she imagined herself donned in the habit of a Carmelite as she rocked to the rhythm of the singing.

"Dana," Mother whispered as she tapped on her shoulder. "The chapel is emptying. It's time to head to the parlor for recreation."

Dana shook her head from side-to-side. "Oh, dear, I must have fallen asleep. The sisters' voices are so relaxing."

"Come along now," Mother said.

Dana followed the nuns into the parlor. Yellow and white roses in pewter vases graced the floor-to-ceiling bookcase. Dana paused to browse the shelves of books. *The Life of Saint Columba, Patron Saint of*

Detectives. She chose a chair by the side windows overlooking the labyrinth. Two sisters were walking through the maze, both deep in prayer. Dana began to read and found herself in the middle of Chapter Six when Sister Agnus Dei came up and sat next to her.

"Humph, even a saint for detectives. What next? Never heard of the man."

"It's actually quite interesting, Sister."

"Another time, perhaps. Don't you think you could better spend your time solving the murder case you came here for than drifting off in some silly book?"

"Guess, we all need time to relax. Wouldn't you agree?"

The nun drew in her breath and released it in a loud huff before speaking again. "How many weeks has it been since you arrived? Has there ever been a case that was beyond your ability to solve?"

"I try not to calculate the time I've spent on a case but, rather, the outcomes. So far, I've solved every case but one." Dana's thoughts went back to the Myra Pembroke case, the one involving a prostitute and her own husband's affair with the woman. Nate died before the case was solved, and she had no desire to resurrect that one again.

"Dana, I've been privy to some talk." The nun brushed her veil over her shoulder.

"Not gossip, Sister?"

The elderly nun ignored Dana's sarcasm. "The nun's eyebrows formed a V with a deep crease in the middle. I'm of the opinion that more needs to be said about Father Tanner. If he fathered that postulant's child, why would he not want her out of his life for good?"

"Granted, Sister, that does make sense, but there's one critical part that doesn't fit."

Sister's eyes widened.

"Why wouldn't Father Tanner do away with the girl once he found out he was the father of the child? I prefer not to work around hypotheses. I'm here to learn the truth, to get the facts."

"Humph, well you might find it difficult around here."

"I'd think a convent would be the most honest of places," Dana said, with a slight laugh in her voice.

"Don't be so sure," the nun said, and walked out of the room.

Chapter Forty-Three

A cool breeze blew in from a crack in the front window. Propped up on a pile of pillows, baby Jewel sat. She rattled a toy shaped like a kitten.

"My it's quite chilly in here," Gertrude said, to the baby. She found the blue sweater Mother Superior had made and placed it on the child. "There now, you should be more comfy," she said, to the infant.

Although Gertrude had no religious affiliation, there had not been a day that she didn't say a prayer of thanks that the baby had been returned safely. Some nights Gertrude woke up screaming reliving the kidnapping experience as if it were a firsthand account. She would see an image of a man in a black leather jacket, his black hair slicked back with Brylcreem. He smelled of Old Gold cigarettes. Jewel was screeching as the man rushed out the backdoor of the jewelry shop. Then, Gertrude would wake up screaming, sweating, her face moist to the touch. Even when she tried to settle down, her legs continued to shake as if she was running after someone.

The stairs squeaked, and Ned came into the room. He reached for Jewel and softly kissed her head. "Doesn't she look like a little princess?" he said. "Where'd the hand-knit sweater come from? I don't remember her wearing this before?"

"Dana came over the other day. Said Mother Superior over at the Carmelite Convent had made it for Jewel."

Ned set the baby down on her blanket. "What? What are you talking about?" His eyes widened as he stared at Gertrude.

"Nothing to get upset about. It's just a gift."

The doctor stepped closer toward Gertrude. He shook his index finger at her. "Wait a minute. What are you talking about?"

Gertrude had never seen the man look so upset. "Settle down, please. Like I said, babies get presents. It happens all the time."

By this time, the doctor tightly held Gertrude's upper arm in his.

"Ned, you're hurting me. Let go."

He did as told, but his eyes glared at Gertrude in an unblinking gaze. Babies get presents, do they?"

"Why, of course. Why are you acting so erratic, Ned?"

"Don't you understand? Can you be so naive?"

"Afraid I am. I have no idea where you're going with this."

Jewel, picking-up the tension in the room, began to cry. She rolled onto her side.

Gertrude stooped to pick-up the baby.

"Leave her alone!"

"But she's upset."

"Do as I say."

Gertrude straightened up and did as the doctor demanded.

In the midst of the baby's escalating cries, the doctor shouted, "Why would you be so stupid as to accept that gift?"

"Stupid? Is that what you're calling me? Far from stupid, I was grateful for the gift. Homemade gifts like this take time and lots of work. Are you that thankless?"

"Don't you see? If that nun made the sweater for Jewel, it means she knows we have a child. Can't you understand that?"

"Most people on Winter Willows know that Martha had a child. Why is this so farfetched?"

"Do you actually believe people accept that as truth?"

Raising her voice and in a sarcastic tone, Gertrude said, "It's not that I've seen anyone come to the door and say the baby is not yours."

His face red, small trails of sweat above his lip, the doctor said, "Have you ever wondered why someone tried to kidnap the child?"

"Ned, you're getting carried away with this. Kidnappings occur. Look at the Lindberg baby. Jewel is not the first."

The man threw his hands up. "Am I speaking to a wall, Gertrude? Someone tried to kidnap Jewel because the person knew the baby was not ours."

"Why, then, did *the person* place Jewel in the trash bin. It's not as if he was trying to return the baby to her rightful owner."

"Quit with your sarcasm. That's just it, Gertrude. Whoever took Jewel knew her mother had been murdered. That Jewel was an illegitimate child. I just bet one of those so-called women of God wanted to do away with her. In the eyes of the church, the child was born soiled, dirty."

"An interesting premise, Ned, but what we're arguing over is not the state of the baby's soul! It's about a baby gift for God's sake."

"A baby gift from someone who knows we have Cindy's child."

"Oh, come on, Ned, you're overreacting to this."

"Am I?" He climbed the stairs to his room and slammed the door.

Gertrude began to think more about what Ned had said. If he was correct in his perception, would someone try again to take the child from them? Equally frightening, would the doctor be convicted of kidnapping? Would she be seen as an accomplice? It wasn't supposed to play out this way. It was only supposed to help Martha with her depressive state. She picked Jewel up, and both of them cried.

Chapter Forty-Four

Dana's shoulders raised and her chest tightened. "How did you get in here?"

"Let's say, if there's a will, there's a way," Sister Magdalene said. She smirked and made herself comfortable on Dana's bed, propping her knees under her chin. "Mind if I have a cigarette?"

Dana crossed her arms against her chest and shook her head in disgust.

"Fine, then I won't."

"Why have you come here?"

"Heard there's someone on our little island who is spreading lies."

"Who?"

"A member of the Grotto. If I were you, Dana, I'd close my ears to nonsense. By now you ought to know, this island is nothing more than a cesspool of rumors, gossip, and lies."

Dana was tempted to say, "You're a fine one to talk" but refrained. "Okay, what is this member of the Grotto saying?"

"Oh, let's get serious, Dana, and cut out the bullshit."

Dana was taken aback by the nun's response. "I don't know who you're referring to."

"Okay, let me be a bit more direct. Have you had the pleasure of meeting Darla Wheeler?"

"Explain why you think she's spreading lies."

"Dana, you're an investigator. You should know what she's been saying." The postulant's eyes narrowed; her tongue moistened her lips. "Loose lips, sink ships, Dana."

"Are you angry because of what she reported to Mr. Mansfield? Are you upset because there happened to be a witness who might have seen something that day at the jewelry store?"

"What do you think? You're the detective."

"As of now, I have no reason to question the woman's integrity."

"Well, maybe you should. Anyone who knows anything around her knows that squirrel is nothing but trouble."

Dana thought Sister Magdalene was a fine one to talk.

"You know, Darla was against Mother taking Cindy into the convent in the first place. She called Cindy all kinds of names behind her back and even said she'd go to the bishop if need be to prevent it."

Dana could feel her eyebrows raise. "Is that so? I've never heard such a thing."

"Think what you like, but Darla has her reasons for the vile she excretes."

Sister Magdalene, with her dark eyes and hollowed out cheeks appeared almost viper like.

Dana, for a moment, almost felt afraid of the young woman. "Think I'd prefer to come to my own conclusions, Sister."

*

During recreation hour, Dana noted Sister Magdalene was not present. When she noticed Sister Seraphim seated in the corner playing a game of Solitaire, Dana approached her. "Hello, Sister, are you winning?"

The nun laughed. "Usually not. My father used to tell me when you play a game alone, you're playing against the devil. He must be swinging his tail right now."

Dana laughed. Although Sister Seraphim was guilty of visiting the Red Barn Tavern, Dana saw the young postulant as someone who involuntarily went along with Sister Magdalene...maybe even coerced or threatened. No matter, Dana felt comfortable in her presence. She wondered where the nun might be. "Sister, I see Magdalene is not here. Know where she might be?"

With her hand partially covering her mouth, Seraphim said, "We are not allowed off our consecrated grounds during recreation hour or for that matter at any time without the strict approval of Mother."

Dana knew that was not the case. More than likely, Mother knew little about the postulant's other lives. "Are you saying sister is gone?"

"I'd check with Sister Agnus Dei if I were you, but I've not seen Sister Magdalene since last night in chapel."

"Thanks, I will speak with sister."

Sister Agnus Dei was slumped in a wingback chair, her mouth open, snoring loudly.

Dana hated to interrupt the woman's sleep, but she was concerned about where the postulant might have gone. She tapped Sister Agnus Dei's arm.

The old woman's mouth closed and opened, a stream of drool on her chin. "Don't leave me. Don't go," the woman babbled; her eyes squeezed shut.

"Sister, it's Dana."

The woman's eyes opened a crack, and she shook herself awake. "Oh, it's you."

"Sister, might you have any idea where Sister Magdalene is?"

"Last night at chapel, I saw her."

"But since then, any word from her? Did you see her?"

"No, why no."

Chapter Forty-Five

Even though she had *fallen* out of her wheel chair recently, Dorothy felt much stronger today. Doctor Vincent stopped by to check on her and helped her into her chair. "No more cleaning windowsills, do you hear me?"

"I've learned my lesson, Doctor."

The doctor left, but Dorothy heard the man speaking to someone outside. She wheeled to the living room window and saw Tanner and the doctor. She overheard Tanner saying, "I'll keep an eye on her. If need be, I'll do the cleaning from now on."

Dorothy figured her son was not about to tell the doctor the truth in the same way that he had lied about her having had a stroke. She reached on the coffee table for her pack of cigarettes when she noticed a book of matches: Red Barn Tavern. "Hmm, that's interesting."

Tanner let the screen door slam. He chewed down on the corner of his lip. "See you've recovered, Mother. So soon, I might add."

"I'm stronger than I look, Son."

Tanner laughed loudly. "Seeing where your ass has landed, I'd doubt that to be the case."

Dorothy knew he was referring to her fall down the basement steps, which landed her partially paralyzed and in a wheelchair for the rest of her life. She puffed on her cigarette.

"Think you'll give those up for Lent, Mother?"

With Lent already gone, she did not bother to respond to his sarcasm. "Got a question for you."

"Oh?"

Dorothy picked up the book of matches. "Where did these come from?"

Tanner read the cover. "Red Barn Tavern? Mother? You haven't been entertaining any men while I'm gone, have you?"

"That would be the day. Who'd want an old lady in a wheelchair?"

"True, Mother. Guess that was a silly question."

"Where do you think the matches came from, Tanner?"

"Seeing I don't smoke, how in the hell would I know?"

Dorothy knew to back off when Tanner's mood turned dark. "Have you ever heard of the place?"

"Who hasn't? Mikowski runs the bar and dance hall. He's Father Merton's favorite. The golden chalices and patens, the royal vestments…where would Father get money like that? Mikowski's a big contributor to the Church and to the convent."

"That still doesn't explain how the book of matches got here."

Tanner grabbed the book and shredded it with his bare hands.

Dorothy looked on in horror. There had to be something wrong with the man, but she would never broach the subject. Even as a young boy, Tanner had had trouble controlling his temper. Often, he'd come home from school with a black eye or scratches on his face. Growing up he never had any friends. Dorothy often wondered if that was his reason for joining the seminary. At least, he would feel a part of something there, included, maybe even accepted. On the other hand, she still questioned whether the fact his uncle was an archbishop and knew Pope Pius XII personally might have had something to do with it. Connections never hurt, she thought.

With the pieces of the match book in the palms of his hands, Tanner let them fall like confetti on a wedding day. "Let's just forget we ever saw these. Right, Mother?"

"Okay, Tanner. Give your Mama a nice big kiss on the cheek."

Tanner turned his mother's face to the side and kissed her.

Dorothy smelled alcohol, and it wasn't wine.

Chapter Forty-Six

The following day, Dana felt strange. She couldn't put her finger on anything specific that added to her mood, but something just didn't feel right. She joined the sisters in the refectory for breakfast. The smell of scrambled eggs and bacon filled the air. Sister Seraphim was distributing the food along with Sister Agnus Dei. Mother stood at the podium as usual, her hands gripping the wooden sides of the lectern.

When all of the dishes had been filled, Mother began to speak. For some reason, Dana feared Mother was about to say something about Sister Magdalene having gone missing. As Dana glanced up-and-down her table and the one across from her, she noticed the nun was still gone. There had to be an explanation. Someone had to have seen her.

Right at the moment when Sister was about to begin her reading for the day, Father Merton, his face flushed, rushed in the dining hall from the side door. He hurried to Mother Anne Baptiste and spoke quietly to her. Mother threw her hands to her face and cried out, "God, no. But who?"

All of the sisters turned their heads in the direction of Mother. Mumbling sounds came from all ends of the room.

Dana was convinced her earlier feeling of doom was soon to be confirmed.

"Sisters, please. No talking. Bow your heads in prayer."

Together the sisters recited the meal blessing, yet none started to eat. Dana felt like the room was ready to burst, the tension of the unknown rising.

Mother spoke, "Sisters, Father Merton has unexpectedly joined us this morning. He has some terrible news to share."

Dana could see from where she was seated that Mother had started to cry.

The nun next to Dana, edged closer to her, and said, "What could possibly have happened? Do you think it has anything to do with Sister Magdalene missing?"

"I have no idea, but I felt like something was wrong the minute I got up."

Mother stared at the two of them. "Please, let Father Merton speak."

The priest cleared his throat. He shook his head. "God be with me, this is tough. I don't know where to begin, how to explain."

The room went silent like a sanctuary at midnight.

"I received word early this morning…. Officer Henning stopped by the rectory, woke me up about five a.m." He cleared his throat again. "This has never happened to me before. I'm sorry. I usually prepare before I speak."

The sisters were rustling in their chairs. An uneasiness enveloped the room.

"Today, early this morning, dear sisters and Miss Greer, the body of Darla Wheeler was found by a fishing vessel near the shore right outside of Willow Fisheries."

The room filled with gasps and sighs.

"Henry Gillion came in from Seattle to examine the body and to determine a cause of death. To paraphrase the coroner, he said, Miss Wheeler was on the dock late last night when she appears to have had a seizure and accidentally fell into the dark waters. Supposedly, she was deceased for less than an hour when her body was found by William Clairiton, captain of the Willow's Fishing Vessel."

Father looked over at Mother. "Would it be possible to exempt the sisters from mandatory breakfast silence, so they may ask any questions they might have?"

Mother appeared none too happy, but she agreed.

One of the nuns near the rear of the room raised her hand. "Father, any explanation for why Miss Wheeler was out so late and, on the dock, no less?"

"According to a witness who happened to be staring out the window of the fishery, he said he often saw the woman on warm evenings strolling on the dock."

Another sister asked, "Was Miss Wheeler known to have seizures?"

"According to our local doctor, Doctor Vincent, she had no medical history of seizures."

The nun seated near to Dana was the next to be addressed. "Father, this is dreadful news, but additionally, we are left wondering where Sister Magdalene might be. She has been missing for almost forty-eight hours."

"Rather than publicly speak of the woman's whereabouts and interfere in her privacy, I can say that Betty Carmichael reported seeing Sister Magdalene last night, and the Sister had intentions of returning to the convent. Has anyone seen her today?"

Dana stood up. "I'd be happy to go to her cell to check on her, Father."

"Very well, Miss Greer."

Dana hurried down the corridor. She was tired of the woman's antics, arrogant attitude, and continual lies. She wrapped on the door to the nun's cell.

"Yes, oh, it's you." The nun kept her head down, not making any eye contact.

Dana did not wait for an invitation to enter but pushed the door open. The room smelled of cigarettes mixed with incense and stale vomit. "Sister, whatever happened? Let me look at your face?" Dana lifted the woman's chin. A purple-black bruise covered her left eye. "Oh, dear, what happened?"

"Nothing."

Dana had had enough. She gently grabbed the woman by her upper arms. "Sister, I think, your game of charades is over. It's time we have a heart-to-heart talk."

Sister lit up a cigarette, what appeared to be dried blood under her nails, and lay on her bed. Still in lay person's clothing, the nun's nylons had a huge hole in them, and the heel of her stiletto was broken. "Have a seat, PI."

"It's about time you do some explaining, Sister. Where have you been for the past forty-eight hours?"

"I report to Sister Agnus Dei, not you!"

"She claims she had no knowledge of your whereabouts."

"She's an old fool. She could care less. Don't know why Mother put her in charge of postulants to begin with."

"I'm not here to listen to your negativity, but I do believe you owe me an explanation."

She puffed on her cigarette, squinting her eyes and focusing on the ceiling. "If you must know I was with Jesse Carmichael. We got into an argument, and this," she pointed to her eye, "is what came out of it. Guess, I lost the fight, huh?"

"What were the two of you arguing about?"

"Jesse and I are a couple. Have been secretly for some time."

"A couple or a blackmailer?"

The nun snuffed her cigarette out on the bedpost "What's that supposed to mean?"

Dana breathed deeply. Her adrenaline pumped; her heart raced. "The day Doctor Vincent's child was kidnapped—."

The nun sat up. "I told you that child is not the doctor's; the infant was Cindy's."

"Was that the motive for the kidnapping?"

"I did not kidnap the child."

Dana took a leap of faith, but her instincts told her she had no choice. "But you know who did. You set Jesse up to take the child from Gertrude while she got preoccupied. And as for Darla Wheeler, did you have Jesse do your dirty work again?"

Sister Magdalene stood up, lit another cigarette, and said, "Get the hell out of here. How dare you make such accusations."

"I'll go a step further. And in your attempt to push Darla off the dock, the woman slugged you in an effort to save her life."

"Holy Mary – Mother of Jesus, I've heard enough."

"Oh, one other thing, Sister. You might want to clean up a bit. Smells like you might have been out drinking during your time away."

At this point, the nun pushed Dana so hard that she almost stumbled into the corridor.

Dana had the answers she came looking for.

Chapter Forty-Seven

The morning Church bells chimed loudly, so loudly Dana was sure the entire island had to have heard them. Surrounding the altar were bouquets of red, yellow, and pink gladiolas. Betty must have been at work early. Crowds began to assemble for the funeral Mass of Darla Wheeler.

The Grim Reaper was one-character Dana had trouble accepting. Something about him coming like a thief in the night...unannounced, pouncing, and stealing life itself. The thought was something she preferred to repress. Although she was forced to stare death in the face with each crime she worked on, the topic was not one she preferred to discuss.

Up the aisle came Father Merton led by Jimmy and Jesse as altar boys. At the foot of the altar stood the closed casket. From what Dana had been told by Mother Superior, Father Merton requested the casket be closed due to the injuries of the deceased woman. It was apparent from what she heard that Darla put up a good fight before she succumbed to her death. The small choir sang "Going Home." Although the cloistered sisters were not allowed to come to the Church for Mass, Dana recognized several of the parishioners: Tim Brownell seated with who must have been his two boys and his wife; Joe Mikowski and a blond woman who looked to be twenty years his junior; Betty sat in the front pew with Dorothy seated in her wheelchair in the center aisle; Mr. and Mrs. Mansfield who had lost their son Gordie to the motorcycle accident; and Charles Filmore, the groundskeeper who had found the body of Sister Mary Margaret, and a grey-haired woman who must have been Tilly, his wife. There were also a handful of men who were dressed in the attire of fishermen who clearly were from the Willows's Fisheries. The last to arrive, in the nick of time, was Henry Gillion dressed in a three-piece Gregory Peck ensemble. He viewed the crowd up-and-down the pews and smiled. His pompous behavior made him appear as if he were the guest of honor. Wrapped around his upper arm was Gertrude. She was sniffling and crying into a lace-edged handkerchief.

Father Merton began to give his sermon, relaying his sorrow at the death of Darla Wheeler. "She was not only a parishioner but a friend, as well. Winter Willows will miss a wonderful contribution to the island."

Hmm, Dana thought. This was quite a contradiction from what Sister Magdalene had told her about the woman. But, then again, Dana gave up putting any faith in what the postulant had to say.

As the Mass ended, Jesse and Jimmy led the way out of the church. Father Merton greeted the people, but the two altar boys went back to the sacristy to change into their civilian clothes. Jesse pushed ahead of his brother, Jimmy. Dana got a quick glance at the boy who bore some significant scratches on his cheek. She decided to wait by the side door of the church, hoping to catch him on his way out.

No sooner did he exit then he lit a king-sized cigarette with one hand and ran his other through his greasy hair. Noticing Dana, he said in a sing-song voice, "Hello, Miss Greer."

"Hello, Jesse, looks like you've been in quite a cat fight."

"Humph. That might be one way of putting it."

"Mind telling me what happened.' "Oh, it ain't nothin', really."

"That's not what I'm thinking. Were you with Sister Magdalene the night Darla Wheeler died?"

"I'd prefer to stay as far away from that nun as possible, but she refuses to do the same. See these here scratches? Her work…all her work."

"You say…*her* work? Don't you mean Darla's work as she fought to save her life?"

Jesse snubbed his cigarette onto the pavement and walked away, whistling some country tune.

*

Mother Anne Baptiste hovered in the corner embroidering what appeared to be an altar linen. "Dana, come have a seat."

The white cloth was embellished with gold, silken threads in the form of crosses.

"How are things coming along with the case, dear?"

"Wish I was further along, but I'm afraid I've a ways to go."

"Pray, dear, pray."

"Yes, Mother."

"Don't mean to pry into your business, Dana, but I heard you found Sister Magdalene in her cell. Is she alright?"

"Quite, Mother, except for a black eye."

The nun dropped her needle onto the cloth. "What?"

"Seems she and Jesse got into a squabble. I noticed at Darla Wheeler's funeral that he had scratches on his face. Neither of them came out looking too great." Dana questioned how the abrasions really got there but needed a bit more evidence.

"I'll be honest, Dana. Magdalene is not fit for the convent. I am known to extend my warnings, especially, when it comes to these young girls who come to the convent right after high school. I've found they usually need quite some time to acclimate, especially, to a cloistered lifestyle. But, Magdalene's behavior has gone on long enough. I've tried speaking with Sister Agnus Dei about it."

"And?"

"She's reluctant to give her opinion, but isn't it clear? I mean, Sister Magdalene isn't quite the cloistered type of woman."

Dana felt sorry for the Mother Superior. It was unfortunate that she had to be put in this situation.

"I'm considering calling the Mother House in Rome. Surely they can advise me."

Dana said nothing.

"There were those who were upset when I decided to take in Sister Mary Margaret…a young girl with no parents and in need of help. Yet, my hands are full with the nonsense of Sister Magdalene." The nun thought for a moment. "Forgive me, Dana, I don't know why I'm gossiping like this. Forgive me, Lord."

Dana smiled. "We all need someone we can speak with, Mother." Dana wished the same for herself. When she had worked on the Bernadette Godfrey case, she had lived with Jay and Loretta, but she had Sergeant McKnight to confer with. During the Douglas Clifford case, she had the company of Elle Banks with whom she lived. This time, living in the confines of the cloistered convent plus being under the contract of the Catholic Church, she didn't feel it would be right to speak with anyone about the case. Yet there was a gnawing feeling that she must reach out to someone.

*

Dana had not officially met Officer Henning nor was she sure she wanted to after all she had heard about him. Seemed he was more the laughingstock of the island. Plus, ever since signing the contract with the Catholic Church, she had been warned not to seek the outside help of law enforcement until there was a pending arrest. Seemed a bit strange, to Dana, but she was told that this is the way the Church had always operated.

Out over the sound on eight concrete stilts, she found the man's office. The small building's wooden sides were warped from the elements, and seaweed, moss, and algae attached to it like hungry parasites. She knocked on the metal door.

Before the need to introduce herself, Office Henning responded with, "My, my. I was wondering how long it would take you to pay me a visit." He pointed to a seat across from his large desk…much too big for the space as he chugged down a stein of beer. "Please."

"What is that supposed to mean?"

"No offense that you're a lady." He burped without excusing himself. "Only saying, a police officer and a private investigator…hey, they go together like a horse and hay."

Hmm. Dana wasn't particularly fond of his analogy but let it go.

"Mind if I get myself another?" he asked, reaching under his desk, where three bottles of gin stood next to several bottles of Pabst Blue Ribbon.

"Help yourself," Dana said, noticing several empty bottles of alcohol in the trash can. She watched the man refill his mug.

He shoved his spindled chair back and put his cowboy boots on top of his desk.

"This sure is the life," he said, as beer foam covered his mouth.

Dana waited until she felt she had the man's full attention before she spoke. "You know that I am hired by the Catholic Church, correct?"

"I do. Does that mean you can't speak with me because I'm a Lutheran?"

Dana laughed. "Obviously, that isn't what I meant. It's just that the Church would rather I not bring in public authorities…the police, to be exact until an actual arrest is evident."

"I get it…to keep things under wraps. Dare someone should realize that sin can as easily occur by Church goers and its leaders as anyone else."

"Certainly. Even the most holy can fall from a pedestal of grace. I agree with that."

"So, Dana, what would you like from me?"

"Nothing really but I do have serious concerns over some of the things that have been happening on the island."

The officer lined up some pencils in a straight line on his desk and tried to balance the remaining ones on top. When they all toppled over with some landing on the cracked linoleum, he said, "Oh shucks! I'll get this right one day."

Dana stood up to leave, her patience wore thin.

"Hey, where you off to?" The palm of his hand lowered. "Have a seat. We still need to discuss what's bothering you, don't we?"

"If you have the interest," Dana said. "I'd appreciate not wasting my time."

"My, my, pretty lady...sure thing." He put his hand to his mouth and belched.

"There have been several felonies. Which do you want to hear first?"

Henning picked at some small stones in the sole of his cowboy boot and threw them on the floor. "You talking about the murder of that nun?"

"Well, that might be a good place to start, but there have been other disturbing things going on around here."

He took another gulp of his beer. "When it comes to that nun, I'd say that's Church business. Now, the kidnapping is quite another."

"What do you know about the kidnapping? You believe Sister Mary Margaret delivered a viable baby?"

"Yeah but to keep things hushed up, it looked better to say the child died. Don't know if you ever met Martha."

"Yes, I did."

"Most were aware the woman should never have a child. She was heavily medicated, and in addition, was more comatose than aware. Suddenly, not only does she have a child, but it's about the same age as the stillborn. I plain don't buy it."

Dana surprised that the man knew as much as he did, asked, "But the death certificate—."

"Yeah, yeah, it's the same way I got away with drinking at the age of thirteen. You can buy anything you like, lady, if you've got the money."

"You're saying the Vincents paid off the coroner to say the baby was stillborn...that he lied?"

"That's what I'm saying. Money talks, and the Vincents sure have their share of it."

"What about Darla Wheeler?"

"Is that why there was a closed casket?" Henning edged closer to his desk and put his feet on the floor.

Dana noticed broken blood vessels around the man's nose, which took over much of his face. His eyes, too, were bloodshot."

"Let me tell you something. Miss Wheeler was quite battered when her body was found. Hardly recognizable, actually."

"But the coroner...Doctor Henry Gillion...said it was ruled an accident."

"To be honest with you, lady, I have no idea how much Gillion made off of that deal...can't imagine."

"Then, who killed Darla?"

"That little island hussie. What's her name...Sister Magdalene?"

"Sister Magdalene?"

Henning nodded.

"But she's a nun. Where would she get that kind of money?"

"Ever hear of the Red Barn Tavern?"

Dana knew what was coming next. "Joe Mikowski?"

"You're one sharp detective. There's not a thing that man wouldn't do for his little ladies."

"Let's get back to Henry Gillion. Why?"

"Simple. He works for the state, but you'd never know it."

"What's that supposed to mean?"

Henning pulled out a cigarette from his back pocket and lit it up. His speech slower, he asked, "Any idea what the state pays?" He puffed away, squinting his eyes. "No way it would come close to paying for that man's lifestyle. The guy's known to live in a mansion on Lake Washington in Seattle, to drive a Ferrari.

"...another example of Joe Mikowski paying off the coroner?"

Henning smiled like a Cheshire cat. "All to keep things hush-hush for the little nun." He stopped and bit down on his thumb. "No, the state wouldn't come even close to that lifestyle."

"I don't know what you could do about the coroner, but as for the local crimes, you represent the police force, why didn't you investigate these?"

"Have you noticed how quickly things get resolved around here? Bodies are put to rest quicker than a blink of the eye. There's a reason for this. Winter Willows has a reputation to keep."

Dana recalled what the sheriff had told her earlier. "…to keep its tourists coming?"

"Exactly, and Gillion does whatever is necessary to keep the sheriff happy. Those two are thicker than thieves when it comes to corruption."

"But you are the face of the police on the island, correct?" Dana could not believe she was asking that question.

"I do represent the force…me, myself, and I. I have to live with these people, Dana. Sometimes, it's better to leave things alone, especially, if it doesn't matter." He snuffed out his cigarette on the edge of his desk.

"Doesn't matter?"

"Look at it this way: the child was given a good home. Sister Mary Margaret is probably singing with the angels in heaven," he paused, to laugh. "And, as for Darla, let the dead rest in peace."

Dana couldn't believe the man was over-simplifying things like this. "Wait a minute. Taking a child that is not yours is called kidnapping and bludgeoning a woman and throwing another woman over the dock is called murder. Shouldn't someone be held responsible?"

Officer Henning's phone rang. "Office Henning, speaking, how might I help?" He shoved the receiver under his chin and reached into his shirt pocket. He pulled out a flask, carefully filling it with gin. He motioned for Dana to stay seated, but she had heard more than enough. It was no wonder no one on the island involved him. He was more concerned with saving face and keeping the Winter Willows's lies under wrap.

Chapter Forty-Eight

Two robins chirped loudly and flew after each other. Dana only wished her life could be that playful and lighthearted. Being immersed in murder cases brought worry and dread. She took a deep breath, closed her eyes, and exhaled. Fiona Wharton had taught her the technique. She said to use the exercise to clear out the cobwebs in the brain. At first, Dana thought the purpose of the technique sounded a bit silly, but at this point, she was willing to try anything to relax her nerves. With her eyes still closed, Dana jumped when she saw Sister Seraphim.

"May I sit with you on the bench for a while?"

"I'd like that, Sister."

The two women sat in silence for what seemed like several minutes before one spoke.

The nun bit down on her lower lip. A lone tear fell down her cheek. "Dana, you told me once that I could trust you."

"Of course, you can. You seem troubled."

Sister Seraphim glanced around the garden, not once but twice.

"We're alone, Sister. Feel free to share whatever might be troubling you."

The sister tucked a strand of her blonde hair under her veil. She grabbed at her right ring finger…the one that would bear a golden band once she made her final vows.

Dana waited in silence until the girl felt comfortable to speak.

"Dana, I've not told anyone this before."

Dana did not know where the nun planned to go with this.

"But I'm planning on leaving the order."

Involuntarily, Dana turned toward the sister and gave her a hug.

The nun cried uncontrollably as if she finally felt comfortable letting the dam break.

"It's okay, Sister. Your words are safe with me." Dana waited a moment until she could tell sister had regained some of her composure. "Why, Sister, do you want to leave?"

Sister Seraphim cast her eyes toward Dana. Her lower lip trembled. "I am not worthy to be here."

Dana could not believe what she was hearing but said nothing.

"Even though, I've not yet made my temporary vows, I believe I am not suited for the order. Sister Magdalene…well, I don't mean to blame her. It's not her fault, but I find myself going along with her…the Red Barn Tavern…dancing, drinking."

Dana held the nun's hands in hers. "Sister, you are young…only eighteen. Perhaps a leave of absence is what you're needing. The things you're doing are no different than other girls your age."

"True but I want to consecrate my life to the Lord, not the world."

"Give yourself time, Sister. Unless you see what the world has to offer, how will you know that you, indeed, have a vocation?"

"I've confessed…confessed to Father Merton…my sins."

"Surely, that must have made you feel better."

"Father says I should give it time, to not be so hard on myself."

"See? Father thinks as I do, but in the end, the decision to leave the order is up to you."

"There's more, Dana."

"Go ahead."

Sister chewed on her knuckle and breathed heavily. "I want to get away from Sister Magdalene."

Dana said nothing about what she and Mother Superior had discussed relative to Mother's desire to have Sister Magdalene removed from the order.

"Not only do I find myself obligated to follow her in sinful ways, but she frightens me, Dana."

"I can see that."

Sister shook her head. "Forgive me. I don't mean to gossip. God in Jesus's name, help me, a poor sinner."

"Listen, Sister. When you speak with a friend, a trusted confidante, that is not gossiping. We all need to share what is burdening our hearts."

"Thanks, Dana. I do consider you a friend." The nun forced a smile between her softly falling tears.

"The other night…the night Darla Wheeler's body was found…I—."

The side door to the convent opened. "Sister, recreational hour is over. Aren't you supposed to be chanting in the chapel?" Mother Superior asked.

In a whispered voice, Dana said, "Let's talk later." She could not help but wonder what the nun had wanted to add about Darla's death.

*

At her desk that night, Dana jotted down what her next steps had to be:

- *See Betty to learn more about Jesse and Sister Magdalene's relationship.*
- *Talk to Tim Brownell about his absence on the flight to Norway.*
- *In addition, that still left Father Tanner, Sister Agnus Dei, and Doctor Vincent on her list of possible suspects. One of them was guilty but who?*

Chapter Forty-Nine

Above the doorway, a bell rang in the *Buds and Blossoms Flower Shop*. The scent of roses, lilies, and sweet peas greeted Dana as she entered the store. Soft music played overhead, and everywhere she looked were garden-type items from engraved stones, bright-colored sprinkling cans, and bags of seeds.

Betty came from the back room. She wore a pink and green striped apron and a badge on the pocket that read: *Welcome to Paradise*. "Hi, Dana." The woman's voice was flat and unwelcoming.

"You don't sound as chipper as I've seen you, Betty."

"Why would I be? If it weren't for my business, which by the way is suffering financially, I'd take my boys and move as far away from Winter Willows as I could."

"Well, thank goodness for your shop. So many on the island depend on you to add some beauty to their lives."

"Nice of you to say, but I'm so tired of the people's treatment of my boy and me."

Dana opened the door to the freezer and took out a small bouquet of red carnations in a crystal vase. She set it on the counter.

Betty busied herself filling small plastic pots with soil. She almost acted oblivious to Dana's presence.

"Betty, about Jesse—."

One of the pots fell onto the floor. Dirt scattered on the tiles and under the freezer door. Rather than finding a broom to sweep the mess, Betty shoved it to the side with the tip of her rubber-soled shoe.

"What about Jesse, Dana? Are you against him, too?'

"No, no, but I would like to discuss something that occurred the other night."

Dana had never seen Betty like this before. Her body stiff…defensive. Her voice hardened and sarcastic. Dana needed to find a way to break through Betty's irritated façade, to speak to her as a friend, not an interrogator. "Why don't we sit down over here?" she said, pointing to a metal garden set with a round table and two chairs.

Betty said nothing but sat down, adjusting her apron.

"I saw Jesse after the funeral Mass for Darla Wheeler. The poor boy's face was scratched and—."

"So, you noticed. What's your point?"

"Jesse told me he'd gotten into a scuffle with Sister Magdalene."

"Huh! That woman never should have been allowed to enter the convent to begin with. Everyone knows she's a liar. I told my Jesse to stay away from her."

"And?"

"She keeps bothering him. She's nothing but trouble."

"The other night, Betty, the night Darla fell from the dock—."

"Are you fool enough to believe that?"

Dana toyed with the top button of her violet-colored sweater. "What do you mean?"

"The death certificate signed by Gillion, the coroner? Listed her death as an accident due to a seizure."

Dana turned her head more in Betty's direction. She did not want to relay what she had heard from Office Henning. "That's what I've heard."

Betty's eyebrows rose. She closed her eyes and opened them wide. "Just like that postulant's infant was stillborn?"

"Are you trying to say—?"

"That's exactly what I'm saying. That explains why Gillion has the lifestyle he does in Seattle. He lives in a twenty-five room mansion overlooking Lake Washington. Add to that he has a butler, a cook, and a live-in maid. I wouldn't doubt he made a couple hundred on the baby's death certificate. And who is dumb enough to believe her child was a stillborn?"

Henning chose to let the crime of kidnapping slide and the possible murder of Darla, all because he chose not to get involved...all in an effort to keep the peace on the island. Gillion wrote up the death of Sister Mary Margaret as an accident...all in an effort to appease the Sheriff and to keep his own job. What Betty said confirmed one thing: Everyone was afraid to confront the truth.

Betty continued. "Darla's death an accident? That's what the coroner wants everyone to believe. He got paid off royally on that one. That little pistol Sister Magdalene saw to that. You can be sure of it."

"But, wait a minute, Betty. Where would Magdalene get enough money to pay off the coroner?" Dana already knew the answer to her question but wanted to see just how much Betty really knew.

Betty ran her dirt-covered fingers through her hair and shoved it behind her ears. Her voice filled with sarcasm, she said. "Where do you think she gets money for make-up, dresses, and those spiked heels she wears on her nights out?"

"Joe Mikowski?"

"You got it. So, if I were you, I'd be the last to put any blame on my boy." The woman picked up a white rose and held it in the air. "Jesse's as innocent and perfect. No one will point a finger at my boy."

Betty made every attempt to clear Jesse of any wrong doings. Of that Dana was confident. She placed her vase on the counter. "How much do I owe you?"

"Forget it. Let's call it your going-away gift. My gift to you to keep you away from my boys and me."

"But, I—."

Betty squeezed Dana's fingers tightly in hers. "I won't have it any other way."

As Dana walked back to the convent, she confirmed what she believed so far about the case. Father Tanner was the father of the nun's baby. More than likely, Dorothy never suspected him of wrongdoing in the same way that Betty defended Jesse. Gillion used the front that he was protecting the island business from ruin, but in actuality, he accepted bribe money to keep up his lavish lifestyle.

Baby Jewel was alive and well while Doctor Vincent basked in the knowledge of the child being his former wife's Martha's. And as for the deaths of Sister Mary Margaret and Darla Wheeler, both were further payoffs to Gillion. Dana paused to relax and to catch her breath. The tide rolled in, lightly splashing the shore. She stood surrounded by the bright colors of the island's spring flowers. In the distance, the ferry glided to the mainland...a large wake left behind. She wished she could be aboard, headed as far from Winter Willows as possible.

*

Only blocks from the convent, Dana passed Winter Willows School. The children, out on recess, were running and screaming, chasing after an over-sized red ball. Others played hopscotch on the pavement while a girl counted to ten as two boys ran to hide somewhere behind the building. As Dana squinted her eyes to get a better view, she recognized a brunette woman, wearing a green pair of pedal pushers and a matching jacket. Once Dana caught a closer look at the woman, she was convinced she was the same woman who was trimming the shrubs in front of the Brownell's house the other day.

The woman blew the whistle around her neck. She did it a second time. "Children, time to line-up." After several more calls, the children did as told and formed a line to the front door of the school.

Dana followed them inside and watched as the students scattered to their respective classrooms. "Quite a job you have there. The name's Dana...Dana Greer. You're Nora Brownell, correct?"

The woman extended her hand to Dana and nodded. "I love children. The last two boys in line are mine. I volunteer at the school once a week."

"Mind if we have a chat, Nora?" Dana pointed to the wooden bench in the hall.

The two sat down.

"I've had the pleasure of meeting your husband, Nora." Dana waited to see if the woman expressed any knowledge of her recent visit with Tim.

Nora smiled and said, "You mean Tejje Hansen?"

"I'm afraid I don't understand."

"My husband's name in Norwegian." She laughed. "He uses that name when he visits family there."

Tejie Hansen instead of Tim Brownell? Was that why he was not listed on the direct flight to Norway on the night Sister Mary Margaret was murdered?

"Dana? Are you okay?" Nora asked.

Dana pushed her bangs off her face. "Sorry, I must have gotten lost in my thoughts. You say your husband has relatives in Norway?"

"We both do. Tim's mother got into a terrible accident about a couple months ago, and he flew in to see her. It's difficult having family far away. What about you Dana? Where do you call home?"

"What? Me?" Dana let her voice trail off, "I'm from Maine. It was nice meeting you, Nora."

The woman made an O face.

Dana stood up to leave.

"Nice meeting you, too," Nora said, in an awkward voice.

Dana could feel the woman staring at her as she left the building.

*

After the evening prayers in the chapel, Dana left her cell and headed to Sister Seraphim's room. About ready to knock on the woman's door, Dana quickly turned to spot a dark shadow slipping by her. Before she could identify the person, she disappeared down one of the side halls. Someone was watching her, following her…Sister Magdalene. Dana reassured herself that she was over-reacting, but her sixth sense told her otherwise.

Sister Seraphim opened the door. Lines of concern covered her face. "Hurry, please. Come in."

"Sorry to barge in like this, Sister, but I hoped we might resume our conversation from the other day."

"I agree. Hurry, come in."

The young nun's cell was much larger than Dana's and had two soft-cushioned chairs, a chest of drawers, and a large, corner writing desk. The women sat down.

"Have you given anymore thought to your plans to leave the order, Sister?"

"If you're asking whether I have spoken to Mother, no, I haven't."

Dana wished she could tell the nun what Mother had plans to do. If she could get rid of Sister Magdalene, Sister Seraphim's worries would be over.

"I have spoken to her, though, about my fears. I'm convinced Mother knows Magdalene is a compulsive liar, but I'm not sure she understands how evil Magdalene is."

"Mind explaining what you mean by evil, Sister?"

The woman cupped her chin in her hand, biting down on her index finger. "You will keep this between you and me, right, Dana?"

"Without a doubt…yes, my lips are sealed."

"The other night…the night Darla was found, Sister Magdalene came to me. She told me she wanted me to cover for her should anyone ask where she went?"

"Wait one minute. Are you talking about the day sister left the convent?"

"Exactly. I lied, Dana. That day at breakfast, I said I had not seen sister since chapel the evening prior."

"But that's the truth, isn't it?"

"A sin of omission…true but not completely. Magdalene told me to say that. She told me she was off to see Jesse."

"Did she say why?"

"Not exactly. Said something about she had some dirty work for him to do."

Jesse's words came back to Dana. He had used the same words when he referred to the kidnapping of Jewel. For some reason, Sister

Magdalene wanted to keep her hands clean. As long as she was the silent partner, no one need think she played a part in anything suspicious.

"Sister, what do you think Magdalene wanted from Jesse?"

"Magdalen was in love with Father Tanner ever since he came to the parish."

"What does that have to do with Darla?"

"A lot. She wanted Darla gone. Darla never cared for Tanner. Magdalene told me the woman spread terrible lies about the young priest. Darla even claimed she would go the bishop and see to it he lost his clerical status."

All of a sudden, the pieces began to fit. Maybe, not enough to make any conviction, but at least, motives were becoming clear. "Are you saying, Sister Magdalene was behind the kidnapping and behind the death of Darla?" Dana knew the answer but wanted sister to confirm her beliefs.

"Yes. Do you see why I'm afraid?"

"You mean, Magdalene expects you to lie for her."

"More than that, Dana. She's threatened me. I do as she says or else. Why, I'm afraid she hates me."

Dana turned her head sideways.

"How can that be? Who could possibly feel that way about you?"

"I'm worried, Dana."

"Go on, Sister."

The nun burst into tears. "I'm so afraid, Dana. I need to get away from here before it is too late."

Dana longed to give the nun some reassurance, some advice, but she had no idea what Sister Seraphim needed to do. From all I've learned from this case, I can understand why you feel the way you do. The more you know, the more likely your own life is in jeopardy."

Chapter Fifty

The morning could not have come quicker. Dana knew what she had to share with Mother would be difficult, so she put on her favorite black pencil skirt and long-sleeved white blouse...one of her outfits that made her feel business-like and professional. She hurried to Mother's office and found the woman behind a stack of papers that read: *Yearly Reviews.*

The woman raised her head. "Dana, nice to see you."

"May I speak with you, Mother. It's important."

"Surely, have a seat." Mother pushed her chair back from her desk.

Dana closed the door to the office. She needed to speak in the strictest of confidence. "About Sister Magdalene...."

Mother tapped a pencil against her lips. "You're inquiring about whether I've made contact with the Mother House?"

"Please don't think I'm prying."

"Why would I think such a thing? After all, it was I who shared my thoughts with you."

Dana could feel her face flush, appreciating that Mother saw her as a friend. "Have you...contacted Rome?"

"Why, yes, I have. Mother Benedicto instructed me as to what I should do. I spoke with her in detail. Although this is not the first time something like this has come up, Mother Benedicto did say that Sister Magdalene is a rare exception. Mother wants me to keep a log of every infraction from this point further that the girl makes."

"What about her behavior up to this point?"

"I hear you. I could write a book. Is that what you're saying?"

"Exactly."

"Well, Dana, I don't expect sister's behavior to change dramatically from what it's been, do you?"

As far as Dana was concerned, Sister Magdalene was involved with the kidnapping of Jewel and the drowning of Darla Wheeler. Could things get any worse? Dana had no choice but to share what she knew with Mother Anne Baptiste. Dana guarded her words, spoke slowly, and gave Mother time to digest the news.

"Dana, dear," Mother stood up, her veil flying over her shoulders. "You're not telling me Sister Mary Margaret's child was taken from her by Doctor Vincent? Are you saying Sister Magdalene instructed Jesse to attempt kidnapping? And, Darla...do you actually think Sister may have been involved in Darla's death?" The woman placed her hand over her heart and breathed heavily. She began to pace the width of her office. "Jesus, Mary, Joseph...how can this be?"

"There's more, Mother."

"Jesus, no. Let me return to my seat." The nun patted her cheeks with the palms of her hands. "How...how can this be?"

"I'm sorry to be the bearer of such news, but you need to be aware. I should have told you this before you called the Mother House."

"Go on. What else could there possibly be?"

"You've heard of the Red Barn Tavern?"

"Joe Mikowski?"

"Yes, Mother. Sister frequents there often."

"Mother ran her hand over her forehead. Her face pale. "With Sister Seraphim, I suppose?"

Dana felt stumped. It was not her intention to mention the other Sister, nor could she tell Mother what Sister Seraphim had recently told her. "It's my belief Sister Magdalene might pressure Sister Seraphim to accompany her."

"I must speak with Sister Agnus Dei at once. She is head of postulants in this convent. She must be made aware." Mother began to jot down a note on a scrap of paper on her desk.

"Please, I don't want to cause any trouble. I tell you all this, so you're aware of what has been happening."

"No, you did the honorable thing. I had no knowledge of any of this. I am shocked and disheartened." Mother closed her eyes and breathed deeply. "It's time the truth came out."

Dana wondered if she had opened a beehive, been guilty of revealing secrets that were more dangerous known than to be kept hidden. She asked herself if she had done the right thing to share these incidents with Mother. She knew there would be repercussions, but she told herself she would find a way to deal with them. "I'm so sorry, Mother."

"Better I have knowledge of these things. Do not worry, dear. No one needs to find out where the information came from."

The image of the black shadow in the corridor crossed Dana's mind.

*

The pain started in the same way it usually did. Dana went back to her cell to lie down until her migraine subsided. Like a ball of yarn, the case was beginning to unravel but not exactly the way Dana had planned. She had come to solve the murder of Sister Mary Margaret but found herself entangled in many directions. In the end, though, she believed these paths would ultimately lead to the solution of the case. She kept reminding herself of this fact until she fell into a deep sleep.

Hours later when she awoke, she saw a blue envelope had been slipped under her door. She tore it open.

> *Dear Dana*
>
> *Thank you for listening to me. I do trust you. However, things have taken a turn for the worse. When Sister Magdalene saw me last night after chapel, she shoved me into a side hall. She told me if she ever sees me near you again, she will deal with it in her own way. I'm afraid, Dana.*
>
> *Sister Seraphim*

The last time Dana had spoken with Sister, it was in her room. Sister Magdalene had to have been watching them.

Chapter Fifty-One

The phone rang sixteen times before Father Tanner picked it up. "I told you not to call me here," he said.

"I need to see you," Sister Magdalene said, her voice like a child's whine.

In a hurry to brush her off, Tanner replied, "Yeah, yeah, maybe I'll see you around the barn sometime."

"No, you don't understand. I want to set up a time."

"Tan, Tanner, who's on the phone, dear?" Dorothy asked.

He could hear the squeaky wheels of his mother's chair heading for the kitchen.

"I gotta go. The old lady's come looking for me."

"Who cares, Tan. Tell her you're speaking with a friend."

He pinched the end of his nose and squinted his eyes. "Gwen, you are not a friend. You're just a nun I happen to know."

"Does it have to stay that way, Tanner? Huh?"

Tanner lifted his chin and squeezed the palm of his hand until his nails dug into his flesh. "I don't see it going anywhere else."

"Tanner, honey, what would you like for dinner?" Dorothy interrupted again.

He put the mouthpiece to the side and yelled to her, "Shut your God-damn mouth, why don't you?"

"What, honey?"

"Listen, Gwen. I've gotta go."

Like a child stomping her feet, Sister said, "No, not so quick. I have something I need to talk to you about."

Tanner looked to the ceiling and rolled his eyes. "Like what?"

"Not over the phone, baby doll. Meet me tonight at the barn, say around eight. We'll talk then."

Before Tanner could reply, the nun hung up the phone.

"Who was that on the phone, Tanner?" Dorothy asked, her chair nestled close to him.

"Some lame dame, Mother."

"That's not nice. Did I teach you to speak that way about the ladies? Furthermore, why are you talking to a lady?" When Tanner did not reply, she continued, "You're a priest, son, a man of God."

"Yeah, yeah," he replied and looked at the clock. It read seven-ten.

Tanner appeased his mother by eating dinner with her and then quickly left by the back door. He could still hear her voice ringing in his ears.

*

When he entered the Red Barn Tavern, he glanced around the dance hall and at the seats lined up against the bar. The nun had not showed up. He'd wait a few minutes and call it a night.

The band took a break, and he bought himself a gin and tonic. He braced himself against the bar when the nun entered. She wore a pink skirt with a black poodle on it and a plunging black top. Her hair was pulled in a tight ponytail to match the image of the girl on her skirt.

"Tan, sorry I'm a bit late."

"Yeah, let's get this over with. Can I get you a drink?"

Sister Magdalene's eyes shone. She smiled, showing her perfectly lined teeth. "Baby, I'd like that. I've got all night. How about a Rum-and-Coke."

Tanner placed the orders, and the two of them found a vacant booth in the corner. "So, what's up, Gwen...er, should I say Sister?"

"I've heard something about that altar boy of yours."

"Jimmy?"

The woman made an upside-down U face. "Not Jimmy, Jesse."

Tanner breathed deeply. "I give, Gwen. What did you hear?" He could hear the disgust in his own voice.

"He was at the dock the night Darla Wheeler supposedly fell in. You don't think...do you?"

"Hey, don't get me involved in this shit. Call that pretty detective."

The nun's shoulders raised, and she smirked. "I think he pushed her, Tan." With her chin raised upward, she blinked. Her eyelashes covered in double-duty black mascara.

"Oh, c'mon, Gwen. You have an over-active mind. Call Henning if it really bothers you."

The nun rolled her eyes. "That goof ball? He sits on his ass all day and wouldn't say anything bad about anyone on Willows."

In a gruff, disgusted voice, Tanner said, "Then, maybe you shouldn't either if you don't know what you're talking about."

"Ah, Tan, that was mean.," she said, in a baby voice. She edged over closer to him. "Plus, I'd like the credit to go to you when everyone finds out I was right all along."

"Listen, Gwen, don't do me any favors."

"Not even a small one?" She pursed her lips and closed her eyes.

"I don't know what you're talking about." Tanner finished his drink as the band came back from their break.

"How 'bout a dance, dreamboat?" By this time, the nun had her arms wrapped around the man's neck.

"No, thanks," he said. He grabbed the nun's arms and roughly pushed them away. He stood up. "I've got a sermon to write tonight."

"Just one…one dance," she begged.

Tanner looked down at her. "See ya around, Gwen." He headed back toward the bar.

Sister stormed out of the barn.

Tanner grabbed a book of matches and ordered himself another drink. He eyed a brunette across the room.

*

The phone rang several times. Dorothy struggled to sit up and reached for the receiver on her night table. In a groggy voice, scratchy from one too many cigarettes, she said, "Hello, may I ask who's calling?"

A woman's voice that almost sounded doll-like responded. "Is Tanner there?"

"Tanner, er…no. He's out for the night."

The caller slammed the receiver down, and the line went dead.

*

When Tanner came in, the house was pitch dark. "Maw, I'm home? Maw?"

No one answered. The house was silent.

"Are you in bed?" He turned on a few lights in the living room and went to the back of the house. The door to Dorothy's room was closed. He knocked. He knocked again. He opened the door a crack. The room was dark. He switched on the overhead light. He gasped. "Oh, my God." Dorothy lay on the floor, blood oozed from her mouth. Tanner called Doctor Vincent. "Please, come. Mother has been hurt." While Tanner waited, he felt for his mother's pulse. There was a faint one. "Hold on, Mother, Doctor is on his way."

*

Twenty minutes later, Doctor Vincent arrived with his black medical bag.

"What's happened?"

"I don't know, Doctor. I was out for the night, came home, and found her like this lying on the floor."

"Give me a hand, Tanner." The two men put Dorothy into her bed.

The doctor wiped the woman's lips with a cloth. He took Dorothy's pulse and blood pressure.

By this time, Dorothy was slowly coming to.

"Dorothy, what's happened?" the Doctor asked.

"I don't know. I can't remember. I was sound asleep. That's when I heard a loud bang."

"From where, Mother?"

"The back door, I think. It banged open. Someone came into my room."

"One person? Did you see who?"

"One, I think. I couldn't see in the dark. I felt something heavy, cold against my face. That's all I remember."

"From the gash on your face, it appears someone hit you on the head with something quite heavy. Then, you were dragged onto the floor. You're one lucky lady, Dorothy. This could have been a lot worse."

"But who…who would do this?"

"I have no idea, Dorothy."

"Do you think it might have been a robbery?" Tanner asked. He scoured Dorothy's closet, her drawers, and her standing jewelry cabinet, opening, closing, and banging. "Nothing appears gone."

"I'm not a detective, but if this were meant to be a robbery, the room certainly does not look disturbed in any way," the Doctor said. "So, why would someone hurt you? It doesn't make sense."

Tanner repeated the question in his mind. "I wonder."

Chapter Fifty-Two

Seemed the only people Dana could trust were Mother Superior and Sister Seraphim. She needed to find a way that she could convince Sister to meet with Mother. This was not a time to keep secrets and to run in fear. Rather than confront Sister Seraphim, Dana sat down to write her a letter:

Dear Sister Seraphim,

Both you and I have had our lives threatened by Sister Magdalene. She is aware we know too much. But the answer is not to resort to fear. Please meet me in Mother's office during recreational hour.

Dana

Dana slipped the note under the door to Sister's cell. It was the only way to relay news to the nun. After the threat of Sister Magdalene, writing a note was the safest recourse.

The door to the office open, Dana could hear the voice of Sister Agnus Dei speaking to Mother. The elderly woman's voice was distinguishable because of its low, manly tone.

Dana stood next to the door but off to the side so as not to be seen.

"Sister I have given you the responsibility to be in charge of our postulants…only the two remaining. I have received word that they have been leaving the cloister at odd hours. Are you aware of this?"

Dana could feel her heart pounding in her ears. Besides Sister Magdalene, there was something about the old nun that made Dana feel uncomfortable, anxious.

The nun cleared her throat and coughed. In a scratchy, deep voice, she said, "I thought we needed to give the girls some freedoms in order to assure us they would not leave the order."

"Freedoms, yes, such as extra time for recreation, perhaps, not wandering outside the cloistered walls unattended. God knows what temptations are out there."

Dana could hear the agitation in Mother's response.

"I hear you, Mother. They have pushed the limits. They have no excuse for their sinful behavior. The girls knew they were joining a cloistered order."

"True, Sister Agnus Dei. A choice needs to be made… in the world or living a life of a cloistered nun, dedicating one's life to sacrifice and prayer."

"Yes, Mother."

"Now, as to the secondary reason I have called you into my office today. We all know, Sister, you, too, were living a sinful life until your dear father paid your dowry to enter the convent."

"That was different. You can't compare me to the postulants."

"Why not, Sister? The only exception is that you let *him* have his way with you, and in the end, *he* had you do away with the consequences."

The nun burst out crying. Mumbling, hardly audible, the nun said, "And a priest, no less."

Dana could not believe what she was over-hearing. This sounded like the same story Dorothy had relayed to her.

Mother continued, "And today a bishop. You see the men get away with their sins; it is the women who are made to pay." Mother pushed her chair away from her desk, scratching sounds on the hardwood floor. "Enough said, Sister. You may leave. But I will have you abide by my orders. The two postulants will not be allowed to leave the sacred grounds of this institution."

Just in the nick of time, Dana slid around the corner...unnoticeable just as the elderly nun left. Dana saw Sister Seraphim coming down the hall. It must be recreation hour, she thought. She hurried into Mother's office and explained that she and the nun desired to meet with her.

Mother's face appeared flushed. She rubbed the side of it. "Please have a seat." She pulled out a linen handkerchief from deep in her pocket and wiped her mouth.

Dana explained she had hoped to tell Mother of their visit, but she did not want to interrupt her meeting with Sister Agnus Dei.

"I wish you had. That woman tries my nerves. You'd think she were the superior of this convent...but she's not."

Dana could not believe the honesty in what Mother had said.

"The purpose...what is the purpose of your visit today?"

Sister Seraphim rushed into the room, sat down, and began to fiddle with the rosary beads at her side. She looked downward.

"Mother, I think, it is about time you know the full truth."

"Go ahead. Guess today is the day for headline news."

"Sister and I have been talking about some things that are of grave concern to us. Sister, would you like to tell Mother?"

The young nun looked sideways at Dana, her face partly hidden by her veil. "Why don't you, Dana."

"Sister and I have been threatened."

"What?"

"Sister Magdalene realized that Sister Seraphim and I have discussed some issues revolving around her. She left a note saying that she will kill us if she finds out we have spoken to each other again."

Mother threw her head back and closed her eyes. "Whatever are you talking about?"

Dana put her hand on Sister Seraphim's. "Why don't you continue, Sister?"

"Dana is correct in what she says. Sister Magdalene expected me to lie…to cover for her…like the time she recently left the convent for almost two days."

"Go on."

"I felt obligated to do as she said. She threated my life if I did not do so."

"And the reason Sister left the convent the other night?"

In a shaky, child-like voice, Sister Seraphim said, "…to be with Jesse. She claims Jesse does her dirty work."

"Sounds like the same story you've relayed to me, Dana. Hard to believe. Jesse always seemed like a decent enough youngster…well, if it weren't for his leather jacket, his chain smoking, and his greasy hair. That's what Betty tells me are his major faults. But maybe Betty doesn't know the extent of his behavior."

"It goes much further than that, Mother," Sister Seraphim said. Her lower lip trembling, she said, "I go out some evenings…to the Red Barn Tavern with Sister Magdalene." Sister quickly turned her head aside…her face a bright coral. "I don't want to, Mother. I want to be a servant of Jesus, to consecrate my life to God, but I'm scared…scared if I would refuse, she might do something to me. You might as well know this, Mother. Sister Magdalene has been in love with Father Tanner ever since he came to Grotto of Lourdes."

Mother bolted from her seat. "Mercy, Jesus. Mercy be upon us. What is all of this? The religious falling in love. Have I not heard enough?" She threw her hands to her face and hurried to the window, where she stood for several moments before sitting down once again. She pulled a handkerchief from deep in the folds of her habit and blew her nose.

Dana knew Mother was referring to what she and Sister Agnus Dei had just discussed. What shocking news…the nun, like Sister Mary Margaret, had had an affair with a priest only Agnus Dei had done away with her child.

"Sorry, Mother, but it is true."

"And it's time the truth be known," Dana added.

Mother said, "This gives me no choice. I must ask Sister to leave the convent at once. She is no longer welcome to be among us. She uses the holy habit to cover for her vices."

"Likewise, I need to alert the authorities. A number of arrests need to be made. There's only one major problem."

"Oh, praise God, Dana, not more!"

"Unfortunately, there is, Mother. Henry Gillion has been involved in accepting bribes to alter the death certificates of both Sister Mary Margaret's child and the nun's, as well as to lie and say Darla Wheeler's death was the result of a fall related to a seizure. Both he and Sheriff Olsen have been intentionally covering up these matters."

Mother paced her office as if she were there alone. Her fingers busily worked their way up-and-down the wooden beads at her side.

"Jesse did play an active role in the kidnapping of baby Jewel, and both he and Sister Magdalene saw to it that Darla was pushed into the deep waters near the Willows's Fisheries."

Mother stopped walking the length of her office and braced herself against the front of her desk. She sighed. "And, Sister Mary Margaret…her death…?" Mother was too out of breath to complete her question.

"It is clear to me now, Mother. I kept going over my list of possible suspects, but the only one who had a motive for removing Sister from the picture was Henry Gillion. He is the one who falsely recorded her child as stillborn. She had to be kept from learning the truth. The Doctor must have paid him off royally in order to acquire a baby for Martha and to do away with Sister Mary Margaret."

"Oh, dear, gracious God. You must call——."

"…the sheriff? Like I said, he was more than happy to keep these crimes off the slate. As he told me once, in the end, it's better for the economy of Winter Willows if people see these occurrences as mere misfortunes, rather than felonies."

"Dreadful," Mother said. "Who can we call?"

"I say we go to the Attorney General of Washington. He needs to see that these two scoundrels, the coroner and the sheriff, are impeached and put behind bars for what they've done."

Chapter Fifty-Three

Dana peeked in the Church doors to see who was having the Mass...Father Tanner. In haste, if she did this right, she could pay a visit to Dorothy before Tanner came home. Dana hurried toward Dorothy's. After speaking with Mother yesterday, there was something troubling her.

When Dorothy opened the door, Dana made an O face. "My gosh, whatever has happened, Dorothy?"

The woman's face was bruised, and a long, dry scab shone from the top of her head.

"This? I can't remember. All I know is Tanner was out last night, and someone broke in the side door. Whoever woke me from a deep sleep."

"A robber? Was anything taken?" Dana asked.

"That's the strange part...nothing. I was hit over my head, and that was the last I remember."

Dana was about to say, "Don't you think you should report this?" but she stopped herself.

"Tanner found me on the floor of my room when he came home. Doctor stopped in to check on me but said I was lucky it wasn't worse."

"But who? But why?"

Dorothy answered with a question, "Who knows?"

"I'm so sorry. First, the fall from your wheelchair and now this."

"Near as I can tell, the person must have had some vendetta to pay. You know, someone who wanted to take it out on me."

"Do you have any idea who that would be?"

"No, dear, I don't. Pretty much keep to myself unless Betty comes for me and takes me to church. Other than that, I stay homebound."

"Tanner…do you know where he went that night?"

"Usually, I'd have no idea, Dana, but once I found a book of matches that read Red Barn Tavern. Guess, it's some kind of beer garden. Could be he went there."

That's it, Dana thought. Magdalene was rebuffed by Tanner and took it out on his poor mother.

"Hmm, I do remember something, though."

"Yes?"

"Before I went to bed that night, a woman called for Tanner. When I said he was out, she hung up the phone. Someone has been calling for him before. Tan gets quite upset. I've heard him ask the woman not to call again."

Bingo! It had to be Magdalene who more than likely did her own dirty work.

Dorothy maneuvered into the kitchen and made a cup of tea for each of them. Out of the pantry she found some stale cookies and put them on a plate. "Not into the sweet things," she said.

Dana sat at the kitchen table and wondered where to begin.

"Was there something you wanted to chat about, Dana?"
Dorothy took a sip of her tea. Lemon and citrus scents warmed the
kitchen.

"Your brother, Dorothy—."

"He's an archbishop in Rome. Been there for more than forty
years."

"Did he always want to be a priest?"

"From a young boy but he had some problems keeping his
hands off the ladies. Adam was such a good-looking lad...well, a lot
like my Tanner."

"I agree with you. Tanner is quite handsome."

"My mother always wished Adam would have given himself
some time. You see, he joined a seminary school right out of eighth
grade. These young men need some time to sprout their wings, see
some of the world."

"Just like Tanner, I suppose."

Dorothy hung her head and did not reply.

"So, you believe Adam was too young to be ordained?"

"Quite!" Dorothy cupped her mouth. "I don't mean to gossip
none, but my brother got himself involved with a young girl who
came from a wealthy family in the parish."

"I see."

"Not exactly sure what all happened. I'm eight years younger
than Adam, but near as I recall, the girl went away for a month or so.

344 – Delphine Boswell

People gossiped she was with child. My brother went back to Rome, and would you believe the girl's family paid a dowry and sent her off to the nunnery? The girl protested, but her father said she had no choice in hell of leaving the convent. He told her she could rot until hell froze over."

"You believe your brother may have gotten the girl pregnant?"

"Adam had her do away with it. He'd never be bishop today with that sin out in public. Listen, I'm not saying it was the right way to handle it. I'm only saying that's what happened."

Dana ran her hand over her forehead. Initially, she thought it too much of a coincidence, hardly likely. What were the chances? Sister Agnus Dei's past coincided with Sister Mary Margaret's other than the baby being taken away from the postulant. Dana could hear Mother Superior's words to the elderly nun, "We all know, Sister, why you're here. You, too, were living a sinful life until your dear father paid your dowry to enter the convent." Wasn't the cliché, like father, like son, but this time is was like uncle, like nephew.

"As always, it was nice talking with you, Dorothy. But I'd better be going; I sure hope you recover soon from the break-in."

*

Dana found Sister Seraphim strolling the labyrinth in the garden. For once not occupied in prayer, the young woman appeared to be enjoying the sunny day as she strolled around the sharply carved paths. When she noticed Dana, she motioned for her to wait.

"Please forgive me, Dana. I'm not trying to gossip but did you hear what happened to Dorothy Bennett? I know the two of you are friends."

"As a matter of fact, that's where I was coming from. She received quite a scare the other night…if that is what you're referring to?"

"Yes, I'm talking about the incident where someone broke in and knocked her out."

"Go on."

Sister dug her nails into the palms of her hands. In a quivering voice, she said, "The other night Sister Magdalene left for the Red Barn Tavern."

Dana listened closely.

"Magdalene sought me out upon her return. She asked me for some bandages to wrap her hand. It was bleeding quite badly. When I asked what had happened…well, I thought maybe she caught a glass of beer as it was falling from the bar…."

Dana was beginning to add two and two.

"Magdalene told me she broke a glass vase." Sister stopped to clear her throat. "When I asked her how, she told me…." The nun wrung her hands. "She told me she had been to Father Tanner's house while he was out. She admitted she hit Dorothy over the head with a glass vase."

"How tragic! Dorothy is such a good-hearted person."

"It wasn't meant to be about Dorothy. She was trying to get back at Father Tanner. She told me he would never hurt her again."

"She's as evil as they come," was all Dana could think to say.

Chapter Fifty-Four

Dana sat at Mother's desk as she dialed the Attorney General's office.

A woman answered the phone in a chirpy voice. "Attorney General's office. May speaking."

"The name's Dana Greer. I am a private investigator working for the Archdiocese of Seattle. I need to speak with the Attorney General at once."

A few seconds later, a man answered the call. "Peter Elliot, Attorney General, speaking.

When Dana explained her need to speak with the man personally, he agreed to arrive on the evening ferry.

While Dana waited, she placed another call to the archbishop to tell him of her plans now that she had resolved the case.

"I will be on the morning ferry, Miss Greer, to personally thank you for all you have done. As for what you believe about the young fellow, Father Tanner Bennett, I'd prefer to deal with this myself. The fact that he found himself the father of the deceased nun's child is a highly confidential matter that I do not intend to be made public. You know, Miss Greer, we do have the Church's reputation to protect."

Another cover-up? Dana thought. She was brought to Winter Willows to solve the murder of Sister Mary Margaret; she would leave Tanner's sin to the Church.

When Dana explained the young priest's behavior at the Red Barn Tavern and his abuse of his own mother, the archbishop abruptly interrupted her. "Miss Greer, I'd prefer you let these matters up to me. I will speak with the man tomorrow."

"But, Archbishop, don't you think his violent behavior with his own mother deserves to be punished?"

"As I said, I'd prefer to speak with the young man myself. I feel confident, I can handle this matter without the authorities."

Dana knew this meant the priest would probably just receive a reprimand; it would go no further.

As for the Attorney General, Dana began to write down exactly what she needed to present to Peter Elliot.

Henry Gillion:
- *Acceptance of bribes in the altering of official documents*
- *Acceptance of bribes in the determination of Darla Wheeler's death*
- *Murder in the first degree of Sister Mary Margaret*

Sheriff Olsen:
- *Cover-up of felonies involving Henry Gillion*

Doctor Ned Vincent:
- *Signing of falsified death certificate*
- *Providing bribes to Henry Gillion*

Sister Magdalene:
- *Involvement with bribes in the kidnapping of baby Jewel and the death of Darla Wheeler*
- *Threats against Sister Seraphim and Dana*
- *Assault and battery of Dorothy Bennett*
- *Murder in the first degree of Darla Wheeler*

Jesse Carmichael:
- *Acceptance of bribes in the kidnapping of Jewel Sullivan and in the death of Darla Wheeler*
- *Kidnapping of Jewel Sullivan*
- *Accomplice in the murder of Darla Wheeler*

Gertrude Mead:
- *Accomplice in the kidnapping of Jewel Sullivan*
- *Cover-up for Henry Gillion's offenses*

Dana went back to her cell, hoping the time would go quickly when she could unload all that she had learned about the case.

*

Charles Filmore drove Peter Elliot, the Attorney General, to the convent while Dana waited out front for the man.

The two shook hands.

Dana led the man to Mother's office, where the woman continued her pacing of the room. Dana introduced the man to Mother and the three of them sat around Mother's desk. The late afternoon sun's rays shone through the window coating the room in a warm golden hue.

Dana provided Mother and the Attorney General with the list she had drawn-up of the perpetrators and the crimes committed.

Mother wrung her hands on her desk. She continually shook her head, her face one of dire disgust.

As for the arrests of Henry Gillion, Sister Magdalene, and Jesse Carmichael, Peter Elliot agreed to return to the island first thing in the morning, via emergency Coast Guard vessel. He would bring officers who officially would make the arrests.

"As for the sheriff, Mr. Elliot?" Dana inquired.

"Unfortunately, there are more sheriffs in this country who fall under the radar for their crimes merely for the fact that they are elected officials. When you don't have a boss over your head, per se, it's amazing how one can abuse power."

Dana explained what Olsen had told her about wanting to keep a clean slate.

"And, that's the truth, Miss Greer. A rosy picture means a re-election. This does not imply that there is a possibility the man could be impeached, however. That would be a civil procedure held in circuit court, possibly with a jury to hear the case."

Dana and Mother thanked the man for his help and agreed to meet back in Mother's office in the a.m.

*

"My sweet, little kitten, you'll worry yourself to death."

"Henry, I have reason," Gertrude whined. "Doctor tells me he worries about that snoopy investigator, too."

"Listen, all we do is stick to our guns. Ned would never put my career in jeopardy, you know that. With the baby, we both came out as winners. He got the child Martha never had, and I got a whopping payoff."

"What about Sister Mary Margaret's death? How do you intend to wiggle your way out of that one?"

Henry jumped up from the couch where they were seated. He threw his arms out at his sides, his face looking like a burning bush. "Gertrude, you don't know when to stop this needless worry. No one was there that night—."

"Other than me!"

"Other than you, there were no witnesses. You needed to be there in order to convince the little nun to come to the cemetery."

"...to help you pull her into the grave."

"That, too, my sweet."

"So, what do you suggest I say, Henry?"

"You were not there that night, know nothing of what happened. You intend to stand by the coroner's report," he looked up with an impish grin, "that the sister accidentally fell to her death. You have no reason to think otherwise, do you hear me?"

Gertrude pulled back at Henry's cold, deep voice. Henry had never spoken to her in such a harsh manner.

The wrinkles on the woman's face slowly started to subside. "Sure, Henry. We can do this. We'll pull this off just fine."

"That's my baby talking. Have you picked out you-know-what, my little kitten?"

"Well, sweetie, I have been down to McFrankle's…just looking."

"And tell me what you found." Henry's eyes twinkled, and he made a mischievous smile."

"So many to choose from. My heart sang, though, when I spotted the oval diamond surrounded with rubies."

"Then, so be it, my love. Instead of worrying your pretty little mind, we need to do some planning." Henry dipped his hand into his trouser pocket. "Ah, hah, here's my calendar. What day were you thinking of, my sweet?"

Gertrude gently pushed the calendar to the floor and began to passionately kiss her future groom.

Chapter Fifty-Five

The following morning in the refectory immediately after the meal prayer, Mother opened a copy of a book that appeared dusty and used. "I'd like to read to you this morning from the book on the origin of the Carmelite order. It's time we all realize what a blessing we have in this order we profess to be a part of." Mother was about to speak when the door to the dining hall banged open and hit the wall behind them.

The sisters "ooh'd" and "aah'd."

Standing before them stood Sister Magdalene. She wore black spiked heels, bare legs, and a tight-fitting yellow linen skirt. Her black-and-while polka-dot blouse was opened at the neck, revealing a long string of pearls. Her black hair hung over her shoulders in a precisioned flip. Over her arms was flung two of the white postulant habits, the two given each sister upon her entry. "Do with these what you like, Mother, she said. She tossed the blessed garb onto the floor and stomped on it with her pointed heels.

"God, bless, no," one of the nuns called out.

"Praise Jesus," another said.

"She's sacrilegious. Pick your habits up now," a third yelled to her.

Mother ran over, picking up the white outfits, kissing them, and asking God's forgiveness for the treatment they were shown.

The room went totally silent. All eyes were on Mother who shivered at the podium, standing with the postulant's habits in her arms.

"There is one more thing before I leave," Magdalene said. "If you're wondering who killed that child…Cindy Sullivan…I'd suggest asking Dorothy. She's the one who bore the demon…the one who calls himself *Father*. Ha! What a blasphemy!"

The sisters, some huddled together in fear, were quiet.

Dana could not believe the spectacle before her eyes. The woman with her bright red lips and black outlined eyes appeared more as a street person than a former nun. Add to her appearance, she falsely accused the man she loved of murder. Who but evil could retaliate in such a manner?

At the moment Magdalene turned to leave the refectory, two police officers, followed by Peter Elliot, pushed the doors open.

Dana jumped and yelled out, "Grab her; this lady is under arrest!"

Magdalene screamed out, "What's this all about? There's been some mistake! Get your hands off me!" She wrestled with the officer until the second police officer cuffed her hands behind her back.

The refectory instantly became like a beehive. The sisters whispering to each other, no idea what was happening or why.

"Mother, I'd better give Betty a call. It's time Jesse admits his guilt in all of this."

Overhearing Dana, Magdalene yelled out, "Leave the boy alone. He's only a kid. Did as he was told."

"But why? Mother asked. "Why did he get himself involved in all of this? He's such a nice boy."

"He did what any kid would do for money."

"Let me guess. The payoff was provided by Joe Mikowski," Dana asked.

"You're smarter than I gave you credit for, investigator," Magdalene sneered.

The doors to the refectory barged open again. In stepped Charles Fillmore...his face covered in sweat, his back arched over. His hand gripped tightly onto Jesse's shoulder. Breathing deeply, Charles said, "Found the damn kid in the cemetery."

The second police officer took hold of the boy by his upper arms. Filmore tried to stand upright as far as was possible with an arthritic back.

Jesse's arms were covered in fresh dirt, streaks of dirt spilled down his sweaty face. His boots were covered in mud.

"Can you explain what you were doing, Jesse?" Dana asked.

The boy glared at Magdalene, and from where he stood, he spat at her.

"Charles, what did you see Jesse doing?" Dana asked.

"Ma'am, the boy was digging with his bare hands into the grave of Sister Mary Margaret, kicking at her tombstone, spitting at it. Why, he was desecrating her resting place; that's what he was doing."

"Tell 'em, Jesse. Tell them the truth," Magdalene screamed.

"I want…I want…my Cindy back." He shoved himself to his knees and kept belting out, "I love you, Cindy. I love you." Tears poured over onto the collar of his shirt.

Pressing forward as if trying to break free from her cuffs, Magdalene said to Jesse, "Give it up. The baby…she was Tanner's, not yours!"

Jesse twisted his head in Magdalene's direction. "What are you talking about? That can't be; that's an outright lie."

"Ask Mother if you don't believe me. Cindy told her the truth."

The police officer nudged Jesse in the back with his knee. "Get the hell up. You and your pretty friend here are under arrest."

As Magdalene and Jesse left the room with the police officers, Charles Filmore shook his head and mumbled, "What the hell is the world coming to?"

The attorney general introduced himself to Charles, Dana, and Mother Superior.

Dana asked the man if he could wait one moment. She went back to her cell and retrieved the broken piece of mausoleum…the first clue in the case. "Think this might be of help to you, Mr. Elliot. Found at the murder site by Charles Filmore."

"Quite an astute eye, Mr. Filmore, and certainly a valuable piece of evidence when it comes to going to court. "You deserve what's known as the citizen of the year award."

Charles blushed and looked down.

Chapter Fifty-Six

The doorbell rang interrupting the Doctor's thoughts as he stood staring out at the bay. "Coming," he said. "Oh, what a surprise, and it isn't even Poker night."

Gertrude and Henry stepped inside, both wearing huge smiles.

"What is the pleasure of your visit?" Ned asked, in a joking way.

"Let's first sit down," Gertrude said.

"So, what's up?" Ned asked.

"We wanted you to be the very first to know," Gertrude said, her arm around Henry's shoulder. "Henry and I have set a date. We're getting married in October."

"My, my," Ned said. "Let me get some champagne, so we can toast. Congratulations are in order."

After they raised their glasses to toast, Ned said, "Does this mean by chance I'll be losing my wonderful nanny?"

"Oh, no. Jewel is the love of my life. You know that, Doctor."

As the three of them sipped on their drinks, Gertrude said, "You look preoccupied. Is everything okay?"

"Hmm? What were you saying?"

"Is something the matter? You seem to be out of sorts today," Henry added.

The Doctor turned to face Henry. The man's eyes were circled in droopy bags. Aside each were deeply etched lines.

"Not getting enough sleep?" Gertrude asked him.

He threw the palms of his hands to cover his mouth, closed his eyes, stood, and wobbled slightly back and forth. "Gertrude, Henry, there's something I need to tell you." His concerned face grew even more serious. "We need to get our stories straight."

A loud bang on the front door interrupted his thought.

A policeman greeted the doctor.

Gertrude, who stood at the doctor's side, said, "What is this about?"

The doctor stretched his arm out as if a gate to prevent Gertrude from going any further.

The policeman identified himself as Officer Rodney Stanwick. "I take it you're Doctor Ned Vincent?"

"Yes, Sir."

"You are under arrest for the offering of bribes, the kidnapping of a Jewel Sullivan, and the payoff in the murder of the child's mother, Cindy Sullivan."

"My wife…she's passed away. Jewel is our child. The birth certificate—."

Henry edged closer to the door and thrust his shoulders back. "I can vouch for that officer. I signed the death certificate on Jewel Sullivan."

"Then, you must be…Henry…Henry Gillion."

"That's correct, Sir."

"Then, you, Mr. Gillion, are under arrest for the acceptance of bribes in the altering of official documents and murder in the first degree of Sister Mary Margaret."

"What?" Ned said. "There has to be some mistake, Officer. Henry would never murder anyone. We've been friends for years. I'm telling, you, you've got the wrong man."

"How can this be, Officer?" Gertrude interrupted. "I am the doctor's nurse. I was present at the birth of Cindy Sullivan's child. Unfortunately, the delivery resulted in a stillborn. Henry Gillion attested to that on the birth certificate. As for Jewel, she is the former Martha Vincent's child, born premature at about the same time as Miss Sullivan's."

"Is that so?" the Office asked, biting down on the inside of his lip. "You can save your words and your breath, lady. Both you and Doctor Vincent can explain that to the judge on your court date. Until then, you, are all coming with me. There's a squad car out front." He grabbed Gertrude by her arm and pulled the gun at his side and pointed it at Henry and Ned. "I suggest you come with me without incidence. I really don't like to use this gun."

Ned's knees felt weak; his head nodded. "My medical license, my profession, over. How can this be?"

"You did it to yourself, Mister," the officer said.

The men, shoulders back stiffly, edged toward the door. Doctor Vincent ducked his head and entered the police cruiser.

Gertrude, by this time, was crying incessantly. "Henry, please, don't leave me…please."

"You can visit him in jail, the police officer said, and snickered.

Henry, turned his back on Gertrude, stepping off the porch and into the police cruiser.

"Let the judge try to prove this. It's his word against yours, Henry," Gertrude said. She was the last to enter the cruiser.

Chapter Fifty-Seven

Dana went to her cell and packed her belongings. The train from Seattle to Denver was scheduled to leave at eleven p.m. She would take the last ferry out of Winter Willows. When she closed the door to her room, the congregation waited for her, forming a large circle of joined hands.

Dana set her suitcase down and threw her hands to her cheeks. She stepped back in surprise.

Mother stepped toward her. "The sisters and I want to present you with a gift in honor of all you have done for us." Mother handed her a small statue. "This is for you, Dana, an image of Saint Columba, the patron of investigators."

The sisters dropped hands and clapped.

Tears welled in Dana's eyes. She glanced around at each and every face before her. She caught her breath and said, "What a bittersweet moment, holy women of God." The circle of women broke apart, and everyone gathered around, taking turns to hug her and to say good-bye.

Charles Filmore waited in his DeSoto out front of the convent to take her to the ferry. "Seems, as though, it was only yesterday I dropped you off here, Dana."

"So, it does," she said.

Epilogue

Six Months Later

Dana was granted another contract by the Catholic Church. This time she found herself at the Saint Ignatius Retreat Center, four hours outside of Denver, Colorado, where a child was found murdered in the library.

As for the community of Winter Willows, Father Merton continued to pastor Grotto of the Lourdes Church along with his dog Francine. He wrote a thank you letter to Dana for her efforts at solving the case of Sister Mary Margaret as did Archbishop Boretti.

Father Tanner was transferred to a residential facility for men who harbor anger issues. When completing his therapy, he will be sent to a new parish in Oregon. His mother, Dorothy, was temporarily being cared for by the former Sister Seraphim, Elaine Reed, who left the convent on a leave of absence.

Doctor Ned Vincent was sentenced to fifteen years in prison for the custodial interference, a lesser crime than kidnapping of Jewel Sullivan. However, due to the payoff to the coroner for the murder of Sister Mary Margaret, he was tried as an accomplice in the murder and sentenced to twenty-five years to be served consecutively.

Henry Gillion received life in prison for the falsifying of documents, the receipt of bribes, and death in the first degree of Sister Mary Margaret.

The state awarded the custody of Jewel Bennett to Mother Anne Baptiste, who is to care for the child until the age of eighteen. To Mother's delight, three new postulants entered the cloister.

Jesse Carmichael was convicted of second-degree murder in the death of Darla Wheeler and an accomplice in the kidnapping of Jewel Sullivan. He, too, was convicted of accepting bribes. Due to being only a minor at the time of the offenses, he was sentenced to twenty years in prison.

Sister Magdalene was convicted of being an accomplice in the kidnapping of Jewel Sullivan. She was charged with taking and passing bribes and with first-degree murder in the death of Darla Wheeler. Sister was sentenced to life, with the possibility of parole in thirty years, at the Women's Correctional Facility in Gig Harbor, Washington.

Gertrude Mead received ten years for her part in the kidnapping of baby Jewel and the cover-up of Henry Gillion's nefarious crimes. Like Sister Magdalene, Gertrude was sentenced to the Women's Correctional Facility in Gig Harbor, Washington.

Joe Mikowski continues to run the Red Barn Tavern and to engage in his illicit gambling exploits, and Office Henning continues to mind his own business and to look the other way.

Betty Carmichael began her new life in Alaska with her son Jimmy who entered the Holy Spirit Seminary High School.

Tim Brownell and his wife, Nora, and their two sons continue to live on the island.

If you enjoyed reading *Bitter Wrath*, please feel free to help me reach other readers, as well.

You could:

- **LEND THE BOOK** to a family member or friend...or even a stranger for that matter!
- **RECOMMEND** the book to others you know; perhaps, you are in a book club, write a blog, or on Instagram.
- **REVIEW** it, by typing the name of the book into www.amazon.com, clicking on the gold stars, and scrolling down to where you can type your own personal thoughts about the book. Amazon values these stars as do writers.

If you're willing to do any of these, please send me an email at delphine.boswell@gmail.com, so I can personally thank you.

Enjoyed reading **Bitter Wrath?** Here's a preview of what's to come in **Delphine Boswell's** fourth novel in the **Dana Greer Mystery Series.**

Whispering Remorse…

At an altitude of 12,000 feet, four hours outside of Denver, Colorado, stands the Saint Ignatius Loyola Retreat House, known as a long-term refuge for prayer. The staff live there year-round; whereas, guests, most from prominent backgrounds, stay upwards of a month at a time and come from all over the country. On a wintry night in December, 1953, nine-year old Isabella Hanka, daughter of one of the employees, mysteriously disappears. After hours of searching, the body of the child is found bludgeoned to death in the library. Dana Greer, PI, signs a contract with the Catholic Church to investigate the crime. Since the Advent guests arrived two days prior to the murder, all guests are quarantined until the case can be solved. There's something about the holy place, isolated in the middle of nowhere, that unsettles Dana. When she learns more about the murdered child, she realizes that although she may be in a center of prayer, there are those around her who are hiding the darkest of sins.

Prologue

Ten Years Earlier – March 18, 1943
San Juan Capistrano, California

In a darkened wine cellar known to the locals as the most content place on earth sat the third-year seminarian enjoying his day off from studies. He swallowed the sweet richness of the grapes and deeply breathed in its robust scent. The seminarian liked coming here as it was one place where no one knew him or his identity. He was considered one of the locals, and beyond that, no one cared to inquire. Sitting near the fireplace, he watched the dancing orange flames and let his past play before him. He came from a large Italian family…the youngest boy in a family of ten with only two sisters. One of the latter became a bride of Christ after taking her final vows in the Dominican Order of Racine, Wisconsin. The rest of his siblings, scattered throughout the United States, he found himself more alone than ever. He often wondered if this might have been his reason for joining the Mission Seminary of Capistrano. He enjoyed the camaraderie of his fellow seminarians yet knowing well that his future depended on where the Jesuit Order decided to send him once he was ordained.

The door to the winery squeaked open and in came a woman with long, black hair held back in a silver clasp. She sat alone at the table next to him and ordered a white wine with a tray of cheese samples. Something about her almond eyes reflecting the dancing flames of the fire caught his attention, and the fact that such an attractive woman would be alone on a Thursday night. His found himself staring at the woman who appeared to be about legal drinking age.

Her scarlet sweater, black skirt, and shiny black heels gave her an air of sophistication along with a silent shyness that reminded him of someone who longed for a friend but had no idea how to go about meeting someone. When the server brought her order and refilled his glass of wine, he quietly stepped over to her table and whispered, "Cheers."

The woman smiled and held up her glass in response.

"Mind if I join you?"

She blushed, something he had not intended. He only wanted to make her feel comfortable, less alone.

"My name's Lorenzo Erranta," he said, holding his hand out. "Friends call me Loren for short." And yours?"

"Sophia Verrico," she said, casting her eyes downward and extending her hand.

Loren kissed the top of her hand and said, "Such a beautiful ring to your name. You, too, must be Italiono, right?"

She nodded. This time she met his eyes.

"Are you from here?" he asked, the typical opener of a stranger.

"No," she said. "I come here once a year on March nineteenth to take in the arrival—."

"Didn't mean to interrupt, but you're referring to the birds of Capistrano.

"Why here of all places?" he asked.

The woman blushed again. "Guess, I believe in miracles."

"Ah, so. Many believe the birds' arrival each year at the same time is, indeed, a miracle."

Her light rose lips smiled. "And you?" she asked, "where are you from?"

He laughed. "It's not the birds that bring me here although, like you say, it is a miraculous sight."

Sophia, pushing a few loose strands of hair off her face, rephrased her question. "Why are you here then?"

"I'm a student," he said, hoping she wouldn't ask the name of the school.

"Surely, you're not studying Italian," she laughed.

"Actually, Latin." He quickly protected his answer with, "I like studying the roots of words."

"Where do you live?" Loren asked.

"I'm from Colorado, outside of Denver."

"What do you do for a living, Sophia? Let me guess. With a name like yours, I bet you're an opera singer."

Sophia smiled. "No, afraid I don't have the voice for that."

"But, it's soft like that of an angel," Loren said. He ran his hand alongside his cheek, warm to the touch.

"Oh, silly me. Would you like some cheese?" she asked.

"Ah, thank you. Nothing like wine with cheese."

They both finished the last of the wine in their glasses.

"Could I get you another?" he asked.

*

Two hours later, they finished the last of the wine in their glasses, giggling and telling each other silly jokes.

"Sophia, what do you say we leave the winery and take a walk?"

"I'd like that."

The two strolled hand-in-hand along the pier, most of the fishing vessels docked for the night.

Loren reminded himself that he was a seminarian, soon to be ordained. The weather, the night, the beautiful woman beside him and he found he could not control his desires. "Sophia, come with me," he said, as he led her toward a grassy knoll.

The two lie down, staring at the starlit sky. A cool breeze blew in from the bay, and Loren embraced Sophia in his arms. The two kissed and then kissed some more.

Beyond controlling their impulses, much too far gone for that, the two found love on a hillside in Capistrano.

It would be ten years before they met again.

CPSIA information can be obtained
at www.ICGtesting.com
Printed in the USA
FSHW011050091119
63840FS